Dear Reader,

Nothing in life can prepare a man for fatherhood. Not
books, prenatal classes or words of advice. One morning
you wake up and there is this doll-size person redefining
life for you. Suddenly, the most important job you have
is to keep that precious little person safe.

Parenting is much easier when it's shared. When our
newborn, Molly, would keep us up half the night, it
was my wife who said, "We can get through this."
When temper tantrums and terrible twos became
household words, my wife said, "It's a stage. It'll pass."
She was the one who had the optimism, the patience
and the uncanny ability to know what was wrong.

Unfortunately, my wife died when Molly was twelve.
Now I find myself a single parent to a sixteen-year-old
and asking myself, "How am I ever going to get
through this?"

Molly thinks I'm overprotective. And she's right. I
want to keep her close to me, but I know she needs
to test her wings, to make her own choices, to become
her own person. That's why I agreed to let her spend
the summer in Montana.

It isn't easy letting her go. It seems like only yesterday
I was giving her piggyback rides to bed and telling her
stories. Now she's driving my car and telling *me* stories.
Is it a stage and will it pass? This father sure hopes so.

Harrison Drake

Please address questions and book requests to: Harlequin Reader Service
U.S.: 3010 Walden Ave., P.O. Box 1325, Buffalo, NY 14269
Canadian: P.O. Box 609, Fort Erie, Ont. L2A 5X3

WESTERN *Lovers*™

PAMELA BAUER

HIS AND HERS

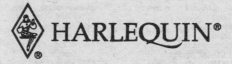

TORONTO • NEW YORK • LONDON
AMSTERDAM • PARIS • SYDNEY • HAMBURG
STOCKHOLM • ATHENS • TOKYO • MILAN • MADRID
PRAGUE • WARSAW • BUDAPEST • AUCKLAND

HARLEQUIN BOOKS
225 Duncan Mill Road, Don Mills,
Ontario, Canada M3B 3K9

ISBN 0-373-30162-6

HIS AND HERS

Copyright © 1987 by Pamela Muelbauer

Visit us at www.eHarlequin.com

Printed in U.S.A.

CHAPTER ONE

"SHE IS NOT COMING with us." Jenna Morgan shoved a plate of bacon and eggs in front of her son with an action that contradicted the equanimity of her tone. Cody caught the sliding plate before it hit the edge of the table.

"Aww, come on, Mom, why not?" he asked, then bit into the whole wheat toast and washed it down with a gulp of orange juice.

"For starters, I barely know the girl, and what I do know doesn't exactly impress me. That girl is aggressive with a capital A. You're going to Cheyenne to ride horses—not romance a girl." A second plate of bacon and eggs slid in the direction of Cody's grandfather, who upon stopping the stoneware, cast a questioning look at its contents.

"Your mother's got a point, Cody," Hank Foster interjected, poking at an egg with his fork. He held a slice of toast in his other hand, ready to mop up what he hoped would be a lightly cooked yolk, but was forced to slap the egg onto the bread when the yolk proved to be solid. He couldn't prevent the disgruntled sigh. "You don't want to be messing your head up with thoughts of a girl when you need your mind to be on the bucking horses."

"She won't be messing up my head, Grandpa," Cody insisted. "Molly knows how important the rodeo is to me, and I want her to be there when I ride."

Something in his tone made Jenna's chest constrict. Cody had never lacked for female attention, but it was uncharacteristic of him to want to have a girl following him around like some rodeo groupie. That was time usually reserved for other cowboys. Never before had he wanted a girl to "be there" for him, but then, never before had he been so adamantly pursued by a girl like Molly Drake, a spoiled little rich girl who was used to having her way with members of the opposite sex.

For six weeks Jenna had been trying to ignore her presence in the small town of Red Lodge, Montana. The young girl had created quite a stir with her Bloomingdale's wardrobe and her private-school colloquialisms. She had used all of her feminine wiles to capture Cody's attention, and Jenna had watched her son slowly succumb to the girl from New York City. Jenna had tried to discourage the relationship, but had been reluctant to show too much disapproval for fear of alienating her son.

However, this trip to Cheyenne was business. And if there was anything Jenna could do to keep Molly from interfering with that business, she wouldn't have any second thoughts about doing it. The Frontier Days Rodeo was one of the top-paying rodeos in the country. A win for Cody would not only establish his name in bronco riding, but would boost his college fund as well. Outwardly Cody was often seen as wild and reckless, but Jenna knew that on the inside he was like his father, gentle and sensitive. What he didn't need was to be taken for a ride by a city girl who would leave Montana at the end of the summer and return to her preppy friends in New York.

"Cody, we booked this rodeo almost a year ago and we are darned lucky to be the trick riders. We're a team—me, you, J.T. and Tracey. It's always been the four of us going down the road. As it is, we barely have enough room for the two of us in the trailer. Where would this girl sleep?" Jenna sat down opposite her son at the wooden kitchen table, a mug of steaming coffee in front of her.

"Mom, she's from New York. She wouldn't want to sleep in a horse trailer. She'd get a motel room."

Cody's inflection on "horse trailer" had Jenna's fingers clenching the blue mug. "Not at this short notice. You know what motel accommodations are like during Frontier Days. There won't be a room to be found. But it doesn't matter." She took a sip of the hot liquid, then set her mug down with a thud that sounded like a judge's gavel. "She's not going."

"Well, then, just maybe I won't go either." Cody got up from the table and threw down his napkin, and with three long strides was out the back door.

Jenna's boots clicked in a staccato rhythm as she stalked across the kitchen to where the screen door bounced back and forth against the doorjamb. "Cody Morgan, you come back here!" she called out into the cool morning air. "It's your turn for KP." But Cody kept on walking until his lanky figure disappeared behind the barn.

When Jenna would have gone after him, a large hand on her shoulder stopped her. "Leave him be, girl," her father's gentle voice urged. "He's just a normal seventeen-year-old boy who's had his head turned by a pretty girl." He watched the play of emotions across her face, the brown eyes unable to hide the frustration, the small white teeth unable to still the trembling lower lip.

"Dad, the last thing Cody needs is a girl chasing him down to Cheyenne."

"Correct me if my memory deceives me, but weren't you about his age when you ran off with one Jack Morgan to the rodeo in Nebraska? Don't you remember how exasperated your mother and I were when you were determined to go after him?"

"I did not run after him." She emphasized each word of the denial. "You're forgetting I was also competing in the rodeo."

"Yup—after turning down the opportunity to make big money in the Texas circuit just so you could go down the road with a bull rider. You were the world-champion barrel racer competing for peanuts, and all because of a man." Hank ambled back over to the table and eased himself down onto the ladderback chair to finish his breakfast.

Jenna's chin rose and she refused to look in her father's direction. After a few moments of silence she said, "If Molly Drake were any of the girls from Red Lodge, you know I wouldn't be objecting. But she has no more interest in Cody's welfare than the broncs he'll be riding in Cheyenne...and she's far more dangerous."

"She's certainly ruffled your feathers, hasn't she?" He finished the remainder of his coffee, then carried his dishes over to the sink. "Personally, I don't think she's so bad."

"Dad!" Jenna turned with her hands on her hips. "You've seen the way she struts around here in her tight blue jeans doing her best to distract Cody from his chores. I bet she phones him at least ten times a day." She crossed the small space separating the two of them. "And I wish you wouldn't do Cody's dishes for him," she added upon seeing her father rinsing the plates. "Just because we have an argument doesn't let him off the hook for his kitchen duties."

Hank dismissed her comments with a shrug of his rounded shoulders and continued to do the dishes. "It seems to me Molly Drake's problem is that she's lonesome. It doesn't sound as though she gets much attention from that father of hers."

"Dad, I've heard all about the governesses and boarding schools," Jenna replied impatiently.

"Did you know that her mother died when she was twelve—the same age Cody was when he lost his father?"

"No, Cody didn't tell me that."

"No, I didn't think he had. Every hair on that pretty little raven-haired head of yours bristles whenever he mentions her name." He looked back over one shoulder as he talked. "The fact that her father's shipped her out here to spend her summer vacation with a woman like Eleanor Fielding must stir a little sympathy in you. Granted, the woman is her great-aunt, but it makes you wonder what kind of father this Mr. Drake is."

"Well, if he's anything like his aunt, then I suppose I could muster up a little sympathy for Molly. If anyone can keep a child in line it's Eleanor Fielding. Rumor has it she used to rap knuckles with a ruler when students wouldn't sit still for piano lessons," Jenna said, frowning. "She must be mellowing as she grows older. The Eleanor Fielding I know would never allow her great-niece to be seen in the company of a Foster. I'm surprised she'd give her permission for Molly to come with us to Cheyenne."

"It does come as somewhat of a surprise, I must admit," her father agreed. "Maybe she's softening in her old age. Just the other day I heard that she's been giving old Barney Waters piano lessons. Can you believe it?"

"Well, who else is there left for her to teach? She's been

through everyone who's anyone in the Red Lodge social register. I'm surprised she never went back East after her husband died. Eleanor's got to be well into her seventies.''

"Seventy-three, according to my calculations," Hank said. "I think the reason she stays here in Montana is because she's afraid she wouldn't fit in with the society folks in New York anymore. Here in Red Lodge she can be the star attraction on the society page and queen bee at the women's club. I would guess that a girl Molly's age, however, would be a lot for her to handle.''

"All the more reason for Molly's father not to send her out here. You and I know what it's like trying to keep a tight rein on a teenager. While Mr. Drake sits in his fancy New York penthouse counting his money, his daughter's on the loose in Red Lodge chasing after my son." Jenna snorted as she cleared the remainder of the dishes from the table.

"Maybe she just needs a little affection," Hank remarked, which brought a click of Jenna's tongue. "Would it be so bad if she went along?"

"Yes, it would," Jenna affirmed. "Cody's seventeen and this is his chance to win big. The money is for his future—the girl isn't. What he needs in Cheyenne is a good horse, not a girl."

"I'm afraid your son doesn't see it that way."

Jenna shrugged. "He'll come around. I'd better go work Snow Velvet." She grabbed her straw hat from the coatrack near the door. "If you're going to do Cody's chores he should at least have to take your turn at cooking breakfast tomorrow."

"I'd rather he took yours. You overcooked the eggs again."

Once more, the screen door teetered back and forth after being slammed shut.

IN A GRAND OLD HOUSE on Main Street, Molly Drake sat at a Steinway piano, her back erect, blond head poised, while her fingers danced across the piano keys. Concentration and determination etched her usually gamine features. She had resolved to give the performance of a lifetime. She would play the Chopin concerto perfectly, for music was the only way to reach the taciturn Eleanor Fielding.

Stealing a surreptitious glance Molly saw that her great-aunt sat entranced in the Louis XIV chair as though she were being transported celestially, her facial expression not unlike those of the saintly images placed strategically about the house. As the final chords faded into silence, Molly dropped her head in a dramatic gesture after seeing the tiniest twitch of a smile on her great-aunt's wrinkled lips.

I ought to get up and curtsy, Molly thought to herself, but chose to wait for the sigh of approval she knew was forthcoming. For whenever Eleanor was extremely satisfied with a piece of music, she emitted a low moaning that might prompt a stranger to reach for the smelling salts, but which, Molly knew, meant ecstatic approval. Just when she thought the crick in her neck would force her to straighten, Eleanor moaned.

"That was lovely, Millicent." She always called Molly by her christened name when she sat at the piano. "I do so wish your father could have witnessed that splendid performance. Then he'd understand why I say you ought to be studying at the conservatory." Eleanor's ample figure shifted in the chair.

The mere mention of the conservatory was enough to cause Molly to shudder inwardly. If there was one subject she didn't want to study, it was piano. Nor did she want to be a musician. But if talk of concert performances and studying with the masters made Eleanor Fielding more approachable, then Molly would oblige. Today she would be willing to feign an interest in tatting if it meant a sympathetic ear from her great-aunt.

After several minutes, Molly finally summoned the courage to approach the subject dearest to her heart.

"Aunt Eleanor, I've been meaning to talk to you about something." She rose from the piano bench and went to sit on the footstool at the older woman's feet.

"About your music, dear?" The voice was unusually eager.

"My music is coming along beautifully." Molly stifled the memories of countless hours of practice she had been enduring since arriving in Red Lodge. "Actually, I wanted to ask your permission to go away for a few days…to Wyoming."

"Wyoming?" Eleanor repeated the name as though Molly had said China.

"Yes. To the Frontier Days Celebration in Cheyenne. It's this wonderful event where they have all sorts of things to do. There's a carnival—"

"I know all about the Frontier Days Celebration," Eleanor cut in, her tone haughty. "It's mainly for cowboys, and quite frankly, I don't think you and your friend Lisa should be around such a rowdy group of people."

"Lisa?"

"You would be going with Lisa and her parents, wouldn't you? I know they go every summer to see the rodeo," she remarked, the distasteful frown making it obvious she didn't understand why.

"I wasn't planning on going with Lisa, Aunt Eleanor." Molly looked down as her fingers began to pleat her voile skirt.

"Well, if it isn't Lisa, then which girlfriend is it?" Eleanor asked, leaning forward slightly.

"It's not one of the girls you introduced me to. It's another friend I met while I was riding. His name is—"

"*His* name? You mean it's a boy?" Eleanor made a noise that sounded to Molly as though she had sucked in a great deal of air. "Oh, my dear! No, Molly. Your father would never approve of you going off to some rodeo with a boy."

"But my father doesn't need to know," Molly blurted out without thinking.

"Doesn't need to know?" Eleanor parroted in a higher octave. "You're sixteen and your father has entrusted you to my care, young lady. Of course he must know. And I'm certain he would never approve of you going away with a boy."

"But it isn't like I'm going away with a boy. Cody's mother would be chaperoning," she pleaded. "You must know Mrs. Morgan—she's the lady who runs the barrel-racing school for girls. Lisa's taken lessons from her."

"Morgan? Jenna Morgan?" Aunt Eleanor nearly choked on the words. "You want to go away with the *Morgans?*" The color drained from her face causing Molly to fear that Eleanor was going to faint. She quickly picked up a piece of newspaper and started fanning the paper-white cheeks.

"Auntie, I don't understand. What's wrong with the Morgans? Cody's the cutest guy in Red Lodge, and his mother—"

"Please, Molly, stop," the older woman interrupted, raising a palm in supplication. "Please, don't mention that name in this house again. I can't allow you to go traipsing off across the country with a family like the Morgans. And that's that." She shrugged off Molly's solicitous arm and stood up. "I'm sorry, but I really can't discuss this any further. Now, while you finish practicing, I'm going to do my correspondence." Straightening the skirt of her paisley dress, she waltzed out of the room as though personally affronted.

Molly could have cried with frustration. And she would have told Aunt Eleanor a thing or two, had it not been for her fear that her father would learn of her involvement with Cody and make her return to New York. And then where would she be? She might never see Cody again. No, what she needed to do was placate her aunt. Above all else, she had to spend the rest of the summer in Montana, for she couldn't bear to think about leaving Cody.

Of all the girls in Red Lodge, she was the one who had succeeded in capturing his attention. But a boy's heart could be fickle and several days in a carnival town could result in losing the only person she had ever truly loved. She simply couldn't let him go alone. One way or another, she was going to Cheyenne.

IT WAS BARELY SUNRISE when Jenna and Cody loaded the horses into the trailer and prepared for the long drive to Cheyenne. Because of the mountainous terrain and the fact that they were transporting horses meant making frequent stops, they were leaving a day early to allow for any unforeseen circumstances that could delay their arrival. If everything went according to schedule, they would reach their destination by dusk. But right now, as Jenna looked to the eastern horizon, rain interrupted the sun's efforts to break through the gray clouds, creating what appeared to be strands of lint in a mellow yellow sky.

"All set?" She glanced at her son who was pulling on a faded denim jacket to ward off the chill in the early-morning air.

Cody nodded, then climbed into the cab of the pickup. He had been sullen since their disagreement several days ago, but Jenna was relieved that at least he was going to the rodeo. For a while she had worried that he would refuse. But the horse trailer was hitched behind his pickup and they were ready to leave.

"I hope it isn't going to rain all the way." She glanced once more at the murky sky. "I suppose we'd better get going if we're going to meet J.T. and Tracey in Casper." Jenna's brother and sister-in-law owned a saddle shop in Red Lodge and usually the four of them traveled together. But this time J.T. and Tracey had decided to visit relatives en route to the rodeo and had arranged for Cody and Jenna to meet them in Casper, which was north of Cheyenne.

"What about Roy?" Hank asked, leaning against the open door, his Stetson tipped far enough back to reveal his receding hairline.

"What about him?" Jenna asked.

"I thought Roy was going to follow you out since J.T. and Tracey left yesterday." He gave her an endearing paternal look that had Jenna smiling to herself.

"Dad, Cody and I can manage just fine." She squeezed his forearm reassuringly. "We don't need anyone following us all the way to Cheyenne…especially not Roy Cooper." Roy had been trying unsuccessfully for years to convince Jenna that they were made for each other. It was true that they shared many common interests, including a love of horses and the rodeo. But what Roy saw as Jenna's stubborn streak was actually her independent nature, a nature that balked at the thought of a man taking charge of her life. If Roy had his way, she would never heave another pitchfork of straw or rope another stray calf. For as much as Roy admired Jenna's equestrian skills, he was a traditional man at heart, insisting that Jenna took on far too many of the ranch responsibilities—responsibilities a man should have. It wasn't that she didn't appreciate his thoughtfulness; she simply didn't need a man who wanted to wrap her in a warm blanket and cosset her.

"Maybe I should be going along this time," Hank suggested, "but I'm not sure if my back would hold out."

Jenna knew that it wasn't his back that kept him from going along, but his memories. The rodeo had been a way of life for her parents ever since she could remember. But after her mother died, her father seemed to lose all interest in the sport. In fact, he had appeared to lose interest in life until one fateful night when Jack Morgan's plane crashed into the side of a mountain. Hank had responded to his daughter's cry for help and ever since had taken his place on the Lost Creek Ranch. But not once had he been to a rodeo.

"You want to give it a try, Dad?" Jenna prodded gently.

"Naw...I'll stay and take care of things here."

"I know you will," she replied, giving him a hug. "We'd better get going." She put her booted foot on the chrome running board and climbed into the pickup. "Wish us luck."

Hank closed the door for her. "I'll be waiting by the radio to hear the results." He walked around and shook hands with Cody. "Good luck, Son, and don't forget—ride 'em high and don't let up on the spurring."

"Thanks, Grandpa."

"I know you'll do well—rodeo's in your blood." And with a salute of his cowboy hat, Hank stepped back and watched the blue and white pickup pull the horse trailer down the dusty road leading from the ranch to the main highway.

Jenna looked curiously at her son and thought about her father's parting words. Rodeo. It had been in their blood for so long, how could Cody not want to be a part of it? Her grandmother had been one of the pioneer women champions, able to compete with men on an equal basis. She had been a trick roper and a trick rider in Buffalo Bill Cody's Wild West Show. Jenna herself had learned to stand on a horse at the age of five, and many days after school she would help her mother break and gentle horses. Now, some thirty years later, she was still riding horses standing up and still competing in barrel racing. Someday she would have to give it up. But the question was, how would she leave it all behind?

She thought about the promising future ahead for Cody, yet

he lacked enthusiasm for this rodeo. Was his reluctance due to Molly Drake's absence? After several miles of silence, Jenna finally broached the subject.

"Cody, you're not still sore at me because I wouldn't let you bring your girlfriend along are you?"

"Nope."

"Are you looking forward to seeing the guys again?"

"Yup."

"Are you sure nothing's bothering you?"

"Nope."

"Well, then, would you stop yupping and noping me and talk to me!" Jenna exclaimed.

"I'm sorry, Mom. It's just that Molly and I broke up."

"Oh." Jenna wasn't sure if she should probe further. "Do you want to talk about it?" she finally asked.

"There's nothing to talk about, really. I simply decided I didn't want to go steady."

Jenna felt a giant wave of relief wash over her. "I think that's a wise decision." She studied his profile, noting the strong chin and hawkish nose. He had Jack's sharp features and tall stature but her coloring and bone structure, which made him a lanky cowboy sought after by many a girl in Red Lodge. Not that he needed to worry; there was plenty of time in the future for girls. First of all there was college to complete, for Jenna knew that the degree in animal science was a must if he wanted to compete in the stock-contracting business. That had been their goal since Jack had died—to furnish livestock to the rodeos. A win at Cheyenne would put them one step closer to that goal. Thank God Molly Drake had been left behind. Once Cody joined the rest of the cowboys he'd forget all about the girl from New York City.

"SHE'S GONE!"

At first Harrison Drake thought he had a poor telephone connection and the crackling sound was due to crossed wires. But then he realized the voice belonged to his aunt and it was her hysterical hiccuping creating the static on the line.

"Did you hear me, Harrison? I said, Molly's gone!"

"What do you mean, she's 'gone'?" He sat up and swung his legs over the edge of the bed.

"She's gone to Wyoming!"

"Wyoming?" he repeated, shrugging his arms into the navy smoking jacket he found at the foot of the bed. "Eleanor, start at the beginning and tell me exactly what happened."

"This morning Molly asked if she could borrow my car to do some shopping, and of course I agreed. She's been such a sweet thing around the house lately and we had been having such a wonderful, productive summer. You should hear her play, Harrison. She's made the most remarkable progress." Her voice broke slightly. "I had no idea that she would pull a stunt like this."

"What stunt, Eleanor?" Harrison asked impatiently.

"Well, when she still wasn't back by dinnertime, I began to worry. So I went and looked in her room and I noticed that her suitcase was missing from the closet and all of her makeup was gone from the vanity. She's run away to Wyoming!"

"Why would she go to Wyoming? You told me last week that everything was going smoothly."

"It was...or at least she fooled me into believing it was. Of all the respectable young gentlemen here in town I don't understand why she had to choose that cowboy for a beau."

"Are you telling me she's run off with a cowboy?" Harrison practically bellowed the words.

"I can't believe it myself," she sobbed. "I should have called you the other day when she asked my permission to travel with this boy to watch him ride in the rodeo. But I had no indication that she'd disobey me and run off with him. I should have realized that a Morgan could corrupt a saint. And everyone in Red Lodge knows that Jenna Morgan can't control that teenage son of hers. He hasn't a father, and with a mother who spends more time with her horses than her son, it's no surprise the boy's a roughneck."

"You're certain Molly's with this boy?"

"She left me a note. Shall I read it to you?"

"If you would." Harrison leaned over, his elbows on his knees, his left palm supporting his forehead.

Dear Auntie

I know you are going to be upset when you read this, but I've gone to Cheyenne. I'm sorry I took your car, but you see, I can't bear to be separated from Cody. Please forgive me.

Molly

P.S. Don't worry, Cody's mother will take care of me.

"That's it? No phone number or address where she can be reached?"

"None."

"Damn!" He swore under his breath. "Have you tried this Morgan woman's home?"

"I did. She left for Wyoming yesterday, according to the boy's grandfather, but I suspect they only left today."

"And you think Molly was with them?"

"He claims she wasn't, but she could have met them in town. After all, it would be just like Jenna Morgan to encourage Molly's defiance. Everyone in Red Lodge knows that son of hers does exactly as he pleases, and with his mother's blessing. I just shudder to think what those two children could be doing under her very own nose."

The images flashing before Harrison's eyes brought a grimace of distaste to the handsome face. He could just picture his daughter under the influence of a rough, tough Annie Oakley type.

"I'm catching the next flight to Cheyenne, Eleanor."

"But how will you ever find them?"

"Believe me, Eleanor, I'll find them. You just let me handle this and try not to worry." His hand shook with anger as he replaced the receiver.

He picked up the silver photo frame from the bedside table and shook his head slowly. Molly was a carbon copy of her mother—in both looks and temperament. After four years he still felt that sick feeling in his gut when he thought of his wife. Would Molly be behaving any differently if Rita were still alive? He'd asked himself that question innumerable times in the past four years. But what good was second-guessing? Rita was gone and never coming back. But Molly... Oh, what was he going to do with Molly? Why was there this huge gulf between the two of them? Sometimes it appeared as though his daughter hated him, and he wondered if Molly was the same child who at seven had ridden him piggyback up the stairs and insisted he read her a bedtime story every night. She was his own flesh and blood yet he couldn't communicate with her. Was it because every time he looked at her he saw Rita and it hurt?

He glanced around the opulently furnished bedroom. They had the best that money could buy. Molly had been educated at prestigious private schools and moved in a social circle where she could date any number of boys who came from the same background as she did. Instead she chose to deliberately flaunt her escapades in his face. First it had been a punk-rock musician and his flock of undesirable companions. Then there was the motorcycle racer who thought carrying Molly's books to class had to be accomplished by riding his Harley-Davidson through the corridors of Bronwyn Academy. That episode had resulted in Molly being asked to find another school at the end of her junior year.

Now she was involved with a rodeo cowboy, and Harrison was going to have to miss what his gut was telling him was going to be one of the biggest days in trading on the stock market. Tomorrow, instead of making multimillion-dollar decisions as the director and executive vice president of one of the country's largest investment management companies, he would be chasing after a cowboy.

He had thought this summer vacation with Aunt Eleanor would be beneficial to both Molly and him. Away from some of her less desirable peer influences Molly would be able to direct her abundant energy into her music and he would be able to clear up several business commitments that had forced him to spend too many nights at the office. Maybe he had been naive. After all, if he couldn't handle her in New York, what made him think an elderly woman would fare any better in the wide-open spaces of the West?

Well, one thing was for certain: he had to bring her back from Montana. He couldn't expect Eleanor to be put through the emotional strain Molly's behavior precipitated.

He punched seven buttons on the phone at his fingertips.

"Diana, it's Harrison. I'm sorry to have to call you at this hour, but something's come up and you're going to have to take over for me at the board meeting tomorrow. I have to fly to Wyoming."

CHAPTER TWO

"HEY, JENNA! Walt sent word over there's some city slicker looking for Cody at the back gate." J. T. Foster's voice carried loudly as he stepped out of the barn into the bright sunlight to where Jenna was walking her Arabian gelding, Snow Velvet.

Jenna automatically glanced across the parking lot to the grandstands and chute area before looking back to her brother. They had only been in Cheyenne two days, yet she would guess that J.T. knew the names of all the rodeo personnel taking part in the Frontier Days celebration. That was part of his effervescent personality. As long as a man liked horses, he was J.T.'s friend.

Being the youngest and the smallest of Jenna's three brothers, he had earned the name The Little Firecracker when as a six-year-old he would ride his Shetland pony and chase after small goats. Growing up in a rodeo-oriented family, he was soon chasing calves and eventually became a five-time world-champion calf roper. Now thirty-one, he had cut back on the number of calf-roping events he entered and concentrated on the art his mother and grandmother had taught him—trick roping. There was only one other person who could match his skills with a rope and that was Jenna, which was why the two of them had decided to create the specialty act. It was a way for both of them to do what they loved most—ride horses and rodeo.

"Cody's probably over at the pens studying his draw. Do you know who this fellow is?" she asked, leading the horse over to her brother.

"Nope. Only that it's some guy dressed as though this was Wall Street rather than Frontier Park." J.T. squinted, then adjusted the straw cowboy hat dyed a bright lime green to match the color of his riding costume.

"Maybe it's a reporter wanting an interview," Jenna suggested.

"If it were someone from the media he would have used his press pass," he reasoned. "Listen, if you want to help Tracey with her rigging, I can go and see what he wants with Cody."

"No, that's all right." Jenna put a hand on his arm. "I'll do it. I've already warmed up Snow Velvet."

"Okay, but don't be wasting any time. By the way, how's the ankle?" He pointed to her left foot.

"Fine."

"I bet. How much tape do you have on it?" He bent down to look at her foot, but she stopped him with a hand on his shoulder.

"James Thomas Foster, I've performed with worse injuries than a little old twist to my ankle. Besides, I could do that somersault and land on one foot if I had to."

J.T. straightened and said, "I wasn't suggesting you not perform."

"I should hope not," she replied indignantly. "I've seen you ride with three cracked ribs."

"I guess we're tough stock, Sis." He smiled his lopsided grin, then aimed a fake punch at her jaw. "You'd better get going, we're on in fifteen minutes," he reminded her as he turned to head back toward the barn.

With a graceful ease, Jenna mounted the Arabian and trotted toward the entrance gate. From a distance she could see Walt McCoy's short, thick figure leaning against the bright gold road barrier, but no sign of any businessman. Then, as Walt noticed her approaching, he waved his arm and from behind the small white booth emerged a tall, fair-haired man dressed in a dark three-piece suit. For a moment Jenna thought it was Robert Redford—Robert Redford the legal eagle, not Robert Redford the electric horseman.

A closer look, however, told her that the resemblance ended with the blond hair and slightly crooked nose. Robert Redford wouldn't have looked out of place ankle-deep in dust, nor would his hair be damp with perspiration. He always managed to appear unflappable, unlike this man whose patience seemed to have disappeared with the shine on his Italian leather shoes. Even with a tight-lipped grimace, Robert Redford looked charming; this man simply looked angry.

With a light flick of her wrist, Jenna brought the horse to a halt in front of the gate.

"This here gentleman is looking for Cody, Jenna." The gate-keeper acknowledged Harrison with a nod.

"It's okay, Walt," she assured him, then watched as he raised the heavy wooden arm of the road barrier for Harrison to pass through.

At that moment Snow Velvet chose to display his impatience, sidestepping with a snort and a smart swish of his tail, which produced an almost comic reaction in the stranger who back-tracked with incredible speed. Jenna's surprised gaze met his, and it was only the look in his blue eyes that kept her amusement in check. She had worked with horses too long not to recognize that look. The illusion was now completely shattered—Robert Redford was not afraid of horses.

"Looks like he's ready to go," Walt commented as Snow Velvet tossed his head.

Jenna glanced over at Harrison who had retreated another foot or so. "You don't have to worry," she said. "He's well broke." Seeing his dubious look, she added, "Really, performing horses have even temperaments. He's just feeling a little edgy because he's ready to work. You don't need to be afraid, Mr.—" The words of reassurance were accompanied by a smile, a smile Harrison thought hid a laugh.

"Drake…Harrison Drake," he supplied tersely. He was hot, dusty and tired, and what he didn't need right now was for some cowgirl—albeit a beautiful cowgirl—to be laughing at his apprehension over a beast that looked as though it wanted to do a tap dance on his chest. He would have preferred for her to climb down from the animal. He could feel his damp shirt clinging to his skin, and with an impatient gesture he shrugged out of the suit coat and slung it over his shoulder before taking a few hesitant steps closer to the horse.

Harrison Drake...Molly's father. Jenna mentally made the connection. Suddenly the three-piece suit and the Italian leather shoes fit. But what was he doing here in Cheyenne, looking as though she had offended him?

"I'm Jenna Morgan, Cody's mother," she said coolly, choosing to remain astride the milk gray gelding. "I understand you're looking for my son, Mr. Drake."

Harrison was momentarily taken aback. He had been expecting a strong, sturdy woman with large hands and sun-weathered skin, not a petite female who wore hot pink lamé like a second skin. She made a striking picture in her trick-riding costume with her honey gold complexion heavily made up for her upcoming performance. The silver-banded hot pink cowboy hat was cocked at an angle, concealing all of her hair except for the long dark braid that trailed down her back.

"I'm looking for your son because I believe Molly is with him."

"Molly's in Cheyenne?"

"Since you're responsible for her being here, I don't know why you should find that such a surprise." Harrison was irritated at having to look up at her as they talked.

"*I'm* responsible? Mr. Drake, the last time I saw your daughter she was in Red Lodge, Montana." Jenna disliked the angle of his strong jaw and the accusing tone of his voice.

"Mrs. Morgan, I happen to know for a fact that you invited my daughter to accompany your son to this—" he grimaced as if the word were distasteful "—this rodeo, even though you knew Mrs. Fielding was opposed to the idea."

"I did no such thing!" Jenna retorted. "Contrary to what Eleanor Fielding may have told you, Mr. Drake, I did not invite Molly along on this trip. Cody asked if she could come with us, but I refused."

"Did your son make the trip with you or on his own?" he questioned.

"Cody traveled with me," she assured him. "Mr. Drake, if Molly were with my son, I think I'd know about it. What makes you so sure she's here in Cheyenne?"

"Eleanor called me last night to tell me that Molly had taken her car, leaving behind a note that indicated she was coming here to Wyoming. Your son must have arranged for her to meet him here.''

"I don't see why. Cody told me he and Molly had broken up.''

"Well, obviously they haven't. Where is your son, Mrs. Morgan? I think I'd better speak to him myself.''

Jenna disliked his implication that Cody had lied to her.

"You'll have to wait until after he rides in his event. I don't want you accusing him of something he didn't do and upsetting his concentration.'' Jenna saw the glint in his eyes and the sideways movement of his jaw but refused to look away from his gaze.

"I think my daughter's welfare is a little more important than your son riding some damn bucking horse,'' he bit out through clenched teeth.

"It's wonderful to see such paternal concern for her welfare,'' she scoffed. "You're the one who shipped her out here like some unruly filly to be tamed by an old biddy like Eleanor Fielding.'' Snow Velvet, as if sensing Jenna's mood, shook his head and pawed the ground.

"Molly doesn't need to be tamed. Nor did she need to be lured into disobeying a gentle old woman by some young, reckless cowboy.''

"Now you wait just a minute, Mr. Drake. My son did not *lure* Molly anywhere. Ever since that daughter of yours flew into Red Lodge she's been chasing after Cody. He can't even go to church on Sunday without her snuggling up next to him in the pew. She's calling him morning, noon and night and following his every move. But the last straw was her begging to come rodeoing with him. At that point I put my foot down, and thank God, Cody saw reason. She didn't come along.''

Jenna's anger only added fuel to Harrison's growing frustration. He stiffened upon hearing his daughter criticized, and like a typical parent, he was unwilling to acknowledge at this point that Jenna could be telling the truth.

"Are you telling me that you don't think your son has seen

my daughter since he's been in Cheyenne?'' he demanded in a voice thick with disbelief.

"I'm telling you your daughter did not come with us. If she came to Cheyenne, it was of her own accord. I haven't seen her, and I doubt Cody has. He's here to compete in the rodeo and as far as I know, he's spent all of his free time with other cowboys, not Molly,'' she replied, shaking aside the tiny niggling of doubt that was trying to burrow its way into her mind.

"I'd like to ask him that myself. Where is he?''

It was then that Jenna heard J.T.'s voice. Turning, she saw Tracey waving in the distance. "Look, I have to go. I'll talk to Cody and see if he knows where Molly is—not that it will do any good.''

"I'm not leaving here until I find out where my daughter is,'' he assured her.

"Very well. I'll speak to Cody as soon as he's finished his ride. If you give me the name of your hotel I'll call you when we're through.''

Harrison withdrew a business card from the inner pocket of his suit coat and penned a number on the back. Jenna reached up and removed the hot pink hat, then tucked the card into the silver braided hatband, before replacing it at the same cocky angle.

"When you do find your daughter, Mr. Morgan, do us all a favor and take her back to the Big Apple.''

Jenna shifted in the saddle, cuing her horse with her weight, her legs and a light touch on the reins. Snow Velvet settled onto his haunches, spun a very precise 180-degree turn and loped away, leaving a frustrated Harrison staring after her, acutely aware of the graceful picture horse and rider made. Jenna Morgan's bright pink figure was a sharp contrast to the milk-colored Arabian, who from a distance appeared to be the purest of whites.

Jenna rode Snow Velvet to an open space under the trees. Looking down and stroking his neck, she smiled softly and said, "We aren't going to let a New Yorker upset us, are we?'' Swinging her right leg over the horse's hindquarters, she dismounted and led him by the reins, studying the way his hooves

struck the ground. Then she walked over to the arena entrance
to wait with Tracey and J.T. for their act to be announced.

"What was that all about, Jenna?" J.T. asked.

"Nothing important," she said a little stiffly. "I'll tell you all
about it later." She adjusted the rhinestone belt around her waist
and double-checked the lacings on her soft leather riding shoes.
She pushed all thoughts of Harrison Drake and his daughter
Molly from her mind. Right now she needed to concentrate on
the mood of her horse and the condition of the ground.

"Snow Velvet's looking a little skittish. Do you think we
ought to scratch the double somersault?" Tracey asked, concern
mirrored in her blue eyes. Although she had been riding for
fifteen of her twenty-four years and loved horses, she possessed
a characteristic she felt her husband and sister-in-law both
lacked—caution.

"No. He's fine...he's just a little wound up." Jenna leaned
over and patted her horse's neck.

Tracey's face revealed her skepticism. "But what about your
ankle? J.T. said you twisted it yesterday in practice. You know
we could do the flag routine instead. The crowd loves that number."

Jenna smiled at the girl she had come to love like a sister.
"Honestly, Trace, there's nothing wrong with my ankle." She
shot her brother a warning glance. "I'm fine and Snow Velvet's
fine. Now let's go out there and put on a good show!"

While the three trick riders were waiting to perform, Harrison
Drake was crossing the dirt parking lot, intent upon finding the
young cowboy he knew would lead him to his daughter. He
wasn't about to sit and wait at some rustic motel for a cowgirl
to call.

"Identification, please," the man dressed in the gray security
uniform called out as Harrison tried to gain access behind the
chutes.

"A Mrs. Morgan asked me to meet her back here," he tried,
but to no avail.

"Uh-uh. Only contestants are allowed back here. No ID, no
admission."

Harrison reached into his pocket and withdrew several bills.

"Look. It's important that I talk to one of the bronc riders who's competing in the rodeo this afternoon. You see, my daughter is with him and there's been a family emergency."

"If he's a bronc rider your daughter ain't with him," the guard said in a matter-of-fact manner, ignoring the proffered money. "No women are allowed back of the chutes. It's rules. Only contestants and stock pass through this gate."

Harrison heaved a sigh of frustration and dragged the back of his hand across his forehead. The heat was enervating, and what he needed right now was a long, cool shower in an air-conditioned room. He just prayed the motel wasn't as big a disappointment as the rental car he was driving. Because of Frontier Days Celebration, the closest motel room available was in a small town called Pine Bluffs, which his travel agent assured him was only an hour's drive from Cheyenne—an hour in a car lacking air-conditioning and looking as though it belonged on a miniature racetrack in some amusement park rather than traversing mountain roads.

"You wouldn't happen to know where these cowboys go after they finish riding?" Harrison asked, trying to restrain the impatience that was gnawing away at his insides.

"Probably back to the trailer park," the guard said in his slow, twangy drawl. "Most of 'em stay across the street either in their vans or travel trailers. Of course, those that win usually go out celebratin' at the Longhorn Saloon. That's just three blocks down off the main highway."

"You're certain I couldn't just slip in and out? Five minutes is all I'd need," Harrison tried once more.

"Rules is rules." The guard turned his angular head and spit a wad of tobacco over the fence. "The only way you're gonna get to see a bronc rider is to buy a ticket and watch from the grandstand."

Harrison stuffed the bills into the guard's chest pocket, then headed for the ticket booth. Once inside the grandstand, he battled his way up to the chain link fence separating the rodeo arena from the spectators. He had hoped that if Molly was prohibited from watching Cody ride from behind the scenes, she would have purchased a ticket to watch from the grandstand bleachers.

But when he saw the size of the crowd, he knew that to search for his daughter would be futile. Quickly scanning the rodeo program, he found Cody's name listed in the bareback-riding event and decided to get something cold to drink while he waited for that phase of the competition.

Standing in the midst of a sea of ten-gallon cowboy hats a few minutes later, Harrison attempted to balance his suit coat, a hot dog smothered in relish, and a cup of draft beer. The loud-speaker was directly overhead the concession area, and he could hear the announcer's good-natured banter with the rodeo clown who had the sell-out crowd exploding with laughter. But it was the conversation of the two men passing by that caught his attention.

"We'd better get back to our seats. They got those trick riders up next and I hear tell they got a couple of the prettiest little things who not only look good but can ride as well."

"Oh…you're talking about Jenna Morgan. I used to watch her when she was just a kid running barrels. Wait till you see the way she…"

They began walking up to the bleachers and the rest of the conversation was inaudible to Harrison. He dumped his empty plastic cup in a waste receptacle and unfolded the rolled-up program he had previously stuck in his pocket. Sure enough. On page fifteen was a large color photo of the Flying Fosters—two women and one man dressed in hot pink, lime green and bright yellow lamé. Each one stood on the back of a horse, arms extended in a V. Harrison immediately recognized the dark-haired beauty on the horse named Snow Velvet. He pushed his way back out into the sweltering July sun, shading his eyes with his hand in an effort to get a glimpse of the performers.

The first two riders had already entered the arena by the time Harrison had elbowed his way to a spot affording him a complete view of the track. The other female—a blonde—was, according to the program, not only an excellent horsewoman, but Jenna's sister-in-law as well. Although she was slim, she appeared to have a larger bone structure and looked to be the stronger of the two. But Harrison was soon to learn how deceptive appearances could be, for the petite woman he had confronted earlier made her grand entrance, suspended by one foot while her delicate limbs hung precariously over one side of the gray gelding, her dark braid brushing the dirt as she came dangerously close to hitting the ground. After circling the arena, she climbed back on top of the horse and showed her appreciation of the crowd's applause by standing at attention as the horse galloped the length of the grandstand.

Harrison was mesmerized by her dazzling performance. She appeared to have the strength of a gymnast yet the grace of a dancer as she performed a series of acrobatic maneuvers that had the crowd rising to its feet in applause. What he couldn't understand was where she found the nerve to perform such dangerous stunts. Well, Aunt Eleanor had said she was a wild thing—gutsy might be a better description, Harrison thought, as once more she astounded the crowd by crawling under the belly of her galloping horse. What Aunt Eleanor hadn't told him was that she was also beautiful. He found he couldn't take his eyes off her—not even as she waited in the background while the other riders performed individually.

When it was time for the trio's grand finale, Harrison felt his stomach contract when he heard the announcer tell the crowd that Jenna was about to execute a double somersault from the back of one horse onto another. No wonder she had snickered at his obvious dislike of horses—she had absolutely no fear of the animals. He watched her leap onto the back of the black gelding called Midnight Dream while Tracey made sure Snow Velvet was loping directly behind. Then J.T. tossed her a red-and-white striped hoop and within seconds she had jumped into the air, somersaulted through the hoop and made a perfect landing on Snow Velvet. While the crowd roared its approval, she swooped down to pick up the hot pink hat, then joined the other two riders in a final parade around the arena, waving and smiling.

"Wooo...eee! Ain't she a high-spirited beauty," a cowboy beside him commented aloud as Jenna passed in front of the grandstand, and Harrison would have wagered the man wasn't talking about the horse. He had a difficult time believing that this daring horsewoman was probably as old as he, with a teen-age son.

JENNA HAD MISSED Cody's first ride of the day, but now that the specialty act was over, she made certain Snow Velvet was cool enough to stand, quickly sponged him off and put him in his stall with a little hay and water. Then she rushed back to the arena to watch the rest of the rodeo with Tracey, while J.T. helped out behind the chutes. Cody had drawn an excellent bucking horse for the afternoon's event, and she was certain that if he could just stay on the required eight seconds, he would move into first place in the standings.

From their special contestants' seats adjacent to the chutes, Jenna caught a glimpse of Cody's black Stetson and the number thirty-three pinned to the back of his light blue shirt as he pre-pared to mount the bucking bronc being temporarily subdued in chute number four. For a woman who fearlessly risked injury in one of the most dangerous careers, she looked uncharacteristi-cally nervous as the horse kicked at the boards, causing Cody to jump to one side of the railing. But then it wasn't as a horse-woman she watched the action, but as a mother—a mother who knew her son's ribs were wrapped with tape because of a pre-vious fall. She could never explain or admit to the momentary panic she experienced each time her son rode the bucking horses. All her life she had watched her father, brothers and her husband compete in the most hazardous events of the rodeo, yet never did she feel for them the trepidation she felt for Cody.

Countless times she had soothed Jack's bruised and broken body after he'd been on the bulls—a body that looked as though it had been in a boxing ring and done a couple of rounds with a heavyweight. She had seen the broken bones and torn liga-ments, the cracked ribs and the dislocated collarbones. Yet she wanted her son to rodeo—even though her heart was in her throat each time he shot out of the chute aboard the side-winding, pitching horses.

After watching two cowboys get bucked off, Jenna could sit no more. "Tracey, I've got to go down front," she told the younger girl, then went to stand against the white wooden fence.

Away from the shade of the bleachers, she pushed her hat back on her forehead in hopes that a stray breeze would blow through her damp bangs. A few minutes later, Tracey was by her side, giving her arm a reassuring squeeze as she said, "Cody's next."

When her son's horse came leaping out of the chute, Jenna jumped up onto the fence, each second seeming to last an eternity as Cody rode the bucking bronc for the full eight seconds. He was bucked off before the pickup men could reach him, and Jenna didn't breathe until she saw him pick himself up and dust off his chaps, a jack-o'-lantern grin lighting up his face. By the time the judges' scores were announced, Cody had retrieved his hat that had gone sailing across the arena, tipping it in acknowledgement of the crowd's cheers. Then, seeing his mother and aunt across the way, he waved and grinned, and Jenna wondered how she could have been so anxious just moments earlier.

"Did you see that score?" he asked excitedly, scaling the fence in a couple of strides. "That horse was bucking like he had a bee stinging him."

"Cody, that was the best ride I've ever seen!" Tracey exclaimed. "I screamed so loud I darn near lost my voice." She placed her palm over her throat. "I'm going to have to get me a soda. What about you, Jenna?"

"I'll take a cherry cola if they've got one," she told Tracey who was waving at a vendor carrying soft drinks. Then she said to her son, "Cody, I think we'd better talk. Can you meet me at the stables."

"But Mom, I've got to get cleaned up right away. A bunch of the guys are waiting for me. We're going over to the carnival."

"Cody, Molly's father is here in Cheyenne looking for her. He seems to think she's with us." Jenna tried to gauge her son's reaction, but could see nothing amiss.

"You told him she wasn't, didn't you, Mom?"

"Is she here, Cody?"

"I thought I already told you," he said a bit impatiently. "We broke up." Just then he turned in response to one of the other cowboys who was calling his name. "Mom, I've got to go. The guys are waiting for me." And before Jenna could protest, he had jumped down from the fence and was returning to the chutes.

"Cody!" she called after him, and when he paused, added, "Great ride." He responded with a grin and a thumbs-up gesture, and once more tipped his hat as he jogged across the dirt arena.

"Unless he falls off tomorrow, that ought to clinch the title for him," Tracey declared, handing Jenna a paper cup. "He sure looks happy."

His disposition *had* perked up since their arrival in Cheyenne, which made Jenna wonder if it was only the rodeo that was pleasing her son.

"Judging by the rides we've seen this afternoon, I'd say there're going to be quite a few cowboys celebrating tonight," Tracey commented. "Your son included."

"Tracey, do you know who Cody's going to the carnival with tonight?" Jenna asked.

"I'm not sure, but I saw him talking to Butch Dugan and Paul Conroy this morning. Why? What's wrong?"

"I'm not sure there is anything wrong." Jenna chewed on her lower lip.

"Then why are you frowning after your son just scored the highest total of the day?" When Jenna didn't reply, Tracey said, "He's not in any trouble, is he, Jen? If he is, we should get J.T. He can straighten out any problem between the cowboys." Her heart-shaped face looked worried.

"It's not that kind of trouble, Tracey." She put her arm around the other woman's shoulder and gave her a grateful hug. "I'll tell you about it on our way back to the stables," Jenna said as they left the grandstand and started walking back to the barn. "That man I was talking to right before the show was Molly Drake's father. He believes she's here in Cheyenne with Cody."

"But Cody didn't bring her with us!"

"No. But apparently Molly borrowed Eleanor Fielding's car and drove here on her own. I told Drake that Cody and Molly had broken up, but he doesn't believe me. He thinks Cody knows where she is."

"Does he?"

"He claims he doesn't."

"And you're not sure if he's telling the truth," Tracey surmised. "I think you ought to trust Cody, Jenna. I've known the two of you for almost five years now, and one thing I've always admired is the honesty in your relationship. There's a mutual respect—something that is lacking between quite a few parents and teenagers."

Tracey's words acted like a douse of cold water on the tiny flame of doubt that Jenna had felt concerning Cody. She shouldn't let Harrison Drake's troubled relationship with his daughter cloud her faith in her own son. While she and Tracey checked on the horses, she decided she would call Mr. Drake as soon as she reached the trailer park and tell him he was mistaken if he thought Cody knew of Molly's whereabouts.

But Jenna didn't have to wait that long to speak to Molly's father; he was waiting for her outside the north gate, and this time when they met, it was face-to-face, with Harrison looking down at Jenna, his tall figure dwarfing her petite one. He had loosened his striped tie and his suit coat still hung from a fingertip over his shoulder.

"I'd like a few words with you, if you don't mind."

Jenna saw the curiosity in Tracey's face as she stepped out of the flow of pedestrian traffic. "Tracey, why don't you go on ahead," she suggested when her sister-in-law hesitated.

"Are you sure?" Tracey asked, then reluctantly left when Jenna nodded.

"Did you find out where my daughter is?" Harrison asked.

"I've talked to Cody, but he told me that he hasn't seen Molly." Up close, she could see the tiny lines of worry in his face, and she felt a rush of sympathy for him—until she heard his next words.

"And you believed him?"

"Of course I believed him!" she replied indignantly.

"Where is your son, Mrs. Morgan?" he demanded, his eyes coldly assessing her.

"He's with friends—male friends. They're going to the carnival. Look, Mr. Drake. I don't know what you expect from us, but neither Cody nor I have seen your daughter.''

"I'd like to come with you to wherever it is you people stay and talk to your son."

"And I've already told you. I've talked to my son and he doesn't know where your daughter is!" The "you people" rubbed Jenna the wrong way. "Now, I've got your card. If I should run into Molly or if Cody happens to run into her, you can be certain I'll contact you." She turned to walk away, but the expletive he uttered had her looking back over her shoulder curiously.

Unaccustomed to sharing the turf he walked on with horses, Harrison hadn't watched where he was stepping. He bent his knee and raised his Gucci shoe to look at the sole, a grimace marring his handsome features. He pulled out a linen handkerchief from inside his jacket pocket, then thought better of it and stuffed the linen back into his pocket. He looked all around, as though he were lost.

Jenna bent down and picked up the remains of a popcorn box, squashing it flat before handing it to him. "I don't think you're going to find any shoeshine boys out here." And before he could reply, she strode off.

CHAPTER THREE

THE COUNTRY-AND-WESTERN music was loud, the air smoky and body room scarce as Harrison pushed his way into the Longhorn Saloon. He had traded his three-piece suit for a pair of khaki slacks and a navy blue sport shirt. But one glance around the bar told him that the only way he wouldn't have looked conspicuous would be to have dressed in Western wear. Even the waitresses wore short shorts made out of denim, bandanna-patterned shirts with the tails tied around their waists, white cowboy hats with feathered hatbands and high-heeled leather boots. Everywhere he looked he saw cowboys...and cowgirls. The walls boasted pictures of rodeo champions along with bulls' heads and cowhides, and Harrison had to duck to avoid walking into the saddle suspended from the ceiling near the horseshoe-shaped bar.

He looked around in confusion, wondering how he was going to find the Morgan woman, and decided to ask one of the few men who wasn't wearing a ten-gallon hat—the bartender. Harrison had little doubt he was either a rodeo cowboy or a professional bodybuilder—no one else would have biceps the size of melons. Across the bulging chest muscles was a T-shirt that read, Steer Wrestlers Get It on the Side, the letters slightly distorted because of the stress on the cotton fabric. Harrison signaled with his forefinger and was surprised to find a frosted mug of draft beer come sailing across the laminated counter in his direction. He placed a couple of bills on the bar, which were quickly snatched up by large knuckles.

"Could I get a bourbon and water?" he asked before the bartender had a chance to move away. Seeing the cold glint in his eyes, Harrison wondered if he had offended the man, who just as quickly snatched the mug of beer from under his nose and replaced it with bourbon.

"Thanks." Harrison slipped another bill onto the counter, and decided he'd better ask his questions before the bartender stepped away. "You wouldn't know where I could find a woman by the name of Jenna Morgan, would you? She was one of the performers in this afternoon's rodeo."

"In the back," he muttered, after subjecting Harrison to a close scrutiny before replying, then returned to drawing draft beer and shooting the mugs across the shiny surface of the bar.

Harrison took but one sip from his drink, leaving the nearly full glass on the bar while he peered over tops of cowboy hats toward the rear of the saloon. It was only after considerable nudging and elbowing that he shouldered his way to the back and found an annex housing a large wooden dance floor. He entered the dimly lit room and slowly made his way around the perimeter, hoping he'd find Jenna seated at one of the numerous square tables.

When he did finally spot her, she was the only female sitting amid several cowboys. She had changed out of her pink lamé into a red suede vest that exposed the golden tanned skin of her arms and shoulders provocatively, and gave a tantalizing view of her generous cleavage. Instead of being braided, her black hair hung loose about her shoulders and around her neck were several gold chains. Harrison knew why the cowboys seemed to be hanging onto her every word: she was downright sexy. This afternoon the excessive makeup had hidden the satiny skin, giving her a hardened show-girl look. But tonight she looked like a luscious kitten. As she laughed, her head tilted seductively and the earrings that reminded him of large golden coins glittered.

Jenna was about to take a sip of beer when she spotted Harrison. "Good grief! How did he find me here?" she wondered aloud, causing her companions to follow the direction of her gaze.

"Mrs. Morgan," Harrison shouted at the same time the band ceased playing, and several more heads turned.

"Is there something I can do for you?" she asked innocently, as though she didn't know why he would have followed her.

"I'd like a few minutes of your time."

"But why? I've already told you I don't know where Molly is," she reminded him.

"And I believe you."

"Then what are you doing here?" Jenna asked a bit impatiently.

"Can't you see the lady's busy and would rather not be talkin' to you?" A big, burly cowboy stood up next to Jenna, his thumbs hooked inside his cowhide belt.

"No, it's all right," Jenna assured her companion, who reluctantly returned to his seat.

"I thought you might like to know where your son is," Harrison replied.

Jenna laughed sarcastically. "Mr. Drake. I know where *my* son is. It's *your* daughter you're looking for, remember?" She ran a bright red fingernail around the rim of her beer mug.

"Yes, and I'll wager that if we find your son we'll find my daughter."

"I thought you just told me you knew where my son is?"

"I did...until he ditched me."

"He ditched you?" she repeated, raising one eyebrow.

"Yes. I was following him because I thought he was going to meet Molly. Maybe you didn't notice, since you're so *busy* here, but your son could have been a walking advertisement for men's cologne. If ever I saw a boy looking for a girl, he's it."

"If he is out looking for a girl, it's for a cowgirl, not some New York debutante," she tossed back at him.

"Don't you think you should find out?"

"My son is seventeen, Mr. Drake. He doesn't need for his mother to be checking up on him. This is his time to have a little fun."

"Even if it's at the expense of a sixteen-year-old girl?"

The niggling of doubt was worming its way into Jenna's head again. As though Harrison knew the direction of her thoughts, he continued.

"Look, if we find Cody and Molly's not with him, you'll be able to prove that I'm wrong. All I want is to find my daughter.

Is that so hard for you to understand?'' The blue eyes held a sincere plea that Jenna was unable to refuse.

"All right," she said softly, then stood up and reached for the black felt hat that was hanging from a wooden peg on the timbered wall behind her. Harrison tried not to notice the tanned skin exposed as the suede vest rose from her waist, or the shapely curves the black denims hugged tightly. She wore a pair of black leather boots that had a shine to match the sheen of her hair, and once again he was surprised by her size. Astride the gray gelding she appeared to be a much larger, more forceful woman, but even with the heel of her boots adding a couple of inches to her height, she still only reached his chin. She would be able to extort a man's protective instincts without any effort.

"I've got to tell a few people I'm leaving," she told him as they started across the now deserted dance floor. Harrison nodded, not realizing that there were few people in the bar who would want Jenna to leave without exchanging a word or two. Several times he was tempted to drag her past the outstretched arms that enveloped her affectionately as she walked by. It seemed there wasn't a cowboy in the bar who didn't stop her, and he could feel the envious eyes looking in his direction as he escorted her through the crowd. He could only assume they were all rodeo people, as he recognized no one except for the blond woman he had seen with Jenna that afternoon. After introducing Harrison to Tracey, Jenna told her sister-in-law where they were going and Harrison felt that finally they were going to make it out the saloon doors.

"Hey! Where are you going?" Harrison watched a large cowboy grab Jenna by the shoulders and plant a hard kiss on her lips.

"I've got to leave, Roy," Jenna explained, extricating herself from the big man's hold.

"But I just got here," he protested, reluctant to relinquish his grip on her shoulder. "And you're looking good enough to eat." He lowered his head for another kiss, but Jenna pushed him away and introduced Harrison.

"Roy, this here is Harrison Drake. Harrison, Roy Cooper, our neighbor in Red Lodge."

Harrison shook the callused hand, noting that Roy Cooper had several notable characteristics...a prominent Adam's apple, a nose that, judging by its hump, had been broken and never set properly, and thick dark eyebrows that nearly grew together under the high forehead. He wore a dark Stetson tipped back off his brow and Harrison could see the snuff tin outlined in the pocket of his Western shirt. He found it hard to believe that a woman like Jenna Morgan would be seriously involved with such a man, although it was obvious that Roy Cooper considered himself more than a neighbor. He was clinging to Jenna's side like an overgrown lovesick puppy.

"I'm sorry, Roy, but I have something I have to take care of," Jenna told him with an apologetic smile.

"You'll be coming back, won't you?"

"I'll see how late it is when I've finished. J.T. and Tracey are over there." She pointed across the bar.

"But you're the one I drove all the way down here to see," he moaned. "I was hoping you'd tell me all about the rodeo— I hear Cody's looking good for the championship."

"Yes, he drew Old Stoneface today and scored an eighty-one."

"He stayed on Old Stoneface?" Roy slapped his thick thigh with his hand. "Hot damn, that must have been some ride. I bet you're mighty proud of that son of yours tonight, eh?"

Jenna exchanged glances with Harrison. "He's a great kid," she said, and watched the glimmer of annoyance come and go in the man's eyes. "Roy, why don't you join the others? If I don't get back tonight, I'll see you tomorrow." She ducked out of his embrace, then waved as she headed for the exit.

"But, Jenna" were the last words Harrison heard as he followed her out the door.

Even though it was a warm summer evening, the air outside felt at least ten degrees cooler than the temperature in the bar. Compared to New York, Cheyenne at night was tranquil. The traffic was minimal, bright lights lit up the business district, but beyond that it was a blackness of wide-open spaces with only an occasional streetlamp and the stars for guidance.

"Well, where do you propose we start?" Jenna asked. She

had donned the black hat at the same angle she had worn the pink one at the rodeo.

"I was hoping you could tell me," Harrison admitted.

"Cody told me he was going to the carnival. We can walk from here—it's only a couple of blocks."

They walked in silence, each of them casting surreptitious glances at the other, until Jenna asked, "Tell me, Mr. Drake, how did you know where to find my son, or for that matter, what he even looked like."

"Why don't you call me Harrison and I'll call you Jenna?" he suggested.

She glanced at his handsome profile and asked, "Doesn't anyone call you Harry?"

"Not to my face," he said with a chuckle. "Actually, my father was a Harry and to make it less confusing at home, I was always called Harrison."

The more Jenna looked at him, the more she realized he definitely wasn't a Harry. "So tell me, Harrison, how you found my son."

"I saw Cody's picture in the rodeo program; it wasn't hard to see the family resemblance." As he gazed at her he thought about how both mother and son exuded a certain power that commanded one's attention; a strength, a grace of motion, like the horses they rode.

"I was on my way over to the trailer park when I spotted Cody leaving. When he caught sight of me, it was only a matter of seconds and he was gone."

"So how was it that Cody was able to lose you? He's never even seen you."

"Who else would be dressed the way I was?" The corners of his mouth broke into a slight smile.

"You've never been to Wyoming before?" she asked, noting how his strong features seemed to relax and soften as they reached the colored lights of the amusement park.

"Only to do some skiing at Jackson Hole—not exactly the same atmosphere that pervades here in the summer."

Jenna could easily picture Harrison in ski wear—Robert Redford, the downhill racer—and a smile tugged at her lips.

"Do you ski much?" she asked.

"I used to, but now I have trouble finding the time." He didn't tell her the true reason; that since Rita had died the sport had lost its appeal.

She found herself wondering what he did have time for other than business. But as they entered the realm of carnival barkers and sideshow entertainers, her thoughts turned to finding her son…or his daughter…or, God forbid, both. They checked out the game booths where large teddy bears and stuffed animals beckoned customers to try their skill, but there was no sign of either teenager. And as the crowd grew denser as they made their way to the carnival rides, Jenna could feel his fingertips on her elbow, or his shoulder coming between her and another body—contact that was rather pleasant when it brought the scent of his after-shave.

After thoroughly combing the carnival grounds, Harrison turned to Jenna. "Have we missed anything?"

She shook her head. "Nor have we missed anyone." All of the cowboys Cody usually ran around with were accounted for. What else could she believe except that her son had deceived her? Unless of course he had already finished his celebrating. He could be sleeping on the cot in the barn, exhausted from today's events and preparing himself for the championship round tomorrow.

"That's it." She snapped her fingers as she looked at Harrison. "We've been expecting the worst and he's probably in the barn with the horses. Come." She grabbed Harrison's hand and began leading him away from the bright lights.

He allowed her to silently lead him across an open field and the dirt parking lot surrounding the stables. When they reached the wide-open doors, she paused to say, "You can wait here if you like."

He spoke not one word but followed her into the barn, being careful to stay in the center of the aisles as they walked past stalls filled with horses. When they came to the blue velvet curtain with a white satin *M* embroidered in the center, Jenna pushed the fabric to one side and gasped. The cot was empty but there were two figures on the bed of straw. Cody sat with his legs stretched out in front of him, his back propped against a bale of hay while Molly sat on his lap, her arms wrapped around his bony shoulders and her cheek nestled against his chest.

If Jenna could have warned Cody she would have, for the thunderous look on Harrison Drake's face was enough to frighten anyone, including Jenna.

"Cody!" Jenna's voice held both disappointment and surprise.

Molly immediately jumped up, running her fingers through the shoulder-length blond hair that was laced with traces of straw. Her stance was defiant as she faced her glowering father. Cody was slower getting to his feet, having to put his boots back on before standing.

Harrison could feel his anger filling his lungs until he thought he would stop breathing. His immediate reaction was to want to see young Morgan on his back in the hay but this time with a bloody nose. Without thinking, he swung back his arm, his fingers balled into a tight fist. Before he could land the blow, however, Jenna's hand closed about his wrist.

"What the hell do you think you're doing?" Her eyes flashed a midnight black.

He stared into those eyes and silently warred a wordless battle of wills. When he realized what he had nearly done, he relaxed his fist and stepped back. He steered Molly out of the wooden stall, his hands gripping her firmly as he positioned her in the aisle.

"What are you doing here?" he demanded angrily.

"It's not what you think, Dad," she insisted.

"Not what I think? First you run away from Aunt Eleanor's, taking her car and causing us to go nearly mad with worry, and now I find you here!" He was forced to turn away momentarily, his anger was so strong.

"But, Dad—" Molly attempted to pacify him, but he shrugged off the arm that touched his.

"I don't want any feeble excuses, Molly." Then he turned and stalked over to Cody.

Seeing him approaching, Jenna stepped in front of her son, as though she could protect him from the venomous look that was radiating from Harrison's eyes.

"I want a word with your son—alone."

"No." She squared her stance, her chin rising defensively. "All you have to do is get your daughter out of here. I'll see to my son."

"It's all right, Mom. I can handle this." Cody tried to step around her, but she stayed in front of him. "Mom, it isn't what you think," he began, only to be interrupted by Jenna.

"Cody, I suggest you go find your pickup and wait for me back at the trailer."

"He's not leaving until I've had a word with him," Harrison insisted, his blue eyes challenging hers.

"Cody, you do as I say." Her gaze never left Harrison's as she spoke.

"But, Mom—"

"Cody, you get your tail out to that truck *now!*"

Harrison was momentarily taken aback by her bold behavior. This was no dainty female needing the protection of a man. It was obvious from her lightning-swift reflexes and the strength of her fingers on his wrist that she *was* as high-spirited as the horses she rode.

Cody picked up his Stetson and boldly marched past Harrison and placed himself in front of Molly. "I'm not leaving unless Molly tells me to."

Jenna inwardly groaned and Harrison grimaced.

"I think you'd better go, Cody," Molly told him in a quiet voice, then watched as he reluctantly walked away.

"Molly, where's Eleanor's car and where are you staying?" Harrison asked as soon as Cody had disappeared.

"The car's parked across the street. I've been staying here," she said in such a timid voice Jenna could hardly believe it was the same girl who had been so aggressively pursuing her son.

"Here? You've been sleeping in a barn?"

It was a toss-up as to whose face looked more horrified, Jenna's or Harrison's.

"Cody let me use his cot and he slept in the hay. Nothing

happened, Dad,'' she assured him. "He only slept here because
he had to watch the horses."

Harrison raised an eyebrow skeptically, then turned his hostile
tongue on Jenna. "And you told me you'd know if your son
was with Molly," he snapped.

The reminder that her son had deceived her cut through her
heart like a hot knife through butter. When she spoke, it wasn't
in anger, but with a voice of maternity that masked her disappointment.

"Obviously our children have misled us; I apologize for my
son's part in this deception. I think you'll agree that the sooner
you take your daughter back to New York, the sooner this un-
fortunate situation will be remedied."

"But Dad, I don't want to go back to New York," Molly
interjected.

"Where are your things?" Harrison ignored her protestation.

"In the car, but Dad—"

"Give me the keys," he demanded.

She reached into her faded denims and produced a heart-
shaped key ring.

"Please, Dad. Can't we just stay in Cheyenne until the finals
tomorrow?" Molly begged.

"I've got a motel room outside the city. We'll spend the night
there and tomorrow we'll take Aunt Eleanor's car back to Red
Lodge."

"If you already have a motel room, couldn't we stay just to
see the rodeo? Please, Dad, if you just let me stay one more day
I promise I'll go back to New York with you."

"You're in no position to be bargaining with me, Molly.
You're going to get a good night's rest in a bed—" he eyed the
canvas cot scornfully "—and tomorrow morning we're leaving."

"But Cody's riding for the championship of Frontier Days
tomorrow," she exclaimed, her eyes bright with tears.

"I don't give a damn if he's riding for the championship of
the world." Once more, the strong jaw was clenched.

Jenna didn't know what prompted her to speak up for the
girl—whether it was the way Harrison had distastefully eyed the

sleeping accommodations in the barn or because she remembered what it had meant to her to watch Jack ride the bulls. Maybe she was worrying about Cody's reaction to Molly's departure.

"Tomorrow is the final performance for Cody's event. I could get you tickets if you wanted to stay," she offered.

The look Harrison gave Jenna would have had a weaker woman knocking at the knees. "I have business that needs my attention; we'll be leaving in the morning." And with a curt goodbye flung in Jenna's direction, he grabbed Molly by the elbow and led her out of the barn.

CODY WAS SITTING with his feet up and drinking a beer when Jenna walked into the trailer. She promptly knocked his feet down from the table and grabbed the can of beer from his hands.

"How could you have lied to me like that?"

Cody shrugged his thin shoulders. "I didn't want to upset you."

"Upset me. Didn't you think I'd find out? My God, Cody, you told me you weren't even seeing Molly anymore and now I find she's been sharing the same stall with you in the barn?" Jenna would have paced but there was no room in the tiny trailer.

"It's not what you're thinking at all. Molly's a nice girl."

"'A nice girl'?" Jenna said in disbelief. "She took her aunt's car, ran away from home and has been sleeping with you in the barn and you tell me she's a nice girl?"

"We weren't sleeping together," he pointed out. "I let her have the cot and I bunked down on the hay."

Jenna's clicking tongue disabused him of any hope that she would believe him.

"Why couldn't you have told me she was here?" she asked, dropping down onto the padded bench beside him.

"Because I knew you wouldn't let her stay with us. And once she was here she couldn't find a hotel room."

Jenna bit back the I-told-you-so. "You said you had broken up. Was that a lie, too?"

"No." He looked down at his hands as he spoke. "We did break up, but then she came all the way down here and now we're back together again. I didn't know she was coming, Mom, but I'm glad she's here. She's the reason I'm riding so well.''

Jenna swallowed back the retort—the one in which she would have told him that he rode well because he was a Morgan, tough and courageous, self-reliant and determined to be the best. She would have loved to criticize and belittle Molly Drake until all of her frustrations and hurt were assuaged. But she had seen the look in her son's eyes as he said Molly's name. And unless she wanted to put more distance between herself and her son, she had to accept his feelings for the girl.

"I'm disappointed, Cody," she finally said. "If you had told me Molly was here we could have worked something out. I could have contacted her father and assured him she was safe. He had every right to be worried and angry."

"I'm sorry, Mom. But if you knew what Molly's father was really like, you'd know why she acted the way she did. Did he tell you where they're staying?"

"He's at some motel over in Pine Bluffs, but they're leaving first thing in the morning."

"She's not going to be here for my ride?"

Jenna shook her head.

"What motel are they at? I've got to talk to her before she goes, Mom." Cody shot forward and pulled on his boots.

"It's called the Lazy C. But Cody, you can't go over there tonight. It's at least forty miles from here and you'll only make things worse if you go see her after what's happened." She put her hand on his forearm.

"I'm not going to go over there, Mom. I'm going to call and leave a message for her. I've got to speak to her tomorrow before she goes back to Red Lodge."

And before Jenna could say another word, he had grabbed his hat and was out the door. Jenna stood in the doorway, watching him run across the park to the phone booth on the corner. With a sigh, she turned to grab a can of soda from the compact fridge and dropped down beside the miniature table. She pulled off her boots and put her feet up on the padded bench seat, leaning her dark head back to stare up at the tiny battery-operated overhead lamp that glowed from above.

God, it wasn't easy being a mother to a teenage son. Why should she feel betrayed because he was interested in a girl? Was it because she remembered the days when he was only a boy and he'd say, "Mama, come watch me ride," the days when *she* was the most important female in his life? Now it was Molly he wanted to watch him ride. And she, Jenna Morgan, whose strength and courage through adversity had earned her the respect of all those who knew her, felt as though she could cry her heart out.

Suddenly she missed Jack more than ever. It had been five years since his death, but it seemed as though it were only yesterday that they had sat in this very trailer at this very same minuscule table discussing what Cody's chances were of winning a junior rodeo event and planning his future with great pride. If Jack were here, what would he be telling Cody on the eve of his championship ride? But more important, how would he handle his son's involvement with Molly Drake? Jack always seemed to be able to put everything in its proper perspective and come up with the right answer. A crystal tear slid down Jenna's cheek and she impatiently swiped at it with the back of her hand.

Well, maybe her perspective was a little colored. Maybe she wouldn't have reacted any differently had the girl been one of her barrel-racing students from Red Lodge. But deep down inside, Jenna knew that Molly and Cody were a mismatch. It was simply an infatuation, and the sooner Harrison Drake took his daughter back to New York, the sooner Cody would forget her.

She heard Cody's boots on the gravel outside the trailer and looked up to see his lanky form loping through the doorway. He reached into the fridge for a soda, popped the top and swallowed nearly half the can in one gulp.

"Well?" Jenna waited for some comment from her son.

"I left a message that I would call her first thing tomorrow morning. I hope that crusty old father of hers at least lets her talk to me before he drags her off with him." He gulped down the remainder of his soda. "I really need to talk to her, Mom. I mean, is it so wrong for me to at least want to say goodbye?"

Jenna swallowed the lump in her throat. "No." She placed her hand on his shoulder and said, "You'd better get some sleep." When he turned toward the door, she stopped him. "You might as well sleep here, Cody."

"But what about Snow Velvet and Sable Rain? I thought you wanted me to keep an eye on them?"

"I'll sleep in the barn. Snow Velvet was a bit skittish today. I should probably check on him anyway." Jenna grabbed her sleeping bag from the overhead berth.

"Here, Mom, I'll walk you over," Cody offered, taking the bundle out of her hands.

Later, Jenna lay awake on the cot, the sounds of the horses a soft medley in the background. Her thoughts were not of Cody or tomorrow's rodeo, but of Harrison Drake. In her line of work she had come across many different kinds of people, but never had she met anyone quite like him.

Why had Cody come up with an adjective like *crusty* to describe him? Maybe to a seventeen-year-old anyone over thirty-five looked crusty. But Harrison Drake was definitely not crusty. He was very attractive—if you went for the conservative type who was afraid of horses. She smiled at the memory of the look on his face when Snow Velvet had startled him. And there was that uncanny resemblance to Robert Redford. And the few times she had seen him smile, she had caught a glimpse of a charm that could warm any woman's heart. She liked his voice—with its clipped distinguished, New York accent. He struck her as the type of man who did everything that was expected of him...a proper gentleman. So why didn't he have a proper wife?

Maybe he was too rigid, too demanding, too pompous, too fussy, too serious—he certainly was too many things too different from her life-style. But he was attractive, and she hadn't missed his appraisal of her in the bar, nor his reaction to Roy Cooper's possessive behavior. Not that it mattered; tomorrow Molly and Harrison Drake would be out of their lives for good, and it was with such a thought that Jenna fell asleep.

It was Cody who woke her the next morning—a jubilant Cody, grinning from ear to ear.

"Mom! She's gonna stay until Sunday!" he exclaimed.

"Cody, what are you talking about?" Jenna raised herself up

on one elbow and brushed her sleep-tousled hair off her fore-head.

"Molly can stay for the finals."

Jenna thought the look on his face matched the exhilaration he had shown after yesterday's ride. "I don't understand. I thought her father was leaving." She was fully awake now and sat up straight.

"Apparently Molly and her father had a long talk last night and after she told him how important this win is to me, he agreed to stay until tomorrow."

"I'm surprised Mr. Drake changed his mind," Jenna said quietly, trying not to let her annoyance show.

"I don't know how Molly did it, but I sure am happy. You can still get them tickets, can't you, Mom?"

"J.T.'s bound to know of someone who has an extra pair," she replied unenthusiastically. "Don't worry about it."

"Great! I'm gonna win, Mom, I just know it!" He gave her a quick hug, then turned to leave. "I've got to go call Molly back and let her know everything's all set. I'll see you later." He was out of the barn like a lightning bolt.

Jenna could only speculate as to why Harrison Drake had agreed to stay another day when last night he had been so ad-amant that they leave. He had indicated that his business needed his immediate attention, yet today he agreed to spend more time away from New York. Maybe Molly's tears could move moun-tains with her father. Whatever the reason, Jenna felt a strange combination of antagonism and pleasure that the Drakes would be at the rodeo today.

CHAPTER FOUR

IF HARRISON HAD THOUGHT the heat had been enervating yesterday, today he thought it positively suffocating. It didn't help that Molly, not wanting to miss a single moment of the festivities, had insisted they arrive early at the rodeo park. Even though their seats for the afternoon performance were in the shade of an overhang, the wind was hot and dry against his cheeks. He had seen the look of smugness on the Morgan woman's face when she had handed him the tickets outside the grandstand gates. She had managed to procure choice seats behind the chute area—how she managed, he could only guess. With a swing of those curvy hips or a pout of that pretty little mouth glossed with shocking pink lipstick she could probably get results a man couldn't; when he had inquired about tickets he had been told all reserved seats were sold out.

Harrison didn't know why he had given in to Molly's tears last night. Attributing his actions to a guilt stemming from not spending enough time with her in recent months, he ignored the tiny voice that urged him to enjoy another glimpse of the little daredevil of a female who jumped on and off horses as easily as a child playing leapfrog.

Although their seats were at an advantageous viewpoint for the action coming out of the chutes, he discovered that the trick riders played to the crowd in the main grandstand across from where they sat. Just as he had yesterday, Harrison found himself fascinated by their performance, especially Jenna Morgan's.

He had allowed his emotions to rule his logic last night, wanting to blame Jenna for his daughter's behavior. But watching her today he realized that she possessed a strength and fortitude that wasn't merely physical. He remembered the way she had undauntedly stepped in front of him and prevented his fist from making contact with Cody's face. And he also remembered her stoic stance when she had admitted her son had deceived her. She hadn't been able to hide her disappointment, yet she had kept her dignity. He had to concede that she was an intriguing woman, and when at the end of the routine, she deliberately rode past their section of bleachers and tipped her hat in Harrison's direction, he couldn't help but smile.

By the time Cody's event was announced, the sun had crossed the sky and Harrison and Molly were now directly in its path. Harrison felt not only hot but dirty, and was convinced that every billowing puff of dust that had erupted from the rodeo action had found its way to his mouth. While one bareback rider was being tossed sky-high, Molly was elbowing her father nervously.

"There he is, Dad."

Harrison followed the direction of her gaze and watched as Cody eased himself onto the platform at the back of the chute, his concentration totally on the sorrel bronc that was pacing in the narrow confines. When Cody lowered himself into the chute and planted his feet on the wooden slats restricting the fidgeting horse, Molly anxiously grabbed at her father's shirtsleeve.

Harrison placed his hand over Molly's and said reassuringly, "He'll be all right."

"He's ridden that horse three times, Dad, and has been bucked off every time." Her voice was apprehensive. "The last time he broke his ribs."

Harrison looked at the delicate features filled with uncertainty and wondered when Molly had changed from a child to a young woman. Had he been that consumed with work that he hadn't realized she was nearly an adult?

Then Cody's name was announced over the loudspeaker system and the gate man was watching Cody's face for the signal to release the latch. As soon as the gate popped open, Molly jumped to her feet as the pounding of hooves and shouts from the cowboys lining the chutes ignited the crowd's reaction. Twisting and lunging in a seesaw motion, the horse did its best to rid itself of the rider, but Cody matched his actions to the wild moves of the horse. The blast of the shotgun was nearly lost in the roar of the cheering crowd, and seconds later Cody was being lifted off the horse by the pickup man and slowly dropped to the ground.

He staggered slightly as he regained his breath, then retrieved his hat that once again had gone sailing across the arena during his ride. When the lights on the scoreboard flashed the judges' verdict, the crowd roared and Cody threw his hat up in the air as jubilant cowboys clustered around him. He had needed an eighty-two to clinch the title and he had scored an eighty-four.

Molly could contain her excitement no longer. She skipped down the bleachers and past the concessions to the area where Jenna, Tracey and J.T. stood leaning on the fence, waving triumphantly and whistling their approval.

Jenna felt a wave of pride and joy, the way she always did whenever she watched Cody ride. As a competitor she knew the emotional high a win could be, and as a mother, she felt once again that enormous relief that not only had her son won, but he had not been injured. When Cody came striding toward the group, Molly jumped up on the bottom board beside Jenna and extended her arms to him. Realizing that Cody wanted to hug Molly, not her, Jenna stepped down from the fence. She tried to mask her disappointment, but she knew the minute she met Harrison's gaze that he had seen the uneasiness in her eyes. There was a respite in the congratulations as Cody proudly accepted his trophy, a silver belt buckle embossed with five circles of laurel leaves. As soon as the award ceremony was over, he jogged back over to the fence.

"This calls for a celebration!" J.T. announced. "Shall we all meet at the Longhorn about nine?" He looked expectantly at the group.

"That'll be great!" Cody enthused, then turned to his mother. "Is it all right if Molly comes along?"

Jenna glanced at Harrison and read disapproval in his expression. "As long as it's okay with her father."

Harrison was standing with both hands in his pockets, a pose that was becoming familiar to Jenna. "Molly is underage." He slanted a mildly reproving look in Jenna's direction.

"Oh, Dad," Molly moaned, partly in protest and partly in embarrassment.

"Both of them are underage, Mr. Drake, but as long as they're with their parents, it shouldn't present a problem," Jenna pointed out in an indulgent tone that had Harrison feeling as though he were waging a battle with her rather than his daughter.

"Besides, Mom knows the bouncer," Cody added with a grin.

"Oh, please can't we go, Dad?" Molly pleaded while the others dropped such lines as "The dancing is great" and "It isn't often a cowboy wins a Frontier Days buckle." Harrison could feel his resolve weakening.

"What about dinner?" he asked.

"I thought Molly and I could get a pizza over at that special place on Main Street," Cody said.

"Hey! That's a great idea! Why don't the four of us go?" Molly suggested, her face animated with excitement. "Come on, Dad. You know you love pizza."

Harrison knew he was cornered and reluctantly agreed. "Very well, we'll go. But we won't be staying late. We're leaving early in the morning," he reminded her.

"What about you two? Do you feel like pizza?" Jenna looked at Tracey and J.T., but they politely declined the invitation and agreed to meet the four of them later at the Longhorn Saloon.

ALTHOUGH CODY TALKED nearly incessantly about his memorable ride and his involvement with the rodeo, Harrison found he had a difficult time concentrating on what was being said as the four of them ate pizza. He tried to focus his attention on Molly and Cody's conversation, but his male instincts were being distracted by the supple body seated next to him in the booth.

If he had thought Jenna dazzling in the hot pink lamé, tonight she was absolutely shimmering in a black suede halter top piped with gold and silver beading. She wore black leather pants and a hip wrap decorated with a large star from which streamers of gold and silver beads dangled as she walked. Her black Stetson had a matching beaded hatband wrapped about the crown, and once again, the tanned skin of her neck was adorned with several delicate gold chains. Harrison found himself having trouble re-

membering that Jenna was the mother of his daughter's boyfriend, and it was only his daughter's affectionate glances at
Cody that reminded him of the reason for his presence.

By the time they arrived at the Longhorn Saloon, he felt he
understood better why Molly was so fascinated with the West.
There was something captivating about the Morgans. Both
mother and son possessed a charisma that was difficult to ignore.

"It's about time you got here." J.T.'s greeting was good-
natured as the four of them made their way back to the dance
floor in the bar. "Everyone's been waiting to toast the champion," he said to Cody, drawing him to the head of a long table
that was actually several smaller ones shoved together.

"This round's on me," J.T. announced proudly, patting Cody
on the back. Harrison could see that the small group gathered
around Cody, clapping and whistling, was a tight one; one
bonded by a mutual love of rodeo and the way of life that went
with it.

"What'll you have, Drake?" J.T. asked in his usual friendly
manner, a waitress in denim shorts at his side.

"Bourbon and water...and a cola for Molly."

"What about you, Sis? The usual?" J.T. turned to Jenna, who
nodded, then indicated to Harrison he should take the chair opposite her.

Harrison glanced uneasily around the crowded room, wishing
he could politely excuse himself. He hated crowds. And even
though he had stopped after the rodeo and purchased a Western-
style shirt and a pair of jeans so that he didn't stick out like a
sore thumb, he still felt uncomfortable. He hesitated briefly, then
wiped off the seat of the chair with his hand before sitting down,
surveying the table laden with half-empty bottles of beer and
straw baskets filled with popcorn.

There were about a dozen people gathered around the table,
all of them friends from the rodeo. Jenna stood and informally
introduced Harrison and Molly to the group, explaining that Harrison was Molly's father and Molly was a friend of Cody's,
which prompted a flurry of welcoming comments. Molly and
Cody took the two empty chairs next to Harrison, so that when
the waitress returned with their order, Cody was seated next to

J.T. As soon as the waitress had slipped out of view, J.T. poured Cody a glass of beer from one of several pitchers on the table, then stood and proposed a toast to Cody's victory.

When the cheers and the sound of clinking glasses diminished, Harrison looked at Cody and said, "Congratulations, Cody. You earned it." He raised his glass in salute, and Jenna felt her heart miss a beat at the approval rather than derision in Harrison's eyes.

"Hey, give that kid another beer," someone nearby called out, but Jenna gently pushed Cody's empty glass aside. "J.T., why don't you order a pitcher of cola with the next round." She didn't miss the surprised expression on Harrison's face, and her heart missed another beat.

Within minutes, the band had begun to play and Molly and Cody scooted out onto the dance floor. Harrison was momentarily taken aback to see his daughter dancing to country-and-western music. He could never convince her to listen to anything but hard rock at home. But then, judging by what he had seen since he arrived in Cheyenne, she would probably do anything to please Cody. The thought was disturbing, and unconsciously he frowned.

Jenna noted the direction of Harrison's gaze and his frown. "They're only dancing," she said a bit defensively, trying not to let the two teenagers disturb her as well. J.T., Tracey and the others had jumped up as soon as the music had started and were dancing to the lively rhythm, leaving Jenna and Harrison alone at the table except for a couple at the far end.

He turned to look at her, trying not to notice how the soft suede of the halter top outlined the swell of her breasts. "You've been watching them just as closely as I have," he replied. "I was just noticing how Molly seems to have adapted to the Western way. I never thought I'd see the day when she'd give up her Reeboks for cowboy boots and wear a straw hat with a pink feather."

"She just wants to fit in," Jenna assured him. "Everyone feels that need on certain occasions." Her cheeks dimpled as she tried unsuccessfully to suppress a grin.

Harrison glanced down at the plaid Western shirt and denims

he had purchased earlier that day, then smiled at her. "I guess everyone does." Her smile was disarming. "I thought if I wore these I might look a little less like a foreigner. But I think I should have gotten a Stetson as well."

"I'm afraid it's your shirt that gives you away."

Harrison lifted one eyebrow. "Snaps instead of buttons, yoked front and back?"

"Nope, it's the short sleeves. Cowboys wear long sleeves— even in summer. Helps prevent sunburn, too." She noticed the reddened skin glowing beneath the blond hair on his arms. It was the middle of summer. She would have thought he would have acquired a little color to his skin, even if he did live in New York City.

"It was quite warm today." Harrison glanced down at his sunburned arms.

"That's the disadvantage of sitting behind the chutes. You get a great view but by the middle of the afternoon the shade is gone."

"They were good seats, and I thank you. From what I understand there were only bleachers available, which meant we would have had to sit in the sun all afternoon. And of course Molly wanted to be close to the action."

"Did you enjoy the rodeo?" Jenna asked, then took a sip of her drink.

"Yes, I did. Does that surprise you?"

"No. Rodeo is the most exciting thing in my life. I can't imagine anyone not enjoying it. But I am surprised that you changed your mind about leaving this morning."

"Surprised and disappointed, I would imagine."

"It did seem like the easiest way of separating the two of them." Jenna nodded toward the dance floor where Cody and Molly were clinging to each other like a couple of entwined vines.

"Sure, and then I could be the heavy and you would be let off the hook. You did offer to get us tickets, if I remember correctly."

Jenna blushed, which was a rare event, and felt chagrined. "Look, I don't know why you changed your mind and decided to stay for the rodeo, but I think we both agree that neither of our children is suited for the other. They're total opposites.''

"I won't argue with that. Unfortunately, opposites attract," he observed dryly. "City girl, country boy. Cody's very different from the boys Molly's met at school.''

"There's no silver spoon in his mouth," Jenna retorted.

"I didn't mean it as a criticism.''

"No?" she challenged.

"No," he averred. A sigh softened his features. He hadn't come this evening to pick a fight with Jenna. "It's rather obvious how we feel about our children's relationship." He looked out across the dance floor before turning to speak to her. "I rather surprised myself when I told Molly we could stay," he admitted. "Maybe it was because the more I thought about it, I didn't see what harm one more day would do. Molly and I haven't exactly had an ideal father-daughter relationship and maybe I wanted to try to understand why all of this was so important to her." He waved his arm in the air in an encompassing gesture.

Once again Jenna could see sincerity in his blue eyes and she felt herself warming toward him. "I don't think there is such a thing as an ideal relationship between a parent and a teenager, do you?''

"I'd settle for a lot less than ideal at this point in our lives. Molly and I are like two magnets with our negative ends trying to come together. The harder we try to communicate with each other, the greater the force is that keeps pushing us apart. I'm afraid my wife was the positive end that drew us together.''

"What happened to Molly's mother?" Jenna asked gently.

"She had a cerebral hemorrhage. One day she was fine, the picture of health, the next day she was gone. Molly took it as well as any twelve-year-old could be expected to, but I haven't been able to fill that need her mother's absence has created.''

"I think every single parent feels that way at times," she observed.

"Molly told me your husband was killed in a plane crash.''

"Mmm. When Cody was twelve—same as Molly. I thought for a while that maybe that was part of the attraction between the two of them. Death is hard enough for adults to deal with, but kids…'' She shrugged helplessly.

Harrison wondered what had prompted him to open up to her the way he had. It wasn't in his nature to talk about his problems with Molly to others—especially not strangers. He was saved from having to say more when a cowboy stopped at the table. He slung his arm around Jenna's shoulder, commented on Cody's win, then complimented Jenna for her performance that afternoon. After he left, Harrison added his compliments, grateful for the opportunity to change the subject.

"Your act is very good. You're quite an equestrian."

"Thank you. I've had a lot of practice," she said with a smile, a smile that had Harrison wanting to ask her more about herself.

"What you were doing in that arena today takes more than practice. I would bet there wasn't a single spectator whose heart didn't leap into his throat at your daring maneuvers." There was a hint of admiration in his voice and Jenna felt a ripple of pleasure.

"It probably looks more dangerous than it really is," she said lightly. "Trick riding is a learned skill."

"A skill that requires a lot of courage," he insisted.

"No guts, no glory—that's the rodeo creed." Her shrug was accompanied by a soft smile.

Harrison returned the smile. "Have you always been a rodeo girl?"

"Ever since I can remember. I've tied ribbons on goats' tails, been a flag bearer and rodeo queen, barrel raced and even played an arena clown once with J.T. That was when I was young and foolish."

He would have asked her more, but they were interrupted again, this time by a man who asked Jenna to dance. Harrison looked away as the man's hand lingered longer than was necessary on Jenna's bare shoulder. But his eyes were drawn to silky smooth skin tanned a golden brown. God, did she have to be so damn sexy? He laughed to himself as he recalled the Annie Oakley image he had of her before making the trip.

"You don't need to sit out because of me," he found himself telling her after she declined the invitation.

"You don't dance out East?" Jenna asked, returning her attention to Harrison.

"Not exactly like that." He nodded toward the wooden dance floor, apprehension unfolding inside him. As if it weren't bad enough that he felt out of place sitting amid the cowboy crowd, now she wanted him to dance to the rhythm of five guys who looked as if they'd just left the film site of an old John Wayne movie.

"You waltz and fox-trot and all that, right?"

He should have said no. Whenever possible, he generally avoided the social scene if it meant ballroom dancing. And the nightclub scene had never held much appeal, either. When she saw him hesitating, she jumped up from the chair and held out her hand to him.

"It's not as difficult as you think. Come, I'll show you how we do the two-step." She flashed him a captivating smile.

Harrison would have refused, but she was already leading him toward the dance floor, and short of making a fool of himself, he had little choice but to follow. And he couldn't deny that the thought of holding her in his arms was attractive.

"Ready?" she asked when they had reached a spot near the edge of the dance floor. She reached up and placed her left arm on his right shoulder and took his right hand in hers.

"Lead away," he returned, placing his hand at her waist where the soft leather of the hip wrap and the suede of her halter top converged.

"Only until you get the hang of it, then you can lead. Just watch my feet for a couple of minutes. It's really simple. Just a one-two, pause, one-two, one-two."

Several couples whizzed by and Harrison wondered what "simple" meant to a woman who rode under the belly of a horse. But within no time at all, he found himself in sync with the music and they were one of the couples whizzing across the dance floor.

"There. You've got it!" She flashed him another captivating smile and Harrison felt like a kid who had just scored the winning run in little league. "They're a great band, aren't they?" she remarked.

"Great," Harrison agreed. What else could he say? Actually, he was surprised to discover that he was enjoying the music— probably because Jenna's eyes were sparkling with an obvious passion for dancing. When the music came to an end, he reluctantly released her. But she made no attempt to return to the table. Almost immediately, the band drifted into another song, and they resumed their positions.

"What's nice about this step is that you can slow it down or speed it up to fit the tempo of the music," Jenna told him, as the twangy whine of the steel guitar established the tone of the love song.

The step might not have changed, but Harrison noticed that the couples who had previously danced with an arm's length between them were now cheek to cheek. When the slightly husky, intriguing voice of the lead singer sang the woeful words of the ballad, it seemed natural for Jenna and Harrison to move closer together, as well.

"Do you do much dancing in New York?" Jenna looked up at him.

"Almost none," he confessed.

"You should, you've got a wonderful sense of rhythm."

Her compliment was like a catalyst to the feelings she was stirring in him. Harrison became disturbingly aware of things he had tried to ignore all evening—the fresh fragrance of her perfume, the bare skin of her back, the rounded fullness of her breasts. Without any conscious effort at all, Jenna was evoking responses from him. But she didn't seem to realize that every sway of her hips was subtly provocative, for when he finally dared to look into her eyes, he didn't see the sexual awareness he was certain would be evident. In fact she was stiffening, and he glanced sideways to follow the direction of her gaze.

Cody and Molly were just a few feet away. They had abandoned the traditional style of dancing for something far slower. Molly's arms were wrapped around Cody's neck and Cody's arms were at her waist—or more accurately, on the seat of her jeans. They were barely moving to the music, swaying back and forth in rhythm.

Harrison saw Jenna's mouth tighten as Cody and Molly exchanged several kisses. She looked as she had earlier that day when Molly had been the one Cody had run to after his victory. He felt a rush of understanding and an unusual desire to protect her.

"You're going to have to let go, Jenna," he said, quietly.

Jenna misunderstood and slackened her hold on him.

"I meant with Cody." She met his gaze with startled eyes. "Are you sure it's just the fact that you think he and Molly are mismatched, or would any girl who's interested in Cody put you on the defensive?"

"Are you going to tell me you're happy with that kind of behavior?" She gestured over to where Cody and Molly were dancing.

"No, but just a short while ago you were the one telling me to relax because they were only dancing," he reminded her. "Besides, after tomorrow they won't be seeing each other."

"Then you've definitely made plans to take Molly back to New York?"

"As soon as we can get her things packed in Red Lodge," he assured her.

Jenna exhaled a sigh of relief.

"That doesn't mean another girl won't take her place, Jenna," he said gently.

"Molly wasn't his first girlfriend and I'm sure she won't be his last, Harrison." She tried to make her voice sound more self-assured than she actually was feeling. It had disturbed her that Harrison had perceptively picked up on feelings she herself had questioned. When the song ended, Jenna didn't linger but headed back to her chair, and Harrison wished that Cody and Molly had stayed on the opposite side of the dance floor, especially when he saw that the group gathered around the large table now included Roy Cooper.

There was no mistaking the jealousy in eyes the color of pea soup, eyes that glared at Harrison when he held Jenna's chair for her as she sat down. Roy Cooper obviously considered Jenna his girl, whether Jenna wanted him to or not. Harrison could feel his predatory instincts surface as Roy slid his own chair alongside hers, draping his thick arm across the back, which prompted Jenna to lean forward and rest her elbows on the table.

Harrison had thought Jenna was strong willed, but he got a chance to see just how capable she was of taking care of herself as she skillfully fended off Roy's advances. He couldn't help but admire the way she was able to control the conversation, always managing to include him when Roy would pointedly try to exclude him.

"When are you leaving for home?" Roy asked Jenna.

"Probably not until Monday." She glanced at Harrison, who interpreted her look as one that said, *That will give you enough time to get Molly packed and gone before we return to Red Lodge.* "We've been asked to perform after the last of the chuck-wagon races tomorrow night," she explained.

"Does that mean you're going to try out the new number with the fire?" Roy asked.

"Fire?" Harrison wondered if he had misunderstood.

"Yeah. Jenna is going to jump her horse through a flaming hoop. It's quite spectacular at night and the crowd loves it," Roy said eagerly.

"Isn't that rather dangerous? I would think the horse would be difficult to handle under those circumstances." Harrison found the thought of Jenna jumping through a flaming hoop very disturbing.

"Hey, we're not talking about an amateur here. We're talking about one of the world's finest horsewomen. Jenna's a three-time women's barrel-racing champion, been voted specialty act of the year four years in a row—"

"Roy, this is supposed to be Cody's special night," Jenna interrupted. She didn't need her one-man fan club broadcasting her accomplishments in the rodeo circuit.

The band took an intermission and she was grateful to see Tracey and J.T. coming back, especially when Tracey said to Roy, "Be a sport, will you, Roy, and slide on over. I need to talk to Jenna for a minute."

Roy reluctantly moved over to the next chair and turned his attention to several cowboys at the other end of the table. However, Tracey didn't have a chance to say much before a clamor of cheers and whistles drew everyone's attention to the front of the bar. Just like Moses parting the Red Sea, a cowboy on horseback was parting the sea of ten-gallon cowboy hats.

"Good grief!" Harrison exclaimed, jumping to his feet with the rest of the people at the table. "This is barbaric." The words were mumbled, but Jenna heard them.

The cowboy slowly walked the horse through the bar, tipping his hat to the cheering crowd.

"That a way, Buford!" Jenna called out, before the cowboy made his exit again.

"You know him?" Harrison asked, his eyes sparkling with amused disbelief.

"Practically everyone knows Buford. He rode one of the meanest bulls in the rodeo today—and stayed on. That's why he just rode his horse into the bar."

"Don't tell me Cody has to do that, too?"

"No one *has* to do anything. But when cowboys start celebrating, who knows what's going to happen?"

"Maybe in the movies, but..." Harrison couldn't hide his disapproval.

"That's why there's a concrete ramp at the entryway," Jenna explained. "It happens every year during Frontier Days. You're not in some posh nightclub in Corporate City, U.S.A., Harrison. Loosen up a little bit. It's all done in fun." She turned and whispered something to J.T., who signaled for the waitress.

Harrison supposed he had made a fuss about nothing and was thankful that at least he hadn't voiced his concern that someone could get hurt. To people who risked injury every time they competed in the rodeo, it would only have made him look even more foolish than he already felt. When the waitress placed a foreign-looking drink in front of him, he glanced questioningly at Jenna.

"It's J.T.'s own special concoction. Go ahead and try it," she urged.

Harrison took a sip of the liquid that resembled darkened orange juice. "Not bad," he commented. "What's in it?"

"Oh, that's J.T.'s secret. He just calls it his Rodeo Special."

"What are you drinking?" he asked.

"A Tootsie Roll—orange juice and crème de cacao."

"A Tootsie Roll, eh?" He smiled and took another sip of his Rodeo Special. As soon as the band started playing, Roy was at Jenna's elbow asking for a dance. It irritated Harrison that the guy just wouldn't give up. With an uncustomary impulsiveness, he stood and reached for Jenna's hand.

"Sorry, Roy. Jenna promised this one to me." He gave the big fellow an annoyingly sweet grin and winked, then led a surprised Jenna out onto the floor. "This is a rock number. I can do it," he whispered in her ear, then wondered what it was about her that made him wish he was raising cattle rather than capital.

Harrison's original plan for the evening had been to stay the minimum time decorum dictated, then politely say good-night and goodbye to the Morgans. That was before Jenna had asked him to dance, before he was introduced to J.T.'s Rodeo Specials, and before he discovered what it was like to sing "Mama, Don't Let Your Babies Grow Up to Be Cowboys" in unison with a hundred people. He was reminded of his original plan as Molly drove him back to the Lazy C Motel.

"I want to thank you, Dad, for staying until closing. Was I imagining things, or did you have a good time?" she asked.

"I confess. I had a good time," he admitted. "What about you? Did you enjoy yourself?"

"It was really great, Dad." Her voice had a dreamy quality to it and Harrison hoped that she wasn't going to start in about not wanting to go home. In his present state, he didn't feel capable of maintaining a logical defense. He listened to his daughter's impressions of the rodeo, until he could keep his eyes open no longer and fell asleep.

SINCE THE LAZY C MOTEL was east of Cheyenne, Harrison had promised Molly they would stop by the trailer park on their way out of town the next morning so that she could say goodbye to Cody. He couldn't recall having agreed to such a request, although he had to admit this morning that the idea was rather appealing. It would be one last chance to see the woman who had been able to penetrate his proper reserve, and strangely, he found he wanted that last chance.

But Jenna was not at the trailer park when they stopped. She had been summoned to the barn where one of her horses needed her attention, and Harrison was disappointed. As he witnessed the emotional goodbyes between Cody and Molly, he felt a pang of regret and the odd feeling that he was closing the door on something he had only had a peek into.

As Eleanor's Buick ate up the miles, Molly sat solemnly, sniffling every now and then to remind her father how unfair she thought his actions were. Despite his daughter's moans and groans, Harrison found the drive back to Red Lodge beautiful. He had never driven through the Big Horn Mountains, and the beauty and the splendor he saw captivated him almost as much as one dark-haired trick rider had last night. There was something mesmerizing about the silent presence of the mountains, with their icy crests etched sharply against the deep blue sky. After several unsuccessful attempts to interest Molly in the scenery, he abandoned his efforts at conversation and allowed his mind to wander over the events of the past two days.

But try as he might, the only images that kept coming to mind were of Jenna—her lithe figure dressed in hot pink as she straddled her horse, the coy expression she wore when she had asked him to dance, the vulnerability she had tried to mask when it came to her son. She was so different from any woman he had ever known. He could just imagine what Diana Elliot would have said had she been sitting in the Longhorn when Buford rode in. Or for that matter, how she would have looked if she had seen him doing an old-fashioned waltz to a band featuring two fiddlers. Diana was a lot like Jenna in many ways. She was determined, career oriented and adept at getting what she wanted out of life. But Jenna was not aggressive, the one quality Diana possessed that had always prevented Harrison from thinking of her as anything other than a business associate.

It was nearly dinnertime when they crossed the border from Wyoming into Montana. It was then that Molly finally broke her silence.

"I suppose we have to leave tomorrow," she said sulkily.

"I do have a job, Molly," Harrison responded dryly.

"Dad, please don't make me go back with you."

"Molly, we've been through all of this before."

"Yes, but you met both Cody and his mother. You know what nice people they are."

An image of raven black hair, honey gold skin and body-hugging leather slid into Harrison's mind. "It's not a question of whether or not the Morgans are nice people."

"But what about my music? Aunt Eleanor will tell you how beautifully I've been playing. She's been thrilled with my progress. Just ask her."

"Don't you realize the worry you've caused your aunt? I think it was a mistake on my part to send you out here for the summer. Eleanor doesn't have the patience or the strength to handle a teenager."

"But I promise I'll do exactly as she says."

"It's probably just as well you return now. Diana's found a school that's willing to grant us an interview. It will be much easier to make the arrangements if you're in New York."

"I can't believe you're trying to ruin my life like this!" she exclaimed.

"I think you're being a bit dramatic, Molly. I would hardly call ending a summer vacation ruining your life."

He was relieved when they reached the small town and drove down the main street of Red Lodge until he came to Eleanor Fielding. She must have been waiting for their arrival, for she burst out the front door, her short, stocky figure waddling as she crossed the walk.

Harrison brought the car to a halt and turned to Molly. "Have some consideration for your aunt's feelings," he warned before she flung the car door open and climbed out.

"Thank goodness you're all right." Eleanor encompassed Molly's slumping figure in a hug. "You gave me such a fright."

"I'm sorry, Auntie." Crying, Molly pulled out of the older woman's arms and ran into the house.

"Harrison, what is going on?" Eleanor demanded, watching him open the trunk and remove their suitcases.

"She's upset because I told her we're leaving for New York tomorrow."

"But what about her music?" Eleanor protested.

"Eleanor, I appreciate all you've tried to do for Molly. I know you've given her a lot of love and you've been a great help with her music, but I really think it's best that she return with me."

"It's because of that Morgan woman and her son, isn't it?" She walked beside him, opening the door for him as he carried the suitcases inside. "Of all the young boys in Red Lodge, I don't understand why she had to choose a boy from that family."

"That family isn't so bad, Eleanor." Harrison dropped the suitcases at the foot of the stairway and stretched his arms.

She looked at him in horror. "You don't know what a tarnished reputation that family has. You don't live here, Harrison, but I've been here almost fifty years. And I've seen the way they live. She practically raised that boy out of a suitcase, dragging him across the country when he should have been in school. Just so she could ride those horses. All of the Foster women were like that—riding horses, roping cattle, sleeping on the ground...just like men." Her tongue clicked in disapproval.

Harrison was tired from the long drive and didn't want to argue with the older woman, especially when he was feeling defensive of Jenna Morgan. "That may be the case, Eleanor, but it really is immaterial now. Tomorrow I'm taking Molly home," he said, a note of resignation in his voice.

"Oh, dear!" Eleanor sighed. "As much as I'm going to hate to see her go, I think you're right in getting her away from the likes of the Morgans."

Harrison only wished he felt as certain.

CHAPTER FIVE

IT WAS LATE Monday afternoon when the Morgans pulled into the Lost Creek Ranch. Hank Foster had been anxiously awaiting their arrival and hurried out to meet them with both congratulations and the news that Molly had called several times that day.

"They were supposed to be gone," Jenna muttered to her father as Cody leaped out of the truck and raced toward the house. Her father could only shrug his shoulders and raise his eyebrows.

Jenna slammed the pickup door and called out, "Cody, these horses need to be let out and walked."

He stopped in his tracks and reluctantly sauntered back. "But Grandpa said Molly wanted me to call as soon as I got home. For all we know she could be leaving any minute. I'll do my share of the work, Mom." His tone was insolent and Jenna could feel her blood pressure rising, but it was Hank who spoke up.

"I don't see any reason for using that tone of voice with your mother, Cody," he admonished in the authoritative voice Jenna remembered from her childhood. "Just because you win a fancy buckle doesn't mean you can ignore your responsibilities."

Cody didn't reply, but walked begrudgingly to the back of the trailer to unhitch the door, with Hank following close behind him.

"I'll help if you'll at least give me a chance to offer proper congratulations," he proposed. Cody went into his grandfather's open arms, accepting his warm embrace. "You did the family proud," Hank said, patting him on the back.

"Thanks, Grandpa. I wish you could have been there. Old

Stoneface really clinched it for me. Once I rode him I knew I could win the title."

"You can tell me all about it at dinner. Let me help your mother with the horses and you go call your girl," he ordered.

Jenna glared at her father as Cody jogged away.

"Don't look at me like that," Hank warned her. "You know just as well as I do that if it were any of his friends from Red Lodge leaving that urgent message you would have unloaded the horses by yourself."

Jenna remained silent while her father opened the trailer doors and pulled out the ramp, then turned her attention to backing Snow Velvet out of the trailer. By the time they had both horses back in their stalls, Jenna had explained to her father the circumstances surrounding Molly's appearance in Cheyenne.

As they headed back toward the house, the sound of tires on gravel had Jenna glancing in the direction of the long driveway. Molly was parking Mrs. Fielding's big blue Buick next to Cody's pickup. Jenna watched Cody leap off the porch and run to greet her.

"Have you ever noticed how she always seems to come when Cody's supposed to be feeding the horses?" Jenna asked her father, as she wearily trudged toward the house.

"Maybe she likes the smell of oats," he suggested.

Jenna chuckled. "All right. I'm not saying another word." She held up her hands defensively. "All I want right now is a long soak in a scented bath to ease my aches and pains."

"Well, don't take too long. Dinner will be ready shortly." Hank pulled open the screen door and motioned for Jenna to enter.

The tantalizing aroma of her father's chicken stewing on the stove was enough to convince Jenna to forsake her leisurely soak for a quick shower. By the time she had finished and walked into the kitchen, Hank was busy at the sink scrubbing dirt off their garden-fresh vegetables.

"Mmm." Jenna lifted the lid of a pan on the stove and sniffed appreciatively. "This smells good."

"It's Cody's favorite," Hank commented, then took the lid from her hand before she could sneak a taste.

"You're a gem, Pa. Thank goodness one of us can cook."
She wrapped her arms around him from behind in a bear hug.

"Your mother should have been much firmer with you when
you were a girl. Instead of letting you run after them horses at
dinnertime she should have made you help with the cooking. I
don't know how you fed Cody before I moved in."

"I didn't. He fed me," she teased, her dark brown eyes dancing. She grabbed a gingham apron from the drawer and tied it
around her waist. "There. Is this better?" She spread her arms
and curtsied. "What can I do to help?"

"You can finish putting the salad together," her father directed, handing her the paring knife. "I've got to make the
dumplings."

"I noticed you added an extra plate to the dinner table,"
Jenna commented, as she sliced a cucumber. "I take it Molly's
staying for dinner?"

"Cody came in and asked while you were cleaning up," Hank
confirmed.

"What about her father and Mrs. Fielding? Aren't they expecting her?"

"Apparently not. Molly said they wouldn't mind."

"I don't understand why she's still here in Red Lodge. Her
father assured me they would be gone by the time we returned."

"Must have changed their plans. What was Molly's father
like?"

"Nice, if you go for the stuffy Wall Street type."

"Nice?" Her father raised one eyebrow.

"Nice," she repeated, carrying the tossed salad over for his
approval. "What do you think? Does it pass inspection?" She
held the glass bowl in front of him.

"I think you should put it on the table, then holler for your
son and his guest to come inside and eat."

Dinner turned out to be a genuinely pleasant meal. Cody filled
his grandfather in on the details of his win in Cheyenne, which
put a rosy glow in Hank Foster's cheeks. They all laughed and
talked together, and once more toasted Cody's triumph. Jenna
learned that the Drakes had been unable to get a flight home
until Tuesday, which explained why Molly was still in Red

Lodge. Each time she caught her son making eyes at Molly she reminded herself that this would be the final night. Besides, it felt too good to be home to worry about surreptitious glances that were probably nothing more than flirtatious gestures. But as soon as dinner was over, Jenna learned the reason for the non-verbal communication that had transpired while they ate.

"Mom, we need to talk to you." Cody and Molly stood hand in hand in front of her.

"What about?" Jenna asked, indicating they should sit down on the sofa.

"We wanted to ask you if you would talk to Molly's dad for us," Cody said after they were all seated.

"What is it you want me to talk to him about?" she asked apprehensively. She knew before she even asked the question she wasn't going to like the answer.

"He thinks Molly should be going back to New York with him."

"And?" she prodded.

"And we want her to stay."

"You want me to ask Molly's dad to let her spend the rest of the summer here?" Jenna couldn't hide her disbelief.

"Please, Mrs. Morgan, you don't know what it's like back in New York." Molly spoke for the first time. "The only reason my father is making me go back is because he thinks I've upset Aunt Eleanor, but he doesn't really want me there."

"Molly, I think you're wrong about that. I'm sure your father loves you very much," Jenna assured her. "It was obvious to me in Cheyenne when he didn't know where you were and was trying to find you."

"Well, if he loves me so much, why does he make me eat dinner alone every night and ignore me when he is home?"

"It can't be all that bad," Jenna chided gently.

"No? You don't think so? Then why don't you call my father and ask him how many evenings we've spent together in the past six months? Even today when I asked him if we could take a ride into the mountains he refused because he had to spend practically the entire day on the phone talking with the indispensable Diana Elliot. Why do you think he makes me attend boarding school? So *he* doesn't have to feel guilty about working late every night.''

At first Jenna thought Molly's distress was only a ploy for sympathy, but she saw an honest sensitivity in the girl's eyes that elicited a rush of compassion for both Molly and her father. The Harrison Drake she had gotten to know in Cheyenne did not seem the kind of man who neglected his daughter, yet he had admitted they were having problems communicating. Did she want to be an intermediary between the two of them?

"A man in your father's position must have many responsibilities demanding his attention. He's a very important man." Jenna sought for an explanation for Harrison's behavior.

"Mrs. Morgan, this summer has been the happiest one of my life. If I go back to New York now I'll spend the entire month of August getting ready for school and keeping appointments Diana's made for me. There'll be no picnics in fields of wildflowers, no wading in clear rushing mountain streams, but worst of all, I won't be able to ride." Molly could see Jenna was vacillating and added, "You know Dad originally intended for me to stay until the end of August. Won't you please talk to him?"

"But what about your Aunt Eleanor?" Jenna inquired.

"She's already said she wants me to stay to finish my piano lessons. It's my father who wants me to go back."

"Will you call him, Mom?" Cody pressed for an answer. "If you don't want to speak on our behalf, at least invite him over so the four of us can sit down and talk."

Jenna wanted to tell Cody that there was nothing to sit down and talk about, but the intensity in their voices reminded her that Molly had already run away from home once to be with her son.

"Why don't you two go for a walk while I think on it awhile," she suggested.

As soon as they were gone, Jenna pulled the telephone book from the desk drawer and flipped through the pages until she came across the listing for Eleanor Fielding. She stared at the number, debating whether she should call. Before she could change her mind, she quickly dialed the number and waited as the phone rang several times before Harrison answered in his proper New York accent. Just the few words of greeting were enough to stir memories of how they had danced together at the Longhorn.

"This is Jenna Morgan." Was that her voice that sounded breathless? "Molly's over here."

There was a long sigh, then he said, "Yes, I know."

"You know?"

"Is there a problem?"

"No," she drawled, "not exactly, but I think maybe the four of us should have a discussion. I know you're leaving in the morning, but would it be possible for you to come over now?"

There was a slight hesitation. "Very well, if you feel it's necessary," he said in a tone that Jenna suspected he used when making concessions at a board meeting, which probably wasn't often. "Unfortunately, Molly took Eleanor's car and I'm without transportation."

"I'll send her back to pick you up." She paused, then added, "I'll see you shortly."

By the time Molly returned with her father, the sun had set and the air had cooled considerably, but it still held a trace of the warmth of the July sun. Jenna suggested they all sit on the large veranda that ran the length of the house. She saw Cody whisper something into Molly's ear as he cuddled next to her on the porch swing, and she quickly shot a sideways glance at Harrison to see if he had noticed. But he was watching her closely, and Jenna was suddenly conscious of her well-worn jeans and recently cleansed face devoid of makeup. He lowered himself onto a rattan chair, and Jenna couldn't help but notice how the fabric of his trousers stretched across his thighs as he crossed his right ankle on his left knee.

"Cody, why don't you get Mr. Drake something cold to drink," she suggested, but Harrison immediately refused the offer.

"No, I'm fine." He gestured with his hand, then steepled his fingers under his chin. "I think we should get on with our discussion."

Jenna expected Molly to begin, but it was Cody who spoke first.

"Mom...Mr. Drake...I know that both of you have been against us from the start. You seem to think that we're mismatched because we come from different backgrounds, and just because you're our parents you think you know what's best for us. But we don't think you understand just how we feel about each other. It's time you realize that we're not kids anymore. I love Molly and she loves me, and we want to be together."

There was silence except for Harrison's swift intake of breath. One look into his eyes told Jenna that he was having just as difficult a time accepting Cody's declaration as she was. But at least he was capable of speaking. She didn't trust herself to open her mouth and speak like a rational human being.

"I think you're not giving us credit for understanding your feelings, Cody," Harrison said in a calm, reasonable tone. "We both know what it's like to be young and in love. I'm certain your mother, just like myself, has experienced a summer romance, and knows how difficult it is when it must come to an end. Now if you called this meeting to try to convince me to let Molly stay the remainder of the summer in Red Lodge, I'm sorry but I'm going to have to say no. Because whether you part tomorrow or four weeks from now, it is going to be painful." Jenna thought he looked as though he could have been reading an annual report to the board of directors, so controlled was his voice.

"That's what you don't understand, Dad." Molly sat with her fingers entwined with Cody's. "This isn't just a summer romance. I love Cody too much to be separated from him. I don't just want to stay in Red Lodge for the rest of the summer, I want to finish my senior year here. I know Aunt Eleanor will let me if you talk to her."

There was no humor in the laughter that rolled out of Harrison's chest. "You can't be serious! You can't finish school here in Red Lodge!" He sat forward in the chair, fidgeting as though he wanted to stand, and Jenna could see that his ears were reddened with anger.

"Why not? They have a fine public high school here in Red Lodge," Molly declared.

"You know my feelings regarding public school." Harrison's poised tone belied the chilling message he delivered. "I've already told you that Diana has arranged for you to be interviewed at a private school in New York and there is nothing further to be said on the subject."

"But I don't want to go to a school Diana Elliot's picked out. I want to go to school with the friends I've made here in Red Lodge," Molly insisted.

Harrison was shaking his head, and Jenna couldn't help but feel sorry for him. The thought of Molly spending the year in Red Lodge wasn't as threatening to her simply because Cody would be going away to college, yet she felt obligated to reinforce Harrison's position.

"Molly, even if you were to stay here in Red Lodge, Cody won't be here. He's going away to college," she pointed out.

"I'm going to come home every weekend, Ma," Cody said a bit impatiently.

"It doesn't matter," Harrison finally said. "It's out of the question, Molly. Diana has worked hard to find the appropriate school and I want you with me in New York. The answer is no."

Molly looked properly chastised, and Jenna found it difficult to believe she would give in so easily. "Is that your final word?" the young girl asked sulkily.

"Yes, I'm afraid it is."

Molly shot a pleading look at Cody who rose from the porch swing and faced his mother and Harrison. "Then I guess I'll just have to find a college in New York that I can attend."

"What?" Jenna cried, jumping up from her chair.

"They must have animal science programs at the New York colleges," Cody stated simply. "I'll find one and enroll."

"But you've already enrolled at Montana State University. You can't just up and move to New York because of some girl. This is your education we're talking about," she protested. "And think of expenses. Out-of-state tuition will eat up your savings just like that." She snapped her fingers in the air. "And what about your rodeoing?"

"All I know is I want to be near Molly." Cody glanced back at Molly who rose from the swing and slipped her hand in his.

"I don't think you two have thought this through clearly," Harrison contended, rising so that the four of them were standing in a small circle.

"But we have. You're the ones who won't accept the fact that we're in love," Cody insisted.

"Mr. Drake has already told you we understand that you have strong feelings for each other. But you have to understand that we are still your parents and only want what's best for you," Jenna explained.

"Then why don't you care about what we want?" Molly cried out, venting her frustration on Jenna. "I thought you said you would try to talk him into letting me stay. Now you're talking as if you're on his side." She pointed an accusing finger at her father. "Well, thanks for nothing. Both of you can try as hard as you want, but you're not going to keep us apart," she threatened. "Come on, Cody." She grabbed him by the arm and disappeared off the porch into the rapidly fading daylight, paying no attention to her father who demanded she stop.

"Well, this is just terrific!" Harrison said with heavy sarcasm, fixing his gaze on Jenna. The calm boardroom voice had vanished. "*You* were going to try to convince me to let her stay? I hope you're satisfied with the mess you've created."

His words fueled her anger. "What do you mean, the mess I created?" Jenna demanded, her brown eyes nearly black with emotion. "None of this would be happening if you had returned to New York immediately. But no, you lingered here in Montana until we had time to trek back, too."

"I didn't realize your son was going to pull a number like this, or believe me, we would have taken a bus back to New York," he said irrationally.

"*My* son? *Your* daughter is just as much to blame. And you're the one who told me you didn't think they were all that serious about each other! Now what are we going to do?"

"I'm doing what I should have done the day I arrived in

Cheyenne: I'm taking Molly home. All *you* have to do is keep your son here. I don't want him trailing after us.''

"My son's not the one who's been doing the chasing. Besides, he's almost eighteen years old. What do you suggest I do? Tie him to the bed? Not that it would help, since that daughter of yours keeps encouraging him to disobey me.''

Harrison's ears darkened to an even deeper red. "Just keep him away from my daughter!'' And with those brusquely spoken parting words, he stalked off. Jenna thought it was as dramatic an exit as in the movies, and she stared out into the dusk taking deep breaths to slow her racing heart. How dare the man act as though everything were Cody's fault?

Within a few minutes Harrison came ambling slowly back to the house, his hands thrust into his pants pockets as he paused on the bottom step and looked up at Jenna. "They took the car,'' he said rather sheepishly.

Jenna's anger dissolved at the sight of him. He wore the same unassuming look he had at the Longhorn Saloon when she had dragged him out onto the dance floor, a look she was beginning to find rather endearing. "It's a long walk into Red Lodge. Of course, you could borrow one of the horses. It's not as far as the crow flies,'' she said with a mischievous grin that added levity to the thin layer of lingering tension.

Slowly a smile emerged on Harrison's face, a full smile that soon became a deep, resonant laughter, a laughter that relaxed the normally sober features and made Jenna realize how good-looking he was without the lines his serious countenance usually possessed.

As the laughter subsided, Harrison dropped down onto the wooden step and ran his fingers through his blond hair. "Raising a teenager certainly can be a humbling experience.''

Jenna nodded. "I think we have two options here, Harrison,'' she said at last. "I can either give you a lift back to Mrs. Fielding's or if you'd like, you can stay until Molly brings Cody home.''

He turned and looked up at her over his shoulder and thought what a tantalizing picture she made silhouetted against the light streaming from the window. In Cheyenne she had worn a glossy glamour, but tonight she was just plain pretty. No black leather or pink lamé, just washed-out denim and cotton. He gazed at her for a long while before he finally said, "I'll stay."

"You look as though you could use a drink. Bourbon and water, right?" Jenna got to her feet and gestured for him to enter the house.

"Tonight I think I'll take it on the rocks." Harrison paused just inside the door, waiting for Jenna to show him into the living room. His first impression was that of a warm country home— the stone fireplace, the dark pine furniture with plaid upholstery and the braided rug covering the polished wooden floor all adding an intimacy and lived-in feeling to the house. Jenna had excused herself to get the ice and while she was gone he did a quick scan of the room, noticing how well she had blended several Western items into the decor. He was looking at the photos on the fireplace mantel when she returned with his drink.

"So what are we going to do with these two kids of ours?" she asked, handing him a tumbler filled with ice and bourbon.

"They think they're in love," he said dryly, taking a sip of his whiskey.

"And you don't think they could be?"

"Were you at that age?" He didn't wait for her to answer, but continued. "What frightens me is that next they'll be saying they want to get married."

"I married my husband when I was seventeen, the June after I graduated from high school," she admitted, her eyes automatically finding her wedding picture on the drop-leaf end table.

Harrison, too, noticed the photo, curious as to what kind of man Jenna had married. Jack Morgan reminded him of Roy Cooper, and the thought was disturbing. "But you were both cowboys, er, what I mean is, you were both rodeo people."

"What is it with you and this 'rodeo people' thing?" Jenna flared. "Do you think we're like a band of gypsies or something? Believe it or not, Mr. Drake, we're as normal as any of the people in New York. We're probably a lot more human. Any cowboy out here would certainly help his neighbor rather than watch him be beaten to death." Jenna crossed the room to stand by the screen door.

Harrison could see that he had offended her and wished he had chosen his words more carefully. He followed her over to the door and stood behind her, searching for the right words.

"I thought we agreed you'd call me Harrison…and I'm sorry," he said gently. "All I meant to say was that you and your husband both had the rodeo background. And you're right about Westerners being friendlier than New Yorkers. It's refreshing to walk down the street and have people greet you with a welcoming smile rather than cold indifference. You don't need to convince me that Cody is a fine young man. The truth is, of all the boys Molly has dated, he's the only one I've liked."

"You like Cody?" She turned and looked up into his eyes.

"Yes. And if I've given you the impression that I believe he's inferior in some way, then I do apologize. But we both know that Cody's future is at Montana State University in animal science and Molly's is at a prep school in New York."

"*We* know that but how do we convince our children?"

"I have to wonder if Molly's attraction to Cody is because she knows I don't approve. If I were to allow her to stay, would the attraction wane? They say absence makes the heart grow fonder."

"And forbidden fruit is more tempting?" Jenna added.

"Maybe we've been going at this from the wrong angle, trying to discourage rather than encourage."

"Are you saying you're considering allowing Molly to stay the remainder of the summer?" Her face mirrored her surprise.

"Would that present a problem to you?"

Jenna's laugh was full of sarcasm. "Remember, I was supposed to be their advocate this evening. Only once they threw their bombshells, I became a little shell-shocked."

"I'm not surprised they solicited your help. Your relationship with your son is much smoother than mine is with my daughter."

His casual compliment put a little lump in her throat. Because of the sensitivity she glimpsed in his eyes whenever he spoke of Molly, she decided against telling him about her conversation with his daughter. She didn't want him to know that Molly believed her father didn't want her with him.

The plaintive howl of a coyote could be heard in the distance and seeing Harrison's attention drawn to the outdoors, she said, "Why don't I get you a refill and we can sit out on the porch? It's much too warm to be inside."

When Jenna rejoined Harrison, he was leaning against the porch railing, gazing at the full moon that bathed the nearby mountains in purple and black shadows.

"I can understand why Molly wants to stay," he told Jenna as she propped herself beside him. "It's everything the travel brochures promise—beautiful, inspirational, tranquil. I don't think I've ever seen so many stars in one sky."

"They're not competing with the lights on all those skyscrapers in New York," Jenna said softly. "Just the big sky of Montana."

"I haven't been here since I was a teenager and I'd forgotten what it's like to absorb the mountains' quiet spell. It's like being a million miles from nowhere."

"But close to the things that count." Jenna's voice was as placid as the glassy surface of the nearby pond that acted as a mirror for the moonlit sky. "I could never live anywhere else. Whenever we've had city engagements where the closest you can get to the stars is a tall building, I feel homesick for these mountains. I miss the wind sighing through the tall straight pines and the sun playing hide-and-seek with snow-capped peaks and lush green valleys." She studied him with growing interest. In the golden shadows created by the house lights, his strong features were relaxed and once again Jenna caught a glimpse of a malcontent. "Have you always lived in the city, Harrison?"

"I grew up on Long Island in an area that wasn't quite as crowded as most of New York. It was only after I married Rita that we moved to Manhattan. She loved New York—the theaters, the restaurants, the shops and especially the social life."

"What about you?"

He shrugged. "It's convenient for my work."

"But do you like it?"

"Not really." He saw the sincere interest in her face and added, "I hate crowds." Out here in the quiet of the mountains with their many secrets and changing moods he could make that admission.

"How can you live in a city like New York if you hate crowds?"

He could see the confusion in her eyes, and it disturbed him. Over the years he had disciplined himself not to ask himself such questions. "You learn to become oblivious to the hordes of people and the endless noise." Sensing her disapproval, he added, "It's the financial center of the world, Jenna, and finances are my business."

"Molly says you work for one of the largest banks in New York."

"Actually, it's a subsidiary of the bank. We're institutional investors, which means we manage corporate pension funds, endowments and foundation money. It's our job to invest pension-fund assets and turn them into profit-making accounts so that companies or employees paying into those funds can contribute less and increase their benefits."

She studied his face for a moment, then said, "I always imagined stock analysts and traders as harried-looking individuals with nervous facial twitches."

Harrison chuckled. "The key to retaining one's sanity is to be an optimist. If the market's down, I consider it's an opportunity to do some good buying. If the market's up, it's an opportunity to do some good selling."

"But it must be a terribly stressful job."

He shrugged. "Raising a teenager can be a stressful job. Did I tell you how much I enjoyed the festivities in Cheyenne?" he asked, deliberately changing the subject.

That brought a smile to Jenna's face. "There's something magical about Frontier Days," she said wistfully. "I don't know anyone who's not affected by it. We've been going for years and we always have a great time."

"I didn't get a chance to thank you for including us in Cody's celebration at the Longhorn. I had a good time...in fact, I probably had a better time than you did. You were rather uptight about the kids."

"I was no worse than you," she protested. "It was just that

once J.T. began filling your glass with his tequila specials, you mellowed out.''

"So it was tequila in those Rodeo Specials. I thought you told me J.T. kept the ingredients a secret?'' he teased.

"I wasn't sure you'd try them if you knew what was in them. You were so serious when you arrived I just wanted you to relax a bit, but I think I owe you an apology. By the end of the evening you were acting like anything but a stuffy New Yorker.''

Harrison smiled at the memories her words triggered. "It was rather fun acting like a cowboy instead of a businessman—even if I looked like a weekend cowboy.''

"You danced very well for a city cowboy in short sleeves,'' she assured him, a teasing lilt to her voice.

He set his glass down on the railing and turned so that he was staring at her delicate profile. "I really did enjoy it, Jenna.''

It was only as she turned her head that she realized how close his face was to hers. She also noticed how a tiny dimple in his cheek creased when he smiled—something he was doing right now, as though he knew an amusing secret.

"What's so funny?'' she asked.

"I've been reprimanding my daughter for letting these mountain nights get to her, yet here I am wanting to kiss you.''

"You can always blame it on mountain magic,'' she whispered, tilting her head invitingly.

It only seemed natural that Harrison should place a gentle kiss on her lips. Her mouth was warm and delicious beneath his, just as he had known it would be. When he lifted his lips from hers, he said, "I don't think I've ever met anyone quite like you, Jenna Morgan.''

Taking him completely by surprise, she reached up and pulled him toward her, claiming his lips in a much more demanding kiss, a kiss that ignited a flame of desire in Harrison and forced him to admit that he liked Mrs. Morgan and not just because she was the mother of his daughter's boyfriend. It was a kiss full of promise, a kiss hinting at the passion that could be theirs, a kiss that was ending just as Harrison's body began to respond to the pressure her supple figure was exerting on his. He stared into her eyes and wondered why she wanted such a kiss to end. Then he heard the sound of a car door slamming, and understanding washed over him. Minutes before Cody and Molly climbed the porch steps he heard her murmur, "I *know* I've never met anyone like you, Harrison Drake."

CHAPTER SIX

THE LAST WEEK IN JULY passed uneventfully, bringing a hot, dry spell to the Beartooth Mountains. Before Harrison had gone back to New York, the four of them had once more sat down and talked. Cody had agreed that if Molly's father allowed her to stay until the end of summer, he would not make any hasty decisions concerning college, and Molly had promised to at least give her new school a try. Jenna felt as though they were in some kind of holding pattern, like a plane circling high above the airport, uncertain as to when it would be clear for landing. She didn't doubt that Molly's and Cody's feelings for each other were strong, but their behavior at times still classified them as juveniles.

Jenna became accustomed to seeing Molly's face around the ranch. Oftentimes, while Cody would be out with the stock, Molly would sit on the corral fence and watch Jenna schooling her barrel horses in figure-eight patterns. After several days of Molly enviously eyeing her as she worked her horses, Jenna finally decided to let Molly ride. Each day thereafter, Molly would be waiting to help her, and each day Jenna would teach her something new about caring for horses. By the end of the week, Molly was not only riding Copper Penny, but grooming him and picking clean his feet without any assistance. At first Jenna suspected that Molly's interest in barrel racing was due to the fact that the Morgan ranch would become home to six girls for the week-long clinic Jenna would be conducting in August. But just as her father's eyes had reflected his fear of horses, Molly's manifested her passion for riding. Still, it didn't surprise Jenna when Cody approached her on Molly's behalf shortly after breakfast one morning.

"Mom, do you think Molly could enroll in the barrels school?"

Figuring it was only a matter of time before the question would arise, Jenna had mentally prepared her defense. "She's an inexperienced rider, Cody. Besides, you know the bunkhouse only sleeps six and I already have my limit."

During the one-week training program, Jenna's students stayed in the small dormitory that was once used for cowhands when the ranch operated on a larger scale. Since then, Jenna had upgraded the building and redecorated until now it appeared to be more of a guest house than a bunk house. Each summer when she would conduct her training schools for barrel racers, it became home to girls ranging in age from eight to twenty, all eager to learn from a champion. Meals were taken with the Morgans, with Jenna hiring a local woman to cook and clean for the young guests.

"She wouldn't have to stay in the bunkhouse," Cody returned. "She only lives a few miles from here."

"But that's part of the fun. Besides, I'm really only equipped for six girls."

"Do you really think one more will make that big a difference?"

"What about our buddy system? The girls are assigned partners as soon as they arrive. She'd be an odd number."

"You could be her partner, Mom."

"Cody, I wish you wouldn't do this to me," she groaned. "You're putting me on the spot."

"But Mom, you've seen how well she rides. And she's not really inexperienced, just a little rusty. Before her mother died she used to ride regularly. She loves horses just like we do."

"But what about her father? We'd need his permission and frankly I'm not sure he'd agree." It had surprised her to hear that Molly's mother rode.

"Why wouldn't he? He knows she's been riding since she came out here. What's for him to object to? Obviously, the cost isn't a problem."

"That's not what I was concerned about." Jenna wondered

what Harrison's feelings were concerning Molly's growing interest in horses.

"You could call and talk to him, couldn't you, Mom?"

Jenna remembered the last time she had agreed to be a champion for the two teenagers and the resulting argument with Harrison. "I presume you and Molly have talked this over quite thoroughly," she said dryly.

"Molly would have asked you herself, but I wanted to talk to you first." He glanced at the kitchen clock. "I'm supposed to pick her up in twenty minutes. If you want, I can bring her back here. Then both of you can talk to her dad."

Jenna sighed in exasperation. "Leave me Mr. Drake's number and I'll call while you're gone." The thought of Molly standing over her shoulder and listening to her conversation with Harrison was not appealing. The memory of his kiss dictated that she make the phone call in private.

"Then you'll do it? Thanks, Mom." He gave her a hug, then dug into his pocket for a slip of paper. "Here's his number at work."

"Maybe we should wait and call him this evening. I don't know if we should be disturbing him at his office."

"Molly says he's always at the office—even in the evenings. It'll only take a few minutes."

As soon as Cody had gone, Jenna curled up on the sofa and reached for the phone. Seconds seemed like minutes as she waited for the long-distance number to ring, during which several opening lines of conversation popped through her mind. "How's everything in the crowded city? Have you done any two-steps lately? Did that kiss affect you as much as it did me?" It was a smooth-speaking secretary who interrupted her thoughts.

"May I speak to Harrison Drake?" Jenna requested in an equally smooth voice.

"Who's calling, please?"

"Jenna Morgan."

There was a smooth thank-you, a pause followed by a click as music played in the background, then Harrison's voice came over the line.

"Hello, Jenna. We must be on the same wavelength. I was just about to call you."

Jenna's heartbeat changed its rhythm. She had forgotten how attractive his New York accent was, and knowing that he had been about to phone her caused her lips to curve into a smile.

"How's everything in the Big Apple?" she asked, wondering if he could hear the smile in her voice.

"Busy, as usual."

Images of Harrison with his sleeves rolled up, his tie loosened and his blond hair mussed, flooded Jenna's mind.

"I take it the reason you're calling has to do with this parental consent form I received this morning by overnight mail," he added.

Jenna's smile faded. He had been about to call her to talk about Molly. What did she expect? That just because they had shared kisses under the starlit sky he would be calling to talk about the two of them?

"You know about the barrel-racing course I'm going to be teaching?" she asked weakly.

"Molly called me earlier this week and at that time I expressed my disapproval. Then this morning I received the application plus a letter that could make Scrooge himself feel guilty if he were to say no to her."

"Cody only discussed it with me this morning and he gave me no indication you even knew about it."

"And you were asked to be their advocate once again?"

She knew that he was remembering that night on the porch, too. "Things haven't changed much since you left, have they?" she asked the rhetorical question. "Do you have serious misgivings about her participating in the school?"

Harrison's response was slow in coming, as though he were being very careful not to offend her. "If she were actually interested in the sport of barrel racing I wouldn't be so reluctant to agree. But my gut feeling is she's just using it to be close to Cody. I'm not sure she'd make a very good pupil if that's the case."

"At first I thought the same thing, especially when you consider there will be six teenage girls living on the ranch for the week. But to be honest with you, Harrison, Molly does ride very well and I think she'd enjoy the course."

"Maybe you should explain to me just what is involved if she enrolls," he suggested.

Jenna detected the note of interest in his voice as she explained the objectives of the program and gave him the details involving the daily schedule, procedures and regulations. "We have a lot of fun, but it's also work."

"It sounds like it might be good for her."

She hadn't expected Harrison to agree so readily. "Does that mean you approve?"

"Yes. I'll sign the consent form and send it back today."

"Molly will be thrilled. I only hope she's as happy once the session begins."

"I'll telephone Eleanor and let her know what's going on so there won't be any confusion at that end." His tone had been that of a caring father up to this point, but then it changed. "It's good to hear your voice, Jenna. I've been meaning to call you ever since I got back to New York."

"It's good to talk to you, too," she said demurely, and wondered where the straightforward Jenna was who normally would have asked, "Why didn't you call?"

"When I arrived back in New York I found myself wishing that I was the one staying in Red Lodge for the rest of the summer."

"There's still three weeks left," she reminded him.

He laughed softly. "Don't tempt me." The words were double-edged.

"Are you planning on coming out to Montana when it's time for Molly to leave?"

"Yes. I'd like to see you again, Jenna."

She wondered if it was Cody's mother he wanted to see or the woman he'd kissed on the porch. Aloud she said, "Do you know what day you'll be flying in?"

"My secretary's making the arrangements. All I have to do is get out from under this pile of work on my desk. Why don't I call you next week and you can let me know how things are progressing with the school?" he suggested.

"I'd like that," Jenna told him. "And don't worry about Molly. I'm sure everything will be just fine."

But Molly's participation in the barrel-racing course got off to a shaky start. She had difficulty in warming to the other girls, partly because all of them were more experienced riders than she. It didn't help that she was late the first day and missed the introductory breakfast. Although Harrison had told his aunt about Molly's enrollment in the school, Eleanor Fielding chose to ignore the fact that Molly was expected at the Lost Creek Ranch by eight o'clock in the morning. Jenna thought she was deliberately sabotaging Molly's participation, using such tactics as insisting that Molly's music lesson be completed before she could leave the house and sending Molly on errands she could have taken care of herself. Surprisingly, Molly acquiesced to her great-aunt's wishes, and Jenna could only guess that after the Cheyenne incident, she dared not provoke her in any way.

But Eleanor Fielding wasn't the only obstacle preventing Molly from enjoying school. Around other girls her own age, Molly became quite insecure, a characteristic Jenna had not expected to find in a girl who outwardly projected such self-assurance. There was a definite vulnerability that surfaced whenever Cody would innocently flirt with the other students, and Jenna found herself mentally berating her son for his insensitivity to Molly's feelings.

She also learned that Molly, not unlike her father, set high standards for herself and had enrolled in the barrel-racing course with the expectation that she would automatically excel at whatever was being taught. Consequently she became very impatient when she couldn't master a technique or didn't come in first place in the trial-run competition. It mattered not to her that most of the other students had been riding since they were small children. She possessed a competitive spirit that Jenna was very familiar with—it had been driving her to compete for almost thirty years.

By the end of August, Jenna could admit to herself that she had been wrong about Molly Drake. She had grown very fond of the girl she had once called aggressive with a capital A—and it wasn't just because she was attracted to her father. She simply

liked Molly, although she still wasn't convinced that she and
Cody were ready for a serious relationship. But even if nothing
else developed between the Drakes and the Morgans, at least
they had all become friends. And she could only hope that those
friendships would flourish in the future.

JENNA WAS NOT the only one reflecting on her relationship with
Molly. While Harrison packed his suitcase in his Manhattan
apartment, he thought of how different this trip to Montana
would be compared to the last time he had flown out West. Four
weeks ago, he had been motivated by anger; today, it was an
eagerness to see Molly. Although he and Molly had been separated for nearly a month, he felt as though they had commu-
nicated better during that time than when they had been under
the same roof. Whether their relationship would continue to im-
prove once he brought her home was his only apprehension.
After all, she had no reason to be sullen and difficult in Red
Lodge—she had gotten her way. Yet, judging by their recent
phone conversations, he had good reason to feel more optimistic
about his daughter's future now than he ever had in the past.

Out of habit, Harrison pulled a navy blue pin-stripe suit from
the closet, intending to slip it into the garment bag. As he passed
in front of the full-length mirror he paused, held the suit in front
of him and muttered, "Stuffy New Yorker, eh?" then returned
it to the closet, grabbing two pairs of jeans instead. Then he
tossed several sport shirts and his Reebok running shoes into the
suitcase with a carefree motion, surprised to discover that he
was actually eager to be away from the office.

He could still hear the excitement in Molly's voice when he
had told her that he was taking a few extra days so the two of
them could spend some time together. It seemed impossible that
in the four years since Rita had died he hadn't taken a vacation
with his own daughter. Their disastrous trip to Walt Disney
World didn't count. He had whisked Molly away from New
York, mistakenly thinking that a trip to fantasyland would ease
the grief of her mother's death. Instead of drawing them closer
together, the trip confirmed Harrison's suspicions: somewhere in
time he and his daughter had drifted apart.

But this time it was going to be different. He had wrapped up all of the pressing business matters, and whatever came up, Diana was perfectly capable of handling in his absence. In many ways Diana Elliot was very much like him, and he knew that had he initiated a personal interest, she would have responded. To those who moved in the fast lane of corporate finances, she appeared to have it all—beauty, intelligence, success, professional respect. She certainly would fit into the Drake family; anyone who graduated from Wellesley was automatically a gem in his mother's eyes. But on the two or three occasions when he had kissed Diana, his body hadn't longed to know hers intimately as it had when he had kissed Jenna Morgan.

It had been a long time since he had felt such an overwhelming desire for a woman. Why it was Jenna, and why it was now, four years after Rita's death, he wasn't sure. But for once in his life he didn't want to analyze reasons. He had spent a lifetime being conservative and methodical, but she made him forget about things like duty and responsibility. It was time now to let his instincts prevail—to lighten up, as Jenna would say. All he knew was that he was attracted to her and he wanted to see her again. And just the thought of her limber body conforming to his sent shivers of anticipation through every vein in his body.

Snapping his suitcase shut, he smiled to himself, unaware that he was humming "Mama, Don't Let Your Babies Grow Up to Be Cowboys."

Harrison hadn't been in Red Lodge but a few hours when Molly insisted he accompany her to the Lost Creek Ranch to see firsthand the progress she had made with her riding. When they arrived at the Morgans', Harrison was surprised at the size of the place. It had been dark on his previous visit, and although he knew Jenna raised horses, he hadn't expected the impressive expanse of corrals and well-kept buildings or the breathtaking beauty of the layout. It appeared as though Jenna Morgan had her own private valley. When he would have taken the gravel road to the house, Molly stopped him.

"Drive on down by the barn, Dad," she instructed. "That's where everybody is at this time of day." But the only person Harrison saw as he parked the car was Cody, who was waving for the two of them to join him at one of the corrals sandwiched between the barn and the arena. "There he is, Dad! Isn't he gorgeous!" Molly ran ahead, and it was only as she reached the fence and stroked the gelding's neck that Harrison realized she was speaking about the horse and not Cody.

"Hi, Mr. Drake!" Cody called out as Harrison approached the corral. "I've got to get Copper Penny saddled for Molly. If you want, you can tell Mom you're here. She's in the arena working out." He gestured with his thumb toward the white building on the other side of the corral.

Harrison acknowledged his message with a wave of his hand, then headed for the arena. Contrary to what he had expected, Jenna was not riding a horse but was jumping on a trampoline, her small figure clad only in a yellow leotard as she twisted and turned with each jump. Harrison's shoes made no sound as he crossed the dirt floor and he was able to admire her for several minutes before she noticed his presence and stopped bouncing.

Within seconds she was standing in front of him, her chest rising and falling from exertion. "Welcome back," she said with a breathless smile, noticing the way Harrison's eyes were drawn to her leotard. She knew the yellow fabric left little to the imagination, and without thinking, tugged at the elastic around her legs. His gaze dropped and she knew she had inadvertently called attention to her legs that were not only bare, but dirty. She reached for the hand towel draped over the edge of the trampoline, then wiped her forehead and face before slinging it around her neck.

"It's good to be back." His smile said more than his words. "Do you do this often?" He gestured toward the trampoline.

"Uh-huh. It's great for working on some of the acrobatic maneuvers we do with the horses." She slipped her feet into a pair of soft leather slippers that looked like ballet shoes to Harrison.

"Shouldn't you have someone in here with you...spotters or something?"

"Normally I do. But today I was just getting some aerobic exercise."

Harrison found her nonchalance irritating. "Why do you take such risks, Jenna?"

"Harrison, life is full of risks. Are you going to tell me investing money doesn't involve risks?" she asked wryly.

"There's a difference between calculated risks and foolish ones." Damn, why had he said that? He wanted to kiss her, not argue with her. He expected her to be angry or hurt or some other feminine emotion, but he didn't expect her to smile.

Coming from any other man, Harrison's comments would have angered her, Jenna thought. But there was something touching about his concern for her safety. His world revolved around responsibility, rules and regulations—a world where volatility was only in the economic market. He didn't take chances unless he was confident of the outcome, which was why he was so successful as a money manager. She remembered how the first time she had looked at his sturdy, solid frame, the adjectives *sensible* and *cautious* had leaped to her mind. But then she remembered his behavior at the Longhorn Saloon and she knew that Harrison Drake could be anything he wanted to be—with the right motivation. She was saved from having to respond to his statement by Cody's appearance.

"Hey! We're ready!" he shouted from the open door of the arena, his lean body silhouetted in the sunlight. "Are you coming?"

"We'll be right there," Jenna shouted back, then motioned to Harrison. "Come. You've got to see what Molly can do." Her voice was filled with enthusiasm. "She's taken to riding like a duck to water."

"Not bad for a city girl, eh?" He fell into step beside her.

"Not bad for anyone who's had little experience with horses. She told me they had English riding at one of the schools she attended, but you chose not to have her participate."

"It didn't seem practical at the time."

"No, I suppose not," Jenna replied pensively.

"She and her mother used to ride...." He let the words trail off.

Both Jenna and Harrison squinted as they stepped out into the bright sunshine. When Molly saw her father approaching the white fence, she yelled for him to hurry.

"I told you she was anxious to show you," Jenna said as they both leaned up against the top rail.

Harrison turned his head to see Molly waiting at the gate, with Cody not far from her at the flag line, his thumb poised over the stopwatch cradled in his hand. Jenna could see the apprehension in Harrison's eyes when Molly came speeding out of the gate and headed for the barrel on her right. There were three white rubber barrels placed in a cloverleaf pattern in the corral, and as she rounded the first barrel going clockwise, she sat straight up in the saddle, then leaned forward, her blond hair flying as she moved to the second barrel, then the third barrel, circling each in a counterclockwise motion before speeding toward the finish. Cody was whistling and shouting as she raced across the finish line, and Jenna could see the relief in Harrison's eyes as Molly gradually slowed Copper Penny and brought him to a halt. Patting the horse's neck, she walked him over to where Harrison and Jenna stood.

"What did you think, Dad?" she asked excitedly.

Jenna found herself awaiting Harrison's answer just as anxiously as Molly.

"That was nice."

"'Nice'?" Molly said aloud exactly what Jenna had said silently to herself, even with the same inflection.

Immediately sensing her disappointment, Harrison quickly added, "That was more than nice, Molly. It was fantastic. I'm very proud of you."

"Thanks, Dad. I told you I'd learn more spending the summer here than in New York."

"Molly really has done extremely well," Jenna pointed out. "It often takes months, even years for a horse and rider to become such a team."

"That's because Copper Penny is such a sweetie." Molly affectionately smoothed the horse's auburn mane. "I'm going to have a hard time leaving him behind. But then, I'm going to have a hard time leaving Montana behind. Dad, it's so pretty here. You should see some of the places we ride to."

"We could show him, Molly. The four of us could ride down to Lost Creek, couldn't we, Mom?" Cody suggested.

Before Jenna could answer, Molly was pleading with her father. "Oh, please say you'll do it, Dad. It'll be so much fun. Please?"

Jenna shot a quick glance at Harrison who was calmly looking at his daughter. "I'm sure there are many beautiful trails in the mountains, but Molly, I don't ride," he reminded her.

"There's really nothing to it, Dad, especially with Cody for a teacher. You could start on the same horse I did, couldn't he Cody?"

"Sure could, Mr. Drake. Golden Girl's a little soft but she's got a big heart. And I've got an extra pair of boots you could wear."

Jenna could see the tiny beads of perspiration on Harrison's temples. "Maybe it would be better if you and Molly rode to the creek and we took the pickup," she suggested. "That would give me time to change my clothes and pack a picnic."

Harrison didn't know what it was about Jenna that elicited his primitive male instincts, but he had this uncontrollable urge to prove his masculinity, and once again, contrary to his usual behavior, he acted impulsively. "You say you've got a horse even a beginner won't have a problem with?"

"You'll have no problem at all, Mr. Drake. Heck, last summer we took Golden Girl over to the senior citizens' fair in Livingston and you should have seen all the old folks that rode her," Cody said with a grin.

Jenna stared at Harrison in disbelief. She had offered him a graceful way out of the situation and he had ignored it. She made one last attempt to get him to change his mind. "I really think it'd be better if the two of us met the kids at the creek," she said, looking directly into his eyes. "It's just as scenic by car as it is on horseback."

But Harrison quickly rebuffed her and his assent was all Molly and Cody needed to race over to the barn and saddle up the horses.

"Are you sure you want to try this?" Jenna asked as soon as the kids were out of sight.

"You don't think I'm capable of sitting on a horse and being led around like one of the old folks?" Harrison was looking at her as though she had challenged him.

"On the contrary, I think you're very capable of doing anything you put your mind to. But I've been around horses all my life and I'm able to recognize when a person is afraid of them."

"Just because I have a cautious regard doesn't mean I have some kind of phobia, Jenna," he protested indignantly.

"Then why are your knuckles clenched white at the prospect?"

Suddenly, more than ever, Harrison decided he was going to conquer his fear of horses, if for nothing else than to prove to this daredevil of a female that he could do it if he chose. "Surely you exaggerate. See? As steady as a rock." He held his hands out in front of him and willed them not to move one centimeter.

"Great," she replied with a lift of one skeptical eyebrow. "I'll just change my clothes and we'll all be off."

"Great" was his equally sarcastic reply.

Jenna felt in need of a shower, but decided that she had better be present when Harrison Drake sat on a horse for the first time in his life. She quickly stepped out of the yellow leotard and into a pair of faded denims and a cotton shirt. She grabbed a pair of socks from her drawer, then hopped on one foot over to the window as she pulled one sock on. From her bedroom window she could see Harrison leaning up against the corral fence, absently kicking at the dirt while Cody led a saddled Golden Girl out of the barn. As soon as Jenna had slipped on the other stocking and jumped into her boots, she flew down the stairs and out the kitchen door, pausing only to grab her hat along the way.

Even from a distance Jenna could see what was going to happen, and worse yet, knew she couldn't prevent the mishap. Molly, in her eagerness to encourage her father, sat astride Copper Penny, not realizing that her horse and Golden Girl were sworn enemies. Golden Girl sensed Harrison's nervousness and Copper Penny's closeness. Harrison had his right hand on the pommel, his left foot in the stirrup and the reins in his left hand as Cody had instructed. He was about to mount the horse when

Copper Penny flattened his ears and kicked out at Golden Girl, who scooted out from under Harrison, sending him tumbling to the ground. If it weren't for the fact that Jenna knew of Harrison's fear, it would have been a comical sight.

Cody quickly had Golden Girl under control, tethered the startled horse to the fence and went to help Harrison to his feet.

"I'm sorry, Mr. Drake. Are you all right?" He offered his hand to Harrison who refused his help and scrambled to his feet of his own accord.

Molly was having difficulty bringing Copper Penny to a halt and it was Jenna who finally settled the horse. Harrison was dusting off his jeans when Molly ran up to him. "What happened, Dad?"

Molly couldn't have chosen three worse words. Frustration, embarrassment and anger overruled discretion and Harrison lashed out at Cody.

"What happened?" he mimicked in disbelief. "Why don't you ask your boyfriend? He couldn't even hold that horse still long enough for me to get on the damn thing."

"Dad, you're being unfair," Molly protested, but Harrison continued to blame Cody for the mishap.

"You call yourself an instructor? My God, I don't believe they'd even let you near those old people if this is the way you help someone mount a horse."

"Molly's right, Harrison. You are being unfair," Jenna finally spoke up. "It was Molly's horse who spooked Golden Girl. But Cody, you know better than to have another horse present when you're giving someone a lesson. Take Copper Penny out of the corral."

"There's no need for that," Harrison said grimly. "The lesson's over."

"Dad, you're not giving up already?" Molly exclaimed, reaching for her father's elbow. "It's not like you got hurt or anything."

Harrison's face reminded Jenna of storm clouds rolling in the sky. "Molly, right now, learning to ride a horse is the last thing I want to do."

He climbed through the rails of the fence and started toward

the car. Jenna, seeing Molly go after him, decided not to inter-
fere, but watched from a distance as the two of them stood in
front of the barn, Molly's slender body leaning toward her father's uncompromising form. She couldn't hear what was being
said, but it was obvious they were arguing. When Molly returned
without her father, Jenna, noticing Harrison's indolent figure
leaning against the car, suggested that Molly and Cody go for
their ride and not worry about Mr. Drake.

Harrison watched as the two teenagers rode off into the mountains and wondered how he could have made such a fool of
himself. Jenna Morgan must think him one sorry stuffed shirt,
which was how he had acted just because he couldn't sit on a
horse the senior citizens of Livingston rode. Other than a bruised
pride, he hadn't even been hurt. The pain had been in Jenna's
witnessing that bruising. She had been the cautious one, offering
him the perfect opportunity to refuse the riding lesson, but he
had acted like some young stud who needed to prove himself to
his girl. And this was to have been his weekend to get to know
her better, to show her how unstuffy he could be. He shoved his
hands into his pockets and sauntered back over to the corral
fence.

"Mr. Drake." Jenna stood with her hands in the back pockets
of her jeans, her expression guarded.

"I wish you'd call me Harrison. We're not in front of our
children now, Jenna." He said her name as though he were
stroking a kitten.

"No, we're not, are we, Harrison. Our children are riding,"
she said with a sugary sweet pointedness.

He half smiled, then said, "I owe you and Cody an apology.
I overreacted and I'm sorry."

"Apology accepted." She smiled and her dimple creased.

"I know it must seem silly to someone like you...my uneasiness around horses."

"No, I don't find it silly at all," she assured him. "Horses
are large animals and it's wise to be cautious around them."

"Well, I had a bad experience as a kid and apparently it's
still with me." He ran one hand across the back of his neck. "It
happened when my grandfather took me to a horse auction. He

warned me to stay close to his side, but like a typical inquisitive kid I managed to wiggle my way into a place I wasn't supposed to be. I got too close to the wrong end of a horse and ended up getting kicked in the stomach.''

"How seriously were you hurt?"

"I had a ruptured spleen and some other internal injuries, but I was fortunate in that everything could be repaired. I've a mean-looking scar to remind me of my carelessness," he said with a lopsided grin that had Jenna's heart fluttering. "I learned two things that day: not to disobey my grandfather and never to trust a horse.''

Jenna wanted to say something soothing, something reassuring about being around horses, but the look on his face told her she would only sound patronizing. Instead, she tactfully changed the subject. "Can I get you something to drink?"

"No, thanks. One of the reasons I came over today was to ask you and Cody to join us tomorrow. Molly may have already told you. I've decided to take a few days off and see some of the sights. I was hoping I could convince you to play tour guide. Molly had mentioned she'd like to see Yellowstone National park." There. He had said it, and he felt relieved.

"Oh, Harrison, I wish we could, but the Flying Fosters have two performances this weekend. We won't be home until Monday." For the first time in her life Jenna found herself wishing she could miss an engagement.

Harrison's stomach plunged. "I understand," he assured her, not wanting his disappointment to show. "It was rather short notice, but I didn't know that I was going to be able to take the time away from work."

"Our act is sometimes booked a year in advance," she explained. "You could come up to Helena for the rodeo—that is, unless you've got your heart set on Yellowstone. Although, to be honest with you, that isn't a fair choice. If you haven't seen Yellowstone, you shouldn't pass up the opportunity. And the drive from here along the Beartooth Highway is said to be the most scenic drive in the country. I only wish we could go with you.''

"I do, too, Jenna. Believe me, I do, too.''

CHAPTER SEVEN

HARRISON WOULD WILLINGLY have consented to spending the weekend in Helena, but it was Molly who chose to explore the scenic wilderness of Yellowstone Park rather than attend the rodeo. And although he had been disappointed to learn that his weekend wasn't going to include Jenna, the fact that his daughter elected to spend the last few days of her holiday with her father instead of her boyfriend gave him hope that their relationship was not as tenuous as he had thought.

So, while Cody and Jenna were rodeoing in Helena, he and Molly were following trails that led to spouting geysers, brilliantly colored hot springs and mud volcanoes. He had forgotten how inquisitive and adventurous she had been as a child, and was delighted with the rapport that developed between the two of them as they explored the natural wonders abounding in the park. It was refreshing to hear excitement in her voice as she spotted an elusive bison or came upon an unexpected panorama that took her breath away. Watching the waning sun drench the mountains with flaming orange, they talked as father and daughter should, and as they hadn't been able to since Molly's mother had died. And Harrison knew that the sixteen-year-old who patiently waited close to an hour for Old Faithful to erupt was not the same sixteen-year-old who had belligerently boarded a plane for Montana at the beginning of summer. He could only wonder if the change wasn't due partly to Jenna Morgan's influence, for Molly talked warmly not only about Cody Morgan, but also of Jenna, and Harrison listened intently. By the time they returned to Red Lodge on Monday morning, they both had a better understanding not only of nature, but of each other.

Later that afternoon, while Eleanor and Molly attended a benefit luncheon for the local dance company, Harrison felt restless and decided to venture into the one room in the old, family house that held the fondest memories for him, his uncle's art studio. It was located on the third floor, which was actually more like a loft due to the gabled roof. He climbed the second flight of stairs, a feeling of expectation hurrying his steps as he remembered the first time his uncle had led him up the narrow risers. He paused when he reached the top landing, noticing the thick layer of dust on the wooden banister.

The door to the studio was closed, but not locked. The minute Harrison pushed it open, he felt as though he had stepped back in time. Everything looked exactly as it had twenty years ago, and he could only assume that his aunt hadn't been able to bring herself to put away her late husband's things. A beam of sunshine poured down through the skylight, creating a spotlight effect around the easel where Charles had loved to work. Harrison could almost feel the presence of his uncle, imagine him sitting on his stool, one foot curled around its leg, the other extended straight out as brush stroked the canvas with a precision Harrison had so admired. On the easel rested a painting of wild horses, and as Harrison gazed at the lifelike images he realized once again that artists like Charles Fielding were indeed rare. It was no wonder that he was represented not only in Western art museums but also in the National Gallery in Washington, D.C., and the Museum of Modern Art in New York.

The memories came flooding back. His uncle setting a blank canvas on the easel. His uncle handing him a palette and brush. His uncle spending hour after hour patiently explaining the basics of his craft. His uncle smiling proudly at his nephew's first attempt at capturing the splendid view that greeted him every day through the floor-to-ceiling windows of the studio.

As though suddenly remembering that view, Harrison crossed the paint-splattered wooden floor, pulled back the heavy green drapes and gasped. A tall building now stood between Charles's studio and the magnificent terrain of snow-capped mountain peaks and richly forested valleys. Harrison sighed and turned away. The breathtaking splendor was gone, as was his dream. Both sacrificed for economic reasons.

Twenty years ago he had returned to New York with his canvas in hand, the one that Uncle Charles had critically appraised as that of a promising artist, ready to enroll in art school. After spending one entire summer vacation studying with his uncle, he had decided to make art a full-time dedication. But being a true Drake—responsible, pragmatic and traditional—he had allowed his parents to dismiss his interest in painting as a passing fancy, a hobby. Instead of majoring in art at college, he had studied economics and business administration, and although he had taken art classes and still painted, he had agreed to follow in the footsteps of the long line of Drakes before him who, with sound financial decisions, had contributed to the growth of America. Now, here in his uncle's studio, Harrison felt like a boy once again and wished he could pick up the palette with its dried stains of color and start over.

Although most of the room appeared to be untouched, several sheets were draped over what Harrison guessed were canvases stacked against the far wall. He remembered that Charles had been planning an exhibition in New York at the time of his death. Curious, Harrison lifted one edge of the sheet. Underneath were Charles Fielding's last paintings, all packed and ready to be shipped. Quickly looking around the room for something to pry open the wooden crates, Harrison could find nothing and decided to try the small cupboard tucked neatly away in the gabled end. He had to stoop down on all fours to peek inside. Fortunately there was a pull chain connected to a very dim light bulb in the tiny closet.

Harrison never knew what purpose the closet had served, but he certainly wasn't expecting to find portraits. On all fours and in near darkness, he was unable to make out the subjects and decided to remove them, one by one, carefully stacking them against the wall as best he could. Then he crawled back out of the cupboard and stood up, brushing the dust from his pant legs.

Picking up the first canvas, he inhaled sharply, for the woman in the portrait looked exactly like Jenna. Harrison stood for several minutes, holding the painting between his extended hands. The woman was beautiful and he couldn't help but feel the love that had captured her beauty. He quickly turned to the remaining portraits and lined them up along the wall opposite the windows. They were by far the best pieces that Harrison had ever seen of his uncle's and he wondered why they were hidden away in a cupboard rather than on display. They were all of the same woman, but different poses—standing on a horse, twirling two ropes simultaneously, splashing her face in a mountain stream, and finally, asleep in a bed of hay. Harrison realized that although the face could easily have been mistaken for Jenna's, the clothes couldn't. They looked like those he and Molly had seen in the historical museum in town.

"Harrison! What are you doing up here!" Eleanor's voice sounded horrified, her wrinkled features pinched with distress.

Startled, he spun around and faced his aunt. "I'm sorry, I didn't think you would mind if I looked around. You know how much I admired Uncle Charles's work."

"But you've been disturbing things," she accused, glaring at the canvases against the wall. She waddled over to the paintings of the horsewoman and began turning them toward the wall. "This is Charles's room. I can't believe you would come up here without asking my permission."

Harrison felt as though he were ten years old and being scolded for not knocking before entering. Had Eleanor not wanted anyone in the room, he thought she would have mentioned it to him, or at least have kept the door locked. But he had expected that she, better than anyone else, would remember how much he had enjoyed his visits to the studio years ago. She had been the one who had urged him to follow in his uncle's footsteps.

"I really am sorry, Eleanor. If I had known it would upset you, I certainly wouldn't have come in. I just wanted to feel his presence again. Don't you remember how I used to sit here and watch him work? He was always so tolerant of my adoration," he said soothingly.

Harrison thought she was about to cry and immediately moved to help spread the large white sheet over the rest of the canvases. He heard her mumble to herself, "No one must know about this," and interpreted it as meaning no one knew that she still kept the studio as it was twenty years ago. He wanted to ask her about the paintings, especially the portraits of the horse-woman who looked so much like Jenna, but instead he found himself pulling the drapery back across the square panes of glass, shutting out the daylight. All that remained was the small ray of light that shone through the skylight, creating a rectangular spotlight about the easel. Eleanor quickly pulled on a large cord and eliminated that, too. When the room was in total darkness, they left.

Downstairs, Molly had made tea and while the three of them sat around the oval dining room table covered with an antique lace tablecloth, Harrison finally asked his aunt about the artwork in the studio.

"Eleanor, I know how painful it is for you to discuss Uncle Charles, but some of his best work is up there in the studio. It seems such a shame no one has ever seen it." His words were gentle, his tone understanding.

"He had arranged an exhibition in New York shortly before he died," she said quietly.

"Have you thought at all about having a showing? You could do it here in Red Lodge," he suggested.

"It's difficult for me...there's so much involved...and I wasn't sure if Charles would have wanted them to be put up for sale." She was hedging, and Harrison didn't understand why.

"But they're wonderful...and probably very valuable. I wish you'd think about doing something with them if for no other reason than safety. You could always lend them to a museum if you're not prepared to sell them."

"Really, Harrison, I'd rather not talk about this. It seems like only yesterday he was up there painting." She raised an embroidered linen hankie to her eye.

"Dad, why don't you tell Auntie about our invitation?" Molly pointedly changed the subject.

"Invitation?" Eleanor's head jerked up.

"Mrs. Morgan has invited us over for a barbecue tomorrow evening at the Lost Creek Ranch," Harrison explained. "Since it's Molly's last evening in Red Lodge, she's invited some of the friends Molly's made this summer for a farewell party."

"You're invited too, Auntie," Molly added.

"Me?" Her face twisted with displeasure. "I'm afraid if you and your father want to eat outdoors with the flies and the ants you'll have to do it without me. My stomach has been bothering me lately, and barbecued food is the last thing I need."

Harrison knew that it wasn't the food but the company Eleanor objected to. Actually, he was a bit relieved she didn't want to go and decided not to argue with her. Eleanor was entitled to her opinions and he felt no need to justify his wanting to spend time with the Morgans...or to be more exact, Jenna. Memories of the last time he had stood on her porch under the starry sky returned and quickened his pulse.

ANY HOPE HE HAD of being alone with Jenna beneath a starry sky seemed remote when he saw the size of the crowd gathered for the Morgans' barbecue. His and Jenna's idea of a "few" were light-years apart. There were pickup trucks and cars lining the gravel driveway, with several vehicles parked on the grassy knoll as well. Harrison figured that to find Jenna he needed merely to look to where the majority of men congregated. But contrary to what he expected, the majority of men were boys about the ages of Molly and Cody. The other adults present were Jenna's father, whom Cody introduced as soon as they arrived, a local ranch hand named Slim Howard, and Jenna's brother and his wife. He suppressed a sigh of disappointment as Molly introduced him to her circle of friends.

Considering the circumstances, Harrison decided it was probably safer with so many teenagers in sight. He'd be flying home in the morning and before long would once again be immersed in corporate finances. A romantic encounter with Jenna at this point would only complicate his life.

A string of colored lights had been mounted across the grassy stretch in back of the house where several picnic tables covered with checkered cloths were arranged in a row not far from a large brick barbecue. Harrison immediately recognized the man with the long apron tied around his waist as Jenna's brother. When J.T. noticed Harrison's presence, he offered his hand.

"You ready to taste the best beef in all of Montana?"

"It looks as though you've got quite a crew to feed," Harrison observed.

"You bet. As soon as the word got out I was tending the grill, they started coming in droves," he boasted with a wink.

Harrison couldn't help but smile. "If that aroma drifts far you're going to have even more, although it looks as though most of Red Lodge is already here."

"Jenna's inside with Tracey. Why don't you go on in?" he suggested. "They're putting the finishing touches on the rest of the meal."

When Harrison hesitated, J.T. called over to his nephew who was getting Molly a soda from an ice-filled washtub. "Cody, take Mr. Drake inside and get him something to drink and tell your mama to hurry up cuz the beef is nearly done."

"What can I get for you, Mr. Drake? A beer?" Cody asked.

"Mr. Drake drinks bourbon and water, Cody," Jenna announced stepping out the door, her hands holding a large bowl of salad. A single file of teenagers followed right behind her, each carrying food or utensils for the picnic. "Hi, Harrison." She smiled such an inviting smile that Harrison felt tongue-tied for a minute.

Cody began to introduce each of the teens to Harrison as they paraded past with biscuits, beans, paper plates, pickles, watermelon and cake. The last person out the door was Tracey, who smiled at Harrison over a bowl of guacamole dip.

"One bourbon and water coming up," Cody declared, then leaped the porch steps two at a time.

"That's all right, Cody." Harrison's voice halted his progress. "I'll just have a cola." With an agility that reminded Harrison of Jenna's, Cody hurdled the porch railing, landing next to the washtub filled with cold pop.

"Have you enjoyed your 'mini' vacation?" Jenna asked, as Harrison came to stand across the picnic table from her and watched her arrange the food banquet-style on the red-checked cloth.

"Yes. Yellowstone was everything you said it would be and more. You're lucky to live so close by." He popped the top on the can and took a swallow. "How was your weekend? I heard Cody won his event."

"He seems to be on a winning streak," she said with a smile, taking the plastic wrap from a plate of relishes. "Are you hungry?"

"It looks like you've got quite a feast," he answered, eyeing the display of food.

"I think everything's ready. I'd better round everyone up." She stepped up onto the porch and hit a metal pipe against a large triangle until everyone had gathered nearby.

"Before we eat, I just want to say a few quick words." She smiled broadly at the crowd. "Molly Drake has been with us for just about three months now and I know you've all come to like her as much as we do here at the Lost Creek." Cody pulled Molly beside him so that she was standing beside Jenna and in the half circle of his arm.

"Tomorrow, Molly goes back to New York." There was a groan from the crowd. "Yes, I know it's sad, but all good things must come to an end...including summer vacation. Speaking on behalf of all of us here, I want to wish her a safe trip home and to say, we're going to miss you, Molly, and anytime you want to come back, you're always welcome." The group of teenagers clapped and whistled and Molly blushed. Then Jenna announced, "Let's eat!"

Molly turned to Jenna and put her arms around her. "Thank you, Mrs. Morgan. I've been wanting to tell you for a long time how sorry I am about following Cody down to Cheyenne. You've really made this a great summer for me, letting me ride Copper Penny and all."

"I think maybe we all just got off on the wrong foot. But everything worked out just fine. I'm happy you were able to spend the summer in Red Lodge," Jenna said sincerely, and Harrison felt his heart turn over at the genuine affection he saw in her eyes. Molly, seeing her father's intense gaze, added, "Thank you, too, Dad, for letting me stay." She kissed his cheek.

As Cody and Molly left to join the others at the food table,

Harrison looked in awe at their retreating figures. "Are you sure that's my daughter?"

"She's nice, Harrison, and I really do like her."

Harrison felt a ridiculously refreshing surge of pride. Had it been that long since he had been proud of his daughter or was it because the compliment came from Jenna? "Do I dare say 'all's well that ends well'?"

"I think so." She grinned and slipped her arm through his. "Come. Let's get something to eat before these ravenous kids clean us out."

Harrison followed Jenna's lead, sampling all of the foods she suggested, carefully balancing his full plate and the can of cola. Instead of sitting at the picnic tables where rock music was blaring from Cody's cassette player, Jenna led him over to an old abandoned haywagon behind the barn. Setting her plate down first, she placed her palms on the weathered wood and prepared to boost herself up. But Harrison grabbed her by the waist and effortlessly lifted her, his hands lingering for a moment on her firm body as his eyes met hers.

"I think you're even lighter than Molly," he said huskily, his fingers fighting the urge to explore the contours that were warm beneath his touch. Instead, he forced his fingers to wrap themselves around the paper plate and hand it to her.

Jenna found herself noticing the small tuft of hairs peeping out of the unbuttoned neck of his sport shirt, and thought of how natural he looked in his jeans and athletic shoes. He probably played touch football in the park or racquetball at the health club after running his ritual three miles every day. He definitely worked out at something; his physique was not that of a forty-year-old man who spent hours at the office and evenings in front of the television. As he hoisted himself up onto the wagon, the denim stretched across his thighs and Jenna tried not to notice the strength and power there.

"This is very good," Harrison complimented as they ate in companionable silence. "It must be quite a job putting on such a spread."

Jenna nodded. "But I usually have lots of help. I always invite

J.T. and Tracey because he's the chef in the family and she loves to putts in the kitchen.''

"'Putts?'"

"Yeah... You know, putter around...putts."

"Ohh," Harrison drawled. *Putts.* He made a face as though a light had suddenly been lit.

"You've never heard that expression, have you? Well, that doesn't surprise me. Sometimes I think my mother invented a language she could call her own...and it wasn't all filled with Western idioms, either.''

"What was she like?"

"A cowgirl," Jenna said with a grin. "A much better cowgirl than me."

"Now that, I find hard to believe."

"No, really, she was." Harrison didn't miss the dreamy look that came into her eyes. "She'd go out on the cattle drives with the rest of the hands, sleep on the ground, tend to the livestock, rope calves, bulldog them down. Even when she was pregnant with us kids, she'd go out on the range. My brother Lee was born out there. She wanted to ride her horse back right after giving birth, but Dad made her ride on the wagon. She was mad at him for days."

"What about you? Do you like to sleep on the ground?"

She laughed, a rather provocative, throaty laugh. "I'll take satin sheets and a soft pillow over a bedroll and lumpy ground any day."

An image of Jenna's dark hair splayed out on satin sheets flashed temptingly in Harrison's mind.

"I think Mama and I were alike in many ways, but she definitely had more grit than I do. When I was pregnant with Cody I still went down the road with Jack, but I made sure there was a hospital nearby at all times. In fact, Cody was born in Cody, Wyoming, which is how he got his name. Jack was riding in the rodeo there the night he was born."

"Hey, you two!"

Jenna turned to see J.T. and Tracey coming around the corner of the barn, and waved.

"This is the only quiet place on the ranch," Jenna explained, patting the wooden board beside her. "Did everyone get fed?"

"I told Cody that if anyone wanted more, he was in charge of the grill." J.T. jumped up beside Jenna after lifting Tracey onto the wagon. "Five more minutes with that music and I wouldn't have been responsible for my actions. Whatever happened to good old country-and-western music?"

"I'm afraid Molly's probably to blame for that," Harrison replied. "It sounded like what she listens to in New York."

"Teenagers are teenagers, whether it's in New York or Montana," J.T. assured him. "So, how're you doing, Harrison?"

"I'm fine and you were right. This is the best beef I've ever tasted. I was just telling Jenna what a great dinner this is."

"Why, thank you, Harrison," Tracey piped up, then burst into laughter with J.T.

"I told you, Tracey takes the credit for the food." Jenna smiled, then finally confessed, "She should. She does it all. You see, Harrison, the reason why these two are laughing at your compliment is because I hate to cook."

"*Can't* would be a better word," teased J.T.

"Can't?" Jenna looked outraged. "J.T., you ought to know by now there isn't a thing I can't do if I put my mind to it."

"Well, Harrison, all I can say is that should you ever be in a situation where your life depends on Jenna's cooking, you'd better hope that she wants to put her mind to it." That quip prompted Jenna to playfully tug on the brim of his Stetson and Tracey to utter an admonishing "J.T.!"

"Considering her other talents, I don't suppose it matters much," Harrison said appreciatively.

Jenna felt uncomfortable as a schoolgirl blush warmed her face.

"Where's Pa?" she asked, anxious to direct the subject from herself. "Did you leave him back there with the kids?" She looked at J.T. as she talked.

"He and Slim like that music," her brother insisted. "That's what comes from riding the bulls too long. The brain deteriorates."

The good-natured bantering and spontaneous laughter continued and Harrison found himself admiring the strong sense of family and genuine affection between brother and sister. When all four of them had finished eating, Jenna suggested they head back to the house for coffee.

"Cody said they're all going on a hayride later," J.T. commented, as they leisurely walked back.

"He spent the afternoon pitching bales of hay up on Pa's wagon," Jenna told him, noting how tall Harrison was, compared to the Fosters. There actually were quite a few things to admire about him besides his physical appearance. She appreciated a man with a sense of humor, a man whose ego didn't need constant pampering, a man who could admit he was wrong. She decided she could appreciate Harrison Drake quite nicely.

"We could probably go along if you two are up to it," Tracey suggested. "I noticed Jeff Borden brought his guitar along and you know that means country music," she added.

"I think I'd rather do dishes," J.T. said dryly.

"Well, maybe Harrison would like to go along," Tracey looked at Harrison questioningly.

"I think I'd rather do dishes, too." He gave her a rather sheepish grin.

"Watch out what you're saying, Harrison. Jenna's not one to let an offer slip by," J.T. warned.

"J.T., you are the worst tease tonight," Jenna insisted. "No one needs to worry about dishes. I already asked Mrs. Jenkins to stay. She's a local woman who helps me with the housekeeping and meals when I have the barrel-racing school," she explained for Harrison's benefit.

When they reached the house, Jenna had a few words with Cody before he led the group of teenagers down to the barn. While the four adults had coffee on the veranda, they watched the wagon full of teenagers roll on by, waving and laughing and singing as they left a trail of hay in their wake. Dusk was rapidly giving way to nightfall, and it wasn't long before J.T. and Tracey were leaving for home and Hank Foster was escorting Mrs. Jenkins back to town. And finally, Harrison was alone with Jenna beneath stars so near he felt he could lift his arms and touch them. It was the moment he had been anticipating for the past five days.

"I want to thank you, Jenna, for all your patience with these two kids this summer. I have to admit, I really didn't want to leave Molly behind last month, and not just because of her romance with Cody. I felt as though I were dumping the problem in your lap, yet I had to return to New York."

"I meant what I said earlier, Harrison. I do like Molly. We may have gotten off on the wrong foot, but looking back now, I think I may have overreacted a bit." Unconsciously, her fingers played with the heavy curtain of dark hair that drifted gracefully around her neck, and Harrison found himself wishing that it was his fingers toying with the silken tresses.

"Does that mean you think it was only a summer romance?"

"Would it bother you if it wasn't?" she asked candidly.

He paused before answering. "No. Should it?"

"I don't think it should." She sighed, then said, "I don't think our plan worked. If anything, I think Molly and Cody are probably more serious about each other now than they were four weeks ago."

"You sound as though you've accepted that."

"I guess I've accepted that I'm not responsible for what Cody's feeling. I'm not sure what's going to happen once you take Molly back to New York, but I hope both of our children will remember this summer fondly." Seeing his empty cup, she said, "You're out of coffee. Why don't you come inside and I'll get you a fresh cup. Then I'll show you around the house."

Harrison declined the offer for more coffee but followed her into the house, this time through the kitchen door where Jenna paused and said, "This is where J.T. would say I spend the least amount of time."

"I can think of a more important room in the house," he replied.

Jenna shot him an unexpected smile over her shoulder that caused his heart to beat erratically, then led him through the old-fashioned kitchen, down a hallway and into a room she called the family room. Harrison thought *museum* would have been more appropriate as it was a veritable showplace of rodeo memorabilia.

His attention was immediately caught by the portrait hanging over the fireplace. It was the same woman as was in his uncle's paintings, only it was obvious that his uncle hadn't been the artist. This woman didn't look nearly as much like Jenna as the other had, and for a moment, Harrison thought it might be someone else. But stepping closer, he saw the tiny mole beneath her left eye and knew that it was the same person. ''She's beautiful,'' he said simply.

Jenna, seeing Harrison's interest in the painting, said, ''That's my grandmother, Harriet Foster. She's the one who got us all into this rodeo business. During the 1920s she was the champion cowgirl at the Frontier Days Celebration, winning the ladies' saddle-bronc riding and the trick and fancy-roping contests.'' She pointed out several photographs amid the collage of pictures and awards covering one entire wall of the room.

''They don't have those ladies' events anymore?''

''Not at men's rodeos. Only barrel racing. Grandma said the official reason given for discontinuing the women's events was lack of contestants, but she claims that it was partly due to the husbands and the boyfriends of the female contestants arguing with the judges.'' She smiled wistfully. ''Back in those days, women could compete with men, and some did. Grandma could rope and tie a steer as fast as any man. But I think what she loved most was traveling with the wild West shows.'' Jenna indicated a colorful poster depicting cowgirls performing various stunts with a picture of Jenna's grandmother in the lower right-hand corner. The caption read Beautiful Daring Western Girls in a Contest of Equine Skill, starring Harriet Foster.

''Do you know you look like her?'' he said, studying her face.

''You think so?'' A few minutes earlier he had said her grandmother was beautiful, she recalled with a thrill of pleasure.

''It's the expression in your eyes, the way you both tilt your head. But she does look physically stronger than you do,'' he said with a grin.

''She was.'' Jenna walked over and picked up a silver photo frame from the console television that seemed like an anachronism in a room filled with relics from another era. "Here, this is my mother." She handed him a photograph of a woman holding a toddler on her lap while three children looked on adoringly. Harrison was surprised at the portly figure sitting so earnestly on the mohair sofa. He had expected another slim, lissome cowgirl, not this sturdy, matronly-looking woman dressed in a cashmere sweater and straight skirt.

"Of course, this was taken by a professional photographer, and Mother hated getting all dressed up for the picture. I remember her telling Dad we should all be lined up sitting on our horses outside in the paddock. But Dad insisted we put on our Sunday clothes for a real picture. That's my two older brothers, Lee and William standing behind Mama."

But Harrison's eyes were drawn not to the gangly adolescent boys, but to a young Jenna, whose puffy crinolined skirt ballooned about her. "You look like a dark-haired Shirley Temple."

"I agreed with Mama. I hated getting dressed up and I would have preferred sitting on a horse, too. As you can see from the rest of these—" she waved her arm in an encompassing gesture "—I usually was."

Harrison felt as though he could have spent hours in this room. So much of Jenna's heritage was here in the awards, the paintings, the photographs. And for every piece he commented on, she had a story.

"Those must be Cody's." He pointed to a pair of bronzed baby cowboy boots.

"His first pair," Jenna admitted with a crooked smile.

"Did you win all of these?" he asked, his mouth nearly agape at the hundreds of belt buckles in a glass display case.

"A Morgan or a Foster did," she replied with pride. "Along with dozens of saddles, horse trailers and even a couple of pickups. Those are outside and in the tack room."

"This room is incredible, Jenna," he said sincerely.

"It's a bit overwhelming, which is why I seldom bring anyone in here. I lose their attention too easily."

"Would you rather I turn my attention to you?" He gazed

into her brown eyes and felt himself being pulled in deeper and deeper.

"What do you think?" The words hung in the air.

"I think I've been wanting to kiss you ever since I arrived back in Montana," he confessed. "Blame it on the mountains or the stars in the big sky."

"There aren't any mountains or stars in this room," she said, her voice as smooth as silk, her mouth curving invitingly.

He laughed softly, and drew her into his arms. "You've got your own kind of magic, Jenna, and it's got nothing to do with this splendid country surrounding you."

"No?" she whispered, wrapping her arms around his neck and threading her fingers into his hair.

"No." He nuzzled her lips, gently at first, wanting to coax every ounce of sweetness from her soft, warm mouth. But Jenna's sigh of longing echoed his own desire and when she parted her lips and pressed herself closer to him, he deepened the kiss, responding to the overwhelming heat that was rushing through him.

His mouth crushed hers as his hands moved slowly across the ribbed knit fabric of her top, finding the narrow strip of hot flesh that was exposed where her summer top had separated from her jeans. As his fingers caressed and teased at the waistband of her jeans, her body trembled, softening against his intuitively.

What started out as one kiss became two, then three, until Harrison admitted to himself that it wasn't just kisses he wanted from Jenna Morgan. He wanted all of her. And he knew she felt it, too. It was there in the trembling softness of her body, in the way her tongue skillfully teased his, in the way her body melted into his.

It was Jenna who finally pulled back, her breath ragged as Harrison continued to nibble at her lower lip. "I'd say you have your own kind of magic, Harrison," she whispered against his mouth.

He lifted his head and looked at the slightly swollen lips and dark brown eyes filled with passion. She was flirting with him, as he had done with her, as he had intended would happen on this vacation. But suddenly he wanted her to be more than a pleasant diversion, more than the mother of his daughter's boy-friend.

The slamming of the screen door and a loud, drawled-out "Ma!" had Harrison and Jenna jumping apart like guilty children. Within seconds, Molly and Cody bounced into the room, unaware of the scene they had nearly interrupted.

"We're back, Dad. How long can I stay out tonight? Can Cody bring me home?" Molly asked in a rush.

Harrison glanced at his watch. "I didn't realize it was so late. We should probably leave, Molly. We've got an early flight tomorrow and it's probably better to say good-night now."

"But a bunch of the others are going to the Lookout. Come on, Dad. It's my last night." Molly's plea had a familiar ring to it and Jenna found herself a little breathless waiting for Harrison's answer.

"The Lookout is a dance club for teens," she explained. "It's only a couple of miles from here and it's well chaperoned."

Harrison looked at the two bodies that were clinging together as though they were Siamese twins joined at the hip. If Jenna wasn't going to object, he wouldn't either. He did breathe a sigh of relief, however, when Jenna reminded Cody of his curfew and neither teen complained.

"Here're the keys," Molly tossed her father Eleanor Fielding's car keys.

As soon as the two had departed, an awkward silence fell between Jenna and Harrison. Their children's presence had been a reminder to why they were together this evening, and the light, flirtatious atmosphere had disappeared. Jenna found herself searching for something to say, anything that wouldn't sound inane.

"I should probably get going," Harrison finally said. "I'm sure my aunt is waiting up for us." He had placed his hands in his pockets.

"Will you have any trouble finding your way back to town in the dark?" Now why had she asked that? Any man who could find his way around Manhattan certainly could navigate one dirt road and highway.

"I think I'll be fine," he said politely.

Jenna led him through the house and out into the black night, the string of colored lights still glowing gaily along the porch. When they reached his car, he turned to her and said, "Thank you for inviting me this evening, Jenna. And for everything you've done for Molly. You're one special lady. Maybe we'll meet again."

"Anytime you're in the neighborhood, stop in." She offered him her hand, but he pulled her into his arms and gave her a lingering kiss.

"You don't know how I wish your neighborhood was closer to mine," he finally groaned next to her ear. Then he released her and before Jenna could recover from the splendor of his kiss, he was driving away.

CHAPTER EIGHT

IF JENNA HAD EXPECTED life to return to normal after Molly's departure, she couldn't have been more mistaken. Cody moped about like a lovesick calf, hounding the postman as though he were waiting for a shipment of gold rather than a love letter. She had hoped that a trip to the university would get his adrenaline flowing and pique his interest in college life. But after registering for his classes and getting a tour of the Bozeman campus, he returned home with the same aloof attitude. Jenna told herself that it would only take time for Cody to snap out of his irascible mood, but when it began to disrupt his work on the ranch, she finally decided to expedite the process.

"The atmosphere around here is worse than it was when we had to put Last Straw to sleep," Jenna commented to her father one morning after Cody had eaten his breakfast with nothing more than a couple of grunts and groans interspersed in the conversation.

"The boy's got it bad," her father stated matter-of-factly. "But he'll get over it."

"Well, I'm going to help him along the way."

"I don't think I like the sound of that." He rubbed the gray stubble on his chin. "Take my advice, Jenna. Let him work it through for himself."

"But, Dad, you've seen the sloppy job he's been doing with his chores. And I shudder to think what the phone bill's going to look like, and it's only been a week."

"Jenna, dear, I know you want to help him, but I really think Cody needs to work this through for himself," Hank cautioned, but Jenna paid no attention.

"What he needs is to have another pretty face looking in his direction. It's about time we had a barn dance," she announced slyly.

"I thought you weren't ever going to have another one after what happened last time. If I remember correctly, your words were: 'Those teenagers aren't going to use my loft for any hanky-panky.'"

"*Those* teenagers were considerably younger. Now they've all graduated from high school and are heading for college." She snapped her fingers and her face lit up. "That's what we'll call it: a going-off-to-college party."

"You think by calling it that, Cody won't want to change his mind about going?"

"Is that what he's said to you?" Her forehead creased with concern.

"I don't think it's anything to worry about. He's experiencing a lot of changes at this time in his life. And I don't think it's just Molly Drake that's got his head in a muddle. I think he's had some real mixed feelings about going to college rather than on the pro rodeo circuit."

"As long as it's not a choice between college and Molly Drake."

"I thought you liked the girl."

"I do." And Molly's father, a little voice inside her heart added. "But the reality is she's city and he's country—not to mention the difference in their family backgrounds." Was she still talking about her son and his girlfriend, or was she trying to convince herself that she and Harrison were opposites? "Well, this barn dance will be just the tonic Cody needs to perk him up. I'll ask Roy to get his nephew's band to play, and there're several girls from the barrel school that I'd like to invite. Oh, it'll be a great party...you'll see," she reassured her father, patting him on the shoulder as she walked away.

And it was a great party, according to all the local residents who clapped their hands and stamped their feet to the fiddling of Ned Cooper and his country rock band. Jenna thought there wasn't a soul in attendance who didn't look as if they were having a good time, not even her son, who despite his obvious efforts to stay on the sidelines, ended up dancing with several different girls. It was good to see him smiling again—a thought Jenna had to keep repeating to herself every time Roy stepped on her toes or swung her around as though she were a rag doll. By the end of the evening, everyone was congratulating her on the success of the party, but it was Cody's parting words that stayed with her as she fell exhausted onto her bed.

"We should have done this while Molly was here."

Jenna lay on her satin sheets, fatigue causing her to giggle softly to herself. Cody was right. They should have had a barn dance while Molly was here. Instead of Roy's clumsy arms dragging her across the floor as she strained to keep her distance, she would have had Harrison's arms drawing her close, her body melting into his as it had on another occasion, an occasion she didn't want to remember, for it resurrected feelings over which she had no control. But what was the sense in dreaming about a man like Harrison Drake when chances were slim she'd ever see him again? She rolled over and buried her face in the pillow, but the memories haunted her well into the night.

"Jenna, you've got a phone call," Hank Foster called out to his daughter as he stepped into the barn.

"Would you take a message, Dad?" she asked wearily, rising from her crouched position in the stall where a tiny colt was resting.

"I think you could use a break," Hank insisted. "I'll finish up here."

"I'm almost too tired to walk back to the house," she moaned, trying to chase away her fatigue with a catlike stretch. After spending most of the past twenty-four hours in the barn while one of her mares foaled, Jenna's body was stiff and sore.

"Well, it's Mr. Drake on the telephone and if he's calling from New York it's costing him money."

"You should have said so right away." She wiped her hands on a towel before tossing it on the side of the stall, then hurried back to the house. Unconsciously her hand smoothed down her tousled hair as she picked up the receiver. "Harrison?"

"Jenna. How's everything in Red Lodge, Montana?"

"With the exception of one gloomy-faced teenager, everything is great. How are things in New York?"

"Busy, crowded, noisy...the usual. Molly's looking rather lost."

"We all miss her. How is she?" Jenna inquired fondly.

"She's pining...as her grandmother calls it. She started her new school last week and it's been a little rough adjusting to the new kids. It's her seventeenth birthday next weekend and I thought I might be able to put the sparkle back in her eyes if I were to invite you and Cody out for the weekend. I know it's short notice, but we'd love to have you as our guests." When Jenna didn't say anything, he asked, "Are you still there?"

His unexpected invitation had taken her by surprise. "Yes. I'm sorry, I had to think for a minute to remember if we had any plans. I know the Flying Fosters aren't booked for this weekend because Tracey and J.T. are going to a wedding in Wyoming. We were going to drive Cody up to Bozeman to get him settled into the college dorm, but I have a feeling he wouldn't mind if we waited until Monday morning to do that."

"Does that mean you'll come?"

"I'd like to. I'll talk to Cody this evening and let you know for sure tomorrow."

"That would be fine. My mother's having a birthday party Friday evening and I know how excited Molly's going to be when she finds out Cody will be here. I also have a favor to ask of you, Jenna," he continued. "I'm planning on getting Molly a horse for her birthday and I was wondering if you'd give me a professional opinion on a gelding I'm considering."

"I'd be happy to. That's a very nice birthday present, Harrison. I'm sure Molly will be thrilled."

"I hope so. I figure Molly will want to show Cody around on Saturday afternoon, which means we'll have time alone to check out the horse."

"Time alone" were the two words Jenna heard most clearly. The thought of spending the weekend in New York at Harrison's apartment sent a shiver of excitement through her.

"It'll be good to see you again, Jenna." Harrison's voice was almost a caress.

"I'm looking forward to seeing you, too," she said softly, as her arms squeezed the accent pillow close to her chest.

As JENNA HAD EXPECTED, Cody was ecstatic about Harrison's invitation. What she hadn't expected was his intention to give Molly a ring as a birthday present. They had driven into Billings and were strolling through a shopping mall when Cody paused in front of a jewelry store and told his mother his plan.

"Cody, what sort of ring are you thinking about buying?" she asked, her heart beating erratically as he leaned over the case displaying engagement and wedding bands.

"Relax, Mom," he said, straightening and moving over to an adjacent case. "We're not getting engaged. I just want to get her something nice—like her birthstone or something."

She chose her words carefully before she replied. "I think the ring is a very sweet idea, Cody, but I'm wondering if, say, a locket wouldn't be a better idea. You know, one of those gold ones that you could have engraved especially for her."

"I don't know, Mom," he said hesitantly. "I kind of had decided on a ring."

"It was just a thought." Jenna gave a dismissive shrug, then wandered over to the cabinet containing watches while Cody continued to browse at the rings. She could feel her palms becoming sweaty as the jeweler opened one of the cases for Cody and removed a velvet tray. Jenna turned and faced the mall, glancing nonchalantly at the mélange of shoppers passing by, fighting the urge to rush over and be a mother. *It's his money, his girlfriend, his present,* she kept repeating to herself and nearly jumped out of her skin when Cody said, "I got it."

"What?" Jenna asked, hoping her expression didn't look as if she had just stepped out of a horror movie.

"Here. Take a look. Then I'm going to have the guy wrap it." He nodded toward the salesman who was discreetly waiting behind the counter.

Too big for a ring, was Jenna's first thought as she accepted the square velvet box from Cody. When she flipped the top, she exhaled a sigh. "It's lovely, Cody." Resting on the satin cloth was a gold chain with a tiny open heart suspended in the center.

"She had one almost identical to it, but she lost it that night of the hayride," he told her. "This one's prettier."

"I'm sure she'll love it," Jenna agreed, resisting the urge to give her son a big hug.

The rest of the day sped by for Jenna as she frantically shopped for just the right clothes to take to New York. There had been few occasions for her to be among what her mother would have called "society folk," but she promised herself that Harrison was going to be in for a surprise if he expected her to look like a cowgirl in Manhattan. It was one thing to carry a purse shaped like a saddle on the rodeo circuit, but New York— at least Harrison's New York—wasn't going to see her sterling-silver belt buckles and brass boot tips.

Both she and Cody had managed to get hair appointments, but when Jenna saw Cody stepping out of the barber shop with his hair trimmed much shorter than usual, her only response was to raise her eyebrows.

"My new look for college," he said with an unabashed grin. "What's your new look for?"

Jenna's answer was to shove a stack of department-store boxes into his arms and lead him to the pickup.

HARRISON LOOKED at his daughter's expectant face and wondered if he wasn't feeling just as anxious as she. Even though he hadn't actually admitted it to himself, deep down inside he knew that he had used Molly's birthday as an excuse to see Jenna Morgan. It wasn't just Molly who had come home starry-eyed from Montana and had been pining away. He had thought that once he got away from the mountains and that Western aura that seemed to drown a person's senses with romanticism, he would forget all about Jenna. But he kept seeing her face, the cowboy hat cocked to one side, that exquisite look of passion in her eyes as she rode her horse. And then there was the way her face had flushed with desire when he had kissed her that last night in Montana.

God, what was he thinking? Here in the middle of the airport the last thing he needed was an arousing thought like that. Well, at least here in New York he would know if the attraction he

felt for her was genuine or had merely been a case of the setting
and the circumstances. After all, with her small, dark beauty
encased in sleek and supple leather, any man would have had
difficulty ignoring her.

"There's Cody!" Molly shot forward, pushing her way
through the small crowd gathered around the terminal gate waiting for passengers disembarking the plane. Harrison's eyes followed her as she ran to the slender cowboy who was wearing a
corduroy sport coat over his jeans. The two figures locked into
an embrace, and Harrison's eyes immediately moved to the
woman behind the pair.

If Harrison had been expecting Jenna Morgan, rodeo star, to
come waltzing off the plane, he couldn't have been more mistaken. The woman coming toward him now could easily have
passed for a chic cosmopolitan female out for a matinee at the
theater or lunch at La Caravelle. In a red silk gabardine suit
belted at the waist and a matching wide-brimmed hat, she would
have stood out in any crowd. Harrison's eyes traveled down the
length of her legs to her feet, which were enclosed not in cowboy
boots, but in a pair of red leather high heels that were open at
the toes. She looked as fragile as a piece of glass.

Jenna felt a moment of triumph at both the surprise and ad-
miration in Harrison's gaze as she stopped in front of him.
"What were you expecting?" she asked with a knowing grin.
"Spurs that jingle?"

Had Harrison not been standing in the middle of a busy airport
with his daughter less than thirty feet away, he might have pulled
Jenna into his arms and kissed her. The thoughts that only
minutes ago had had his blood stirring now seemed minor compared to the overwhelming desire swamping him. He gave her
his most suave smile and said, "Welcome to the Big Apple,
Mrs. Morgan."

"It's a pleasure to be here, Mr. Drake."

For several seconds they stood staring into each other's eyes,
as though silently communicating a private message. Then Cody
and Molly were beside them, anxious to be away from the
crowded terminal.

With the ease of an experienced traveler familiar with La

Guardia Airport, Harrison had them through the baggage claim and out into his car in short time. Although Jenna knew little about New York City, when Harrison drove his Lincoln Town Car past Central Park and turned down a side street lined with exquisite brownstone buildings, and finally into the circular drive of a posh apartment complex, she knew the Drakes resided in one of the most expensive and exclusive neighborhoods. A concierge opened the door for them, then carried their luggage up the canopied steps into a lavishly furnished lobby, where mirrored doors slid open as they stepped in front of the gilded elevator. She began to have second thoughts about her visit when the man placed a key in the panel on the elevator wall and they began their ascent to the penthouse level. Within seconds, the doors were sliding apart once more and Harrison was ushering them into an elegantly furnished apartment.

Posh was the only word that came to Jenna's mind. It could have been right off the pages of some glossy magazine, the sort of home Jenna always thought looked as though no one could possibly live in it because there was never a thing out of place. She expelled a sigh of relief as her eyes made a sweep of the room and she saw schoolbooks tossed on the cushions of the white leather sofa, a pair of Reeboks peeking out from under a chrome-and-glass coffee table where several financial magazines were neatly aligned, a pop can sitting on the matching end table, and sheet music carelessly tossed across the Steinway piano.

She cast a quick glance at Cody, who appeared to be as bemused by the opulent surroundings as she. His only comment was "You live here?" before Molly pulled him by the hand into the sunken living room.

"What do you think of New York?" she asked, opening a pair of vertical blinds to reveal a view of the city Jenna guessed few New Yorkers ever saw.

As Cody marveled at the panorama, Jenna could feel a sense of vertigo threatening to weaken her legs. She could climb some of the tallest mountains with much more breathtaking views without a doubt, yet up here in this man-made structure, looking out at miles and miles of crowded pavements, she felt trapped.

"Isn't this great, Mom?" Cody asked.

Drawing a deep breath, Jenna turned and said, "Yes. It's wonderful." She glanced over to where Harrison had just tipped the concierge who had deposited the luggage down a hallway Jenna assumed led to the bedrooms. He was looking at her as though he were waiting for her verdict of his home. He walked toward her, the unasked question evident in his eyes.

She smiled and said, "It's very nice, Harrison. Thank you for inviting us." And she meant every word. The apartment was nice, and as Harrison showed her around she saw that despite the *Better Homes and Gardens* appearance, the penthouse was a home. The fact that it sat atop a tall building in a very crowded city she would ignore. But what a contrast it was to her place in Montana!

They truly did come from two completely different worlds, and when he told her they would be dining with his mother before Molly's party, Jenna felt a momentary sense of panic. The evening ahead loomed long and intimidating, and she wondered if she would have anything at all in common with the Drakes' guests. She came from a background where the only bloodlines that mattered belonged to animals, and if someone mentioned the market it was in reference to what oats and feed were going on the agri market, not the Dow Jones Industrial. The world of country clubs, stately dinners and private yachts was foreign to her. It was like mixing champagne and caviar with beer and pretzels.

But then Harrison was showing her to her room, looking at her as though she were the finest lady he had ever entertained. And while she showered and dressed for dinner, she prayed that there wouldn't be too many people at the Drake home, then silently berated herself for her lack of self-confidence. What would her mother say if she saw her only daughter wincing at the thought of meeting people? For someone who had spent as much time on the road as she had, she seldom worried about having to walk into a room full of strangers. But if she were honest with herself, she knew it wasn't so much the roomful of strangers, but Harrison Drake's reaction to her presence that had her nervous.

Jenna took a good, long look in the cheval mirror, pleased

with the results of her fussing. The royal blue silk dress fit her perfectly, clinging in all the right places yet falling softly to below the knee. It was a very proper-looking dress, until she walked and the sarong skirt revealed a sensuous length of her right leg. She clipped on the large silver earrings her father had said looked like door knockers and fastened a sterling-silver choker around her neck. A smile came to her lips as she thought of how the sophisticated image could change with a simple switch in belts—her sterling-silver buckle for the black leather sash. An impish urge tempted her to wear the cowboy boots she couldn't resist bringing along. Instead, she slipped her stocking feet into the thin black straps of a pair of high heels and gave herself one final look before going out to meet the others.

When Jenna saw Harrison's appraisal, she was glad she hadn't let the impish urge overrule common sense. The look in his eye was worth every penny she had paid for the dress.

"I didn't think they wore dresses like that back in Montana," he said with admiration in his voice.

"They don't." She pivoted gracefully. "Do they in New York?"

"If they don't, they should." He was gazing at her with a feral look, a look that made Jenna's blood go a little wild, too. She was saved from answering by the entrance of Molly and Cody.

Jenna thought the girl's grandmother would whole-heartedly approve of the way Molly looked. She was dressed in a pink taffeta dress with a dropped waist, lots of ruffles, and a large bow at the shoulder. Her bare arms were striped with several different colored bracelets, her long legs covered with silk stockings that had a tiny pattern threaded in, and on her feet were matching pink leather flats. Her blond hair was pulled back with two jeweled combs—Jenna guessed they were real jewels—and she wore only a slight dusting of blush and lipstick. Around her neck was the heart Cody had given her.

"You look lovely, Molly," Jenna said sincerely.

"Thank you, Mrs. Morgan. You do, too." Jenna thought she detected a note of caution in her tone, but then decided she had imagined the girl's disapproval.

After seeing Harrison in formal evening attire, Jenna was happy that she had insisted Cody bring his one suit along—the one she had bought for his high school graduation. She felt a surge of maternal pride as he stood next to Molly, and she pushed aside any doubts she had about either herself or her son feeling out of place with the Drakes' guests.

Harrison's mother lived in an exclusive area on Long Island known as Oyster Bay, where Jenna thought the homes should have been called mansions rather than houses. When Harrison drove his car through ornate iron gates and up a long driveway, Jenna felt as though she were visiting someone from *Lifestyles of the Rich and Famous*. The grounds were exquisitely kept, every tree perfectly shaped, the emerald lawn resembling a plush carpet. And when the car came to a stop in front of a huge Georgian mansion, Jenna wished she were back in Red Lodge. She tossed a quick glance over her shoulder at Cody who was peering up at the well-lit facade and wondered if she looked as intimidated as he did. Oh, why had she agreed to this visit? They were two ordinary people who celebrated birthdays in blue jeans and leather, not silk and starched linen.

Once again Molly was pulling Cody by the hand, this time up the wide steps to the double front doors while Jenna waited for Harrison to come around to her car door. Some of her trepidation must have shown in her face, because when he took her hand in his, he said, "It's really much more imposing from the outside than it is on the inside."

"Harrison, just how important is your family?" When he gave her a quizzical look, she added, "I guess what I'm trying to say is, I'm not familiar with New York society and I don't want to address anyone incorrectly." Unconsciously she bit her lip.

Her insecurity was touching. Never in his life had Harrison wanted to protect a woman more than at that moment. All the other times they had been together she had been so bold, so full of self-confidence, it hadn't even crossed his mind that she might feel out of place with his family. He took both her hands in his and gave them a reassuring squeeze. "Jenna, it doesn't matter where my family came from or who they are. They're just people…like you and me."

But when the double oak doors opened and a uniformed servant greeted them, Jenna knew Harrison was wrong. She was entering a world that was totally foreign to her…a world of crystal chandeliers, sterling silver and imported crystal. Mrs. Drake had more original paintings hanging in her foyer than were in the entire art museum in Red Lodge. Harrison tucked her hand neatly in the crook of his arm and led her into an elegantly furnished room filled with at least half a dozen people.

All eyes turned in their direction and a tall gray-haired woman with graceful carriage came forward with her arms extended.

"Molly, darling. Happy Birthday." Harrison's mother wrapped her arms around her granddaughter and placed a kiss on her cheek, then turned to Harrison.

"Hello, Mother. I'd like you to meet Jenna Morgan and her son, Cody. Jenna, Cody, my mother, Amelia Drake." He smoothly made the introductions.

"How do you do?" Molly's grandmother said pleasantly. "I've heard so much about both of you I feel as though I already know you."

Several words popped into Jenna's mind as she took the delicate hand Amelia offered. Gracious. Genteel. Sincere. There was a smile in the woman's eyes as well as on her face, and Jenna, noting the resemblance to Harrison, returned the smile warmly. If Amelia Drake disapproved of Molly's relationship with Cody, she certainly wasn't letting it show. Harrison introduced them to the others in the room, which included his sister Anne and her husband, Amelia's brother Edgar and his wife, and Molly's maternal grandmother.

Dinner turned out to be less of an ordeal than Jenna had expected. She had given Cody a crash course in table etiquette, assuring him that if he simply worked his way from the outside in with the silverware, he would look as though he were used to eating off Limoges china with a servant placing food in front of him. But he seemed to have no problem at all with the formal dinner. He was laughing and getting along wonderfully with Molly's grandmother. And contrary to what Jenna had expected, there was no talk of commodities and trade deficits, but rather of high school and Molly's summer vacation.

It wasn't long after dinner that the party guests began arriving, and everyone moved into the adjoining ballroom where a small orchestra was tuning up.

"I thought you told me this was a small party," Jenna said to Harrison as the spacious room began to fill up.

"Just some of Mother's close friends," he reassured her. "Mostly old, thank goodness. I don't need any competition this evening."

Jenna's heart fluttered. "Any of them like horses?" she asked teasingly.

"If they do, I'm not going to introduce you to them." The predatory look in his eyes changed the flutter to a pounding.

Jenna would have responded but several people were saying hello to Harrison, among them a tall, beautiful woman with dark red hair swept back from her face in a very classical style. Everything about her spoke of money and success, and Jenna caught just a glimmer of surprise in her cool, hazel eyes as they noticed Harrison's hand resting protectively at Jenna's waist. Then, as introductions were made and pleasantries were exchanged, Jenna learned the reason for the woman's brief but thorough scrutiny. She was Diana Elliot, and all of Jenna's feminine instincts indicated her interest in Harrison was more than professional.

Jenna smiled warmly, shook hands with everyone, including Diana Elliot, and made the appropriate responses to the introductions, all the while trying to gauge Harrison's reaction to Diana's subtle yet proprietary manner. Among the small group gathered were a congressman and a well-known government economist, and when the conversation turned to a topic unfamiliar to Jenna, she began to wish she hadn't come.

But then the music started up, and as if on cue, the crowd drifted toward the perimeter of the room and several couples moved into the vacated space. And Jenna didn't care whether Diana knew what the analysts expected the consumer price index to do because Harrison was asking her, Jenna Morgan, trick rider, to dance. She felt his touch on her elbow and smiled as she accepted his invitation, thinking of how different the setting was from the last time they had danced at the Longhorn Saloon.

Harrison must have been thinking along the same lines, for he said, "I hope you like the big-band-era music. Mother always has this orchestra play because she says they were Dad's favorite."

"You don't think they know any country—is that what you're trying to tell me?" she said with a smile as they joined the other couples who were pairing off on the dance floor.

"No, but they do know how to play a mean fox-trot." He pulled her into his arms, his smile enticing as the sensuous rhythm began.

Jenna didn't say a word, but allowed herself to be pulled close to him, feeling his hand caress the middle of her back as the silky fabric allowed the warmth of him to heat her skin. All of the insecurities she was feeling only minutes ago dissolved as her eyes met the urgent blue gaze of the man who was beginning to generate deeper emotions within her the more she was with him.

They danced well together, shoulders and hips swaying in rhythm, their steps perfectly matched. The high heels added enough to her height that Harrison didn't have to stoop, but rather cradled her tenderly in his arms.

When the tempo of the music slowed, he rejected the traditional manner of dancing, bringing both of her arms up around his neck and letting his hands drop to her hips, a gesture that evoked dozens of sensations in Jenna...all of them pleasurable. She was acutely aware of the strength in his solid chest, and she wondered what it would be like, always to have the protection and warmth of his arms. It frightened her for just a moment— that feeling of wanting a man to wrap her in his embrace and never let her go. But that moment of reality was whisked aside by more primitive emotions. He was an attractive, masculine man, and feelings she thought she had successfully hidden awoke with a vengeance, and she found herself molding her body to his, answering his radar with a message of her own. Unlike the time they danced in Wyoming, where he had been hesitant in leading, Harrison was now in his domain and in control. After several slow numbers, he led her away from the dance floor, his arm resting around her waist possessively. Before guiding her through the open doorway, he grabbed two glasses of champagne from a passing waiter, handed her one, then said, "Come. I want to show you something."

"Where are the kids?" Jenna looked around for some sign of either Cody or Molly as they passed through the foyer and dining room.

"My guess is they're probably playing pool in the billiards room, but I can guarantee you they'll mystically reappear at the orchestra's intermission. That's when Molly gets to play her tape player and the teenagers can dance to their kind of music." He grimaced. "My mother's idea."

"Your mother has a lovely home, Harrison," she told him as he led her through what Jenna thought was a maze of hallways. "Is this where you were raised?"

He nodded. "It was built by my great-grandfather in the late 1800s, and renovated several times since then. It's always been inhabited by a Drake."

"It's very grand," she commented.

"Too grand for my taste."

"Is that why you and Molly live in an apartment?"

"Partly. It's also easier for me to get to work, too. I don't know what I would do with a monstrosity like this…I'm not much for entertaining. That's my mother's forte." He opened a door that admitted them into an immense kitchen where several servants were busy at work. Harrison bestowed several charming smiles on the staff as he escorted her through the kitchen and out the back door. They took a stone walkway leading away from the house until the noise and the lights faded into the background. They hadn't gone far when they came to a greenhouse, where Harrison reached up over the sill and produced a key.

"This was my grandmother's contribution to the renovation," he told Jenna as he held the door open for her to enter. "After she died, Mother took it over." The only lights on inside were the ultraviolet plant lights that combined with the moonbeams flooding the room to create an iridescent glow over the rows of flowers.

"It's breathtaking!" Jenna couldn't believe the number of flowers in the building. "Does she do this all by herself?" Jenna asked, wandering between rows of roses.

Harrison nodded. "The regular garden staff aren't allowed in unless she's with them. She's very protective of her flowers."

"I can see why. They smell heavenly." Jenna leaned down to inhale the fragrant aroma of an exquisite red rose. "The scent here is so wonderful it's almost intoxicating." When she straightened, Harrison had stepped closer so that her face met his ruffled shirt front.

"Yes, it is intoxicating," he agreed, but Jenna knew he wasn't referring to the flowers, and she felt a bolt of excitement when she glanced up into his eyes and saw the desire burning there. "But no more so than the way you looked when you stepped off that airplane, or the way you felt when your body melted into mine while we were dancing." His words were a soft caress and she felt a tingling heat unfolding deep inside her.

"I thought maybe I had imagined that," she said lightly.

Harrison took the champagne glass from her hand and set it beside his on a small ledge above the flowers. "You're not imagining this," he said, slowly moving his hands down the length of her back, stroking, caressing, until she gently melted against him. He lifted her until her mouth was on a level with his, then gently brushed his lips against hers. "Do you know what I would have done had they played one more slow song?"

"What?" she asked, wrapping her arms about his neck and running her fingers through his hair.

"This." The word was a careless whisper before his mouth captured hers in a seductive kiss that had Jenna parting her lips beneath the persuasive pressure of his. She savored the taste of him as his tongue slid over hers, setting her senses afire with a burning response. She was oblivious to the sweet fragrance of the roses, their aroma paling in significance compared to the sweet sensations swirling through her. She was consumed by the strength and the heat of his passion, and returned his kiss with equal fervor. When the kiss finally ended, he let her slide down his body until her dainty feet touched the floor.

"Maybe we should only slow-dance in private," she said huskily, her slightly swollen lips tempting him as she moistened them with her tongue. She tilted her chin as she spoke, and Harrison tenderly cupped her face in his hands.

"Jenna, I..." he began in a husky whisper. *I what?* he thought to himself. How did he tell her that he would dance every dance with her for the rest of the evening if he thought he could keep from caressing her in public? Or that he wanted to take her home and into his bed but their two teenage children stopped him? He dropped down onto a wooden bench beside the flowers and pulled her down onto his knee. The action caused the sarong skirt of her dress to fall away from her thigh, and Harrison couldn't resist the temptation to run his hand along the silk-stockinged leg.

Jenna shuddered and buried her lips into the hot skin of Harrison's neck, pressing her breasts into his chest, her legs unconsciously spreading as his hand began an erotic journey up her thigh. She thought there could be no more exquisite a sensation than a man's hand through silk stockings. Her breath dissolved into pleasurable exhalations of air until Harrison captured her mouth in a hard, deep kiss that left little doubt as to the effect she was having upon him as well. When her fingers found their way inside the crisp white shirt, Harrison could feel his self-control ebbing. If he didn't pull back now, there would be no stopping him. With an almost inhuman sigh, he lifted his mouth from hers, Jenna reluctantly removing her fingers from inside his shirt, her eyes silently asking him why.

"Only because there's a small crowd of people at the house and because this greenhouse has glass walls," he told her gently, responding to her unanswered question.

Jenna felt herself blush as she realized that her hunger for him had risen so quickly she hadn't given a second thought as to where they were. She hadn't meant for things to go so far, nor had she expected he would awaken such an intense need in her.

Harrison took her chin in his fingertips and said, "It excites me to think that I had you senseless." He planted a quick hard kiss on her mouth, then with a groan, lifted her to her feet.

Jenna couldn't resist reaching up to wipe the lipstick from his mouth. Her eyes had darkened with unrelieved tension as her body protested logic's intrusion. She wondered if he could read the thoughts running through her head, and quickly glanced downward just in case he could. Although everything had seemed so right between them, she wasn't quite sure if she was ready for him to know she wanted to make love with him.

Jenna smoothed down the silky fabric of her dress and straightened her belt. "Am I mussed?" she asked, a hand flicking at her dark curls.

"We can say we've been for a walk." He smiled. "I'll be the only one who'll know the wind wasn't responsible for your tousled curls." Taking her by the hand, he led her into the cool night air.

"Harrison?"

"Umm-hmm?"

"You'd better button your shirt."

NORMALLY HARRISON was a heavy sleeper. Thunder could rumble, the wind could howl, Molly could play her rock music and he would still sleep soundly. But tonight, not only had he had difficulty falling asleep, but when he finally drifted off, it was a restless slumber that soon had him prowling about his room like an impatient parent waiting for a truant child to return. Only his child was safely tucked in bed—which was the reason he was awake. Because he had a sixteen-year-old daughter asleep in the room across the hall, he was sleeping alone, instead of with the woman he longed to have lying next to him. Sighing impatiently at the direction his thoughts kept taking, he picked up the latest bestselling business-management book and tried to immerse himself in the economics of foreign markets.

"I'm hopeless," he told himself aloud, tossing the book onto the nightstand after rereading the same page three times. He propped his pillow up against the headboard and leaned back, giving in to the thoughts he had been trying to shut out.

It had been a wonderful evening, and Molly's birthday party had been a success. She was happy because Cody was here in New York with her; Harrison was happy because Jenna was here. Both Molly and Cody had been silent on the way home, probably due to fatigue, and Jenna, too, had been content to ride home in silence. For Harrison, the journey had seemed to go on forever. Every time he had glanced at Jenna he had wanted to shower her with compliments, yet she seemed so distant, as though they hadn't nearly made love in the greenhouse.

He had hoped that she would sit up and talk with him once they had returned home, but much to his disappointment, she had said good-night at the same time Cody had. Not that it would have done them any good to be alone. He was hardly likely to make love to her in the middle of the living room. It probably was a good thing that one of them had used common sense. Maybe she was still awake, too. He nearly leaped off the mattress and headed toward her room, but then wondered what he would tell Cody if he should find him knocking on his mother's door at 3:00 a.m. After all, maybe she was sound asleep, her dark hair spread out across the pillow, her sexy body covered in…covered in what? Did she sleep in a nightgown or naked? The thought brought an instant reaction in him and when he looked down at the bulge in his pajama bottoms the aching became worse than ever.

He rolled over to turn off the light and as he did he saw the small oval brass frame with Rita's picture inside. He hadn't exactly been celibate since her death, but then neither had he felt as though he had made love, either. He had satisfied physical needs, but never had he wanted to possess another woman the way he wanted Jenna. The feeling brought a twinge of guilt. Once he made love to Jenna, he would close the door on what now seemed like another lifetime. Loving her would be that important. And for the first time in four years, when he looked at Rita's picture, the hurting was gone.

CHAPTER NINE

"YOU'RE JUST IN TIME," Harrison announced as Jenna walked into the kitchen where Cody and Molly were already having breakfast at the island countertop. "Eggs Benedict or an omelet?"

Jenna's heart did a little flop at the sight of Harrison with frying pan and oven mitt in hand. Jack, too, had always liked to cook breakfast, only his favorites had been pancakes and scrambled eggs.

"Just coffee is fine for me," she replied weakly, remembering how she had lain awake last night comparing Jack and Harrison. They were alike in so many ways, yet so different. Harrison was so conservative, so cautious, so methodical, unlike Jack who was always so happy-go-lucky, living one day at a time.

"You'd better eat, Mrs. Morgan, or Dad will have to deliver his 'breakfast is the most important meal of the day' lecture." Molly grinned, then added, "He does make a great omelet."

"Want to give me a try?" Harrison asked, his question filled with innuendo that seemed lost on Molly and Cody.

"Mom'll eat anything as long as someone else is cooking," Cody said with a grin, oblivious of the undercurrents in the conversation.

"Cody!" Jenna said in mock indignation. "It's really not necessary, Harrison. I usually only have coffee and toast in the morning."

"You'll be doing me a favor. Otherwise I have to eat alone. The kids are nearly finished and then they're off."

"Off? Where to?" Jenna asked, climbing onto one of the leather stools at the counter.

"I've got to show Cody around," Molly explained, clearing

away the dirty plates and placing them in the dishwasher. "We've got to go shopping and then we're going to a couple of places where my friends all hang out." Molly's summer tan had faded a bit and she was back to looking very preppy in an oversize oxford shirt and denims. Jenna knew the weathered and washed-out look of her jeans hadn't come from being laundered and hung out to dry.

"Mr. Drake said he would show you around New York if you want, Mom," Cody said apologetically.

Jenna's eyes met Harrison's. "That's fine, Cody. You two go and have a good time. I'm sure we'll find plenty to do."

The minute the elevator doors slid shut, Harrison leaned across the island and planted a kiss on Jenna's surprised mouth.

"Good morning, Jenna."

She smiled, then placed an equally tempting kiss on his lips and said, "Good morning, Harrison."

"Did you sleep well?" he asked, returning his attention to the eggs he was whisking in a bowl.

"Like a baby. And you?"

"Same," he lied, trying to keep his eyes on the task in front of him and not on the body-hugging red fabric of her shirt. It would be just his luck to botch the omelet. "I never hear a peep once I close my eyes."

"Would you like any help?" she asked, when the only sound to be heard was the sizzling in the frying pan.

He gave her an incandescent smile that had her breath catching in her throat. "If you'll just get the coffee? Oh, and there's kiwi fruit in the refrigerator."

"Sure." Jenna slid off the leather stool and walked around into the kitchen, her eyes taking in all the modern conveniences at Harrison's fingertips, including several gourmet appliances. She couldn't help but wonder if this had been Rita's domain.

"You look as though you enjoy being in the kitchen," she commented as she poured two cups of coffee.

"Does that surprise you?"

"No, I find it charming."

"Charming?" he asked, placing the perfectly cooked omelets across from each other and motioning for her to sit down. He had on a long-sleeved dress shirt with the cuffs turned back and faded denims, and he most certainly did look charming to Jenna.

"Yes, charming," she repeated with a dimpled grin. She took a taste of the omelet and gave a sigh of satisfaction. "It's wonderful."

"A way to a woman's heart is through her stomach," he teased.

"J.T.'s already told you I'm not exactly Julia Child in the kitchen."

"Molly finds that one of your most endearing qualities. She doesn't like to cook either, which is why I'm usually the one doing breakfast."

"I thought you'd have a housekeeper or something."

"Oh, I do Monday through Friday. On weekends Molly and I fend for ourselves. Only Molly would just as soon skip a meal rather than have to cook. And I'm not one for fast food, so I cook."

"You're very good," Jenna complimented. "You're welcome at the Lost Creek Ranch anytime."

"I just might take you up on that," he said with a grin.

While they ate she told him about her childhood and her life in the rodeo, how during the peak of her barrel-racing career she had spent nearly nine months out of the year on the road. Harrison absorbed her stories with interest, envying her freedom from the demands and pressures of a career such as his. He found himself reluctant to talk about his work, for she seemed to have the ability to read his emotions quite well.

When they had finished eating, Jenna thought of how companionable breakfast had been. They had talked like two friends rather than as the parents of two friends. And she was happy that Molly and Cody had made plans of their own. When Harrison mentioned that he needed to change his clothes before they left for the horse farm, Jenna offered to clear away the dishes.

"I may not be the greatest cook, but I am good at cleaning up," Jenna assured him, grateful for the opportunity to look about the expertly designed kitchen. She peeked in cupboards to find all the canned goods neatly aligned and noticed that some food items were hand dated. As she suspected, every drawer was meticulously arranged, and she knew they were indicative of his life-style—everything in Harrison's life was ordered.

"Ready?"

She winced when his voice sounded close to her ear. Turning, she looked at him and couldn't suppress the grin. "I like your new shoes." Harrison was wearing a pair of faded denims, a sweatshirt and a shiny new pair of Wellington boots.

"I've kept them hidden in the closet. I didn't want Molly getting any hint of her surprise. I only hope you approve of the horse as easily as you did the boots."

THE HORSE WAS BEAUTIFUL, as was the Bennet Quarter Horse Farm, which reminded Jenna of her brother's farm in Kentucky. With Harrison's limited experience of horses, she had been worried that he might be buying an expensive, well-bred horse without really knowing what kind of animal he was getting. Often she had seen parents make the mistake of being in too much of a hurry to get a horse for a child, with the result that they bought the first one that looked good. But Harrison had surprised her. On the way to the farm she had discovered why he was such a successful businessman. He had done his research well, and had even hired a veterinarian to check over the horse.

"What do you think?" he asked as Mr. Bennet brought the gelding over to the corral fence.

"He's a beauty," she said, rubbing her hand affectionately down the sorrel coat of the horse. "He's got good bone structure and straight legs. Nice high withers, too." She turned to Mr. Bennet. "There's thoroughbred back there somewhere."

Mr. Bennet smiled. "You're right, Mrs. Morgan. Great-grandsire."

"How's his temperament?"

"Mellow, but he's no deadhead. Not the type you want to go to sleep on."

Mr. Bennet handed Jenna the reins. She mounted the gelding and worked him in a figure-eight pattern, then checked how he handled with some slide stops and rollbacks. Harrison stood back, admiring the rider as well as the horse. When she returned to the rail, her cheeks were glowing with the sparkle Harrison was coming to recognize.

"Fine horse," Jenna said, patting his neck. "I think he'd suit Molly, Harrison. He's got an easygoing stride and he's alert without being too hot about it."

Mr. Bennet waited with the stoic patience of a horse trader, then bartered amicably with Jenna until she got him to a price she felt was fair.

"We've got a deal," Mr. Bennet confirmed to Jenna, a twinkle in his eye. "Mr. Drake, your friend's a smart horse-trader."

Harrison smiled, shaking the gentleman's hand. "I'd like to bring my daughter down tomorrow, as we agreed upon."

Jenna walked the sorrel gelding while Harrison and Mr. Bennet completed the arrangements. He was such a fine, well-mannered horse, how could anyone not like him? Yet she had seen the apprehension in Harrison's eyes when she had reined up close to him. Still, she hadn't missed the glimmer of desire in his eyes when he watched her from a distance. No matter how much Harrison personally disliked horses, the sight of her astride one aroused him.

After stopping for lunch on the way back to the city, Harrison told Jenna there was one more stop he wanted to make. Parking his car in front of an old brick building that appeared to house a used bookstore and antique shop, he led her into a side door and up a flight of stairs to a door that read Uptown Gallery.

"This is one of my favorite places. The fellow who runs it is an old college friend of mine," he told her, pushing open the door for her. "I thought you'd be interested in seeing some of the pieces here."

When Jenna stepped into the gallery, the first thing she noticed was the six-foot-tall sculpture of an eagle by a well-known wildlife artist. Although the atmosphere was very low-key, the art was high quality.

"Many of my uncle's paintings were shown here," Harrison told her as they wandered through the gallery. "Whenever he visited New York, he'd bring me down here and tell me all sorts of stories about the old West."

"He was well respected in Red Lodge, and of course everyone knows of his reputation in the art world."

"Did you ever meet him?" Harrison said curiously.

"Only once. I was sixteen and I had just won my first world championship. He came to see me. He told me he had watched me race and asked if I would mind if he painted me. I could hardly believe that an artist like Charles Fielding would want to paint me."

"And did you sit for him?"

She shook her head. "He told me he would contact me during summer vacation, but unfortunately he died that spring. Did you see him often?"

"Not as often as I wanted. He and Aunt Eleanor left New York before I was born. I'm afraid that when you come from the kind of background I do and you decide you're going to be an artist rather than a banker, you're looked upon as a black sheep. Once my parents found out I was fascinated with Uncle Charles's studio, the visits became fewer."

"But it's obvious your mother is a great patron of the arts," Jenna said, somewhat puzzled.

"You have to remember that my uncle didn't become a success overnight. At the time he left New York he was very young, and I think the Fieldings thought he was acting like a spoiled little rich kid who was defying his parents and playing at being an artist. They hoped that he would one day come back to New York and take his proper place in the financial world."

"Thank goodness he didn't," Jenna exclaimed. "Look what we would have missed. Is that why your aunt never went back to New York after his death?"

"According to Mother, Eleanor never wanted to leave New York in the first place. Apparently she used to beg Uncle Charles to take her back. That was before she got involved in her charity work and opened the music studio. Now you couldn't drag her back to New York."

They stopped in front of an abstract landscape painting. "What do you think?" Harrison asked.

Jenna studied the painting with a pensive look on her face.

"I like the bold, yellow strokes, but it looks a little out of place with the rest of this Western art," she replied honestly.

Harrison laughed and shook his head. "But look at the title."

"Sunrise in the Rockies," Jenna read aloud and again studied the confusion of color. She leaned closer to get a look at the artist's signature, her eyes squinting in an attempt to decipher the barely discernible initials. "It's signed H.A.D. Maybe that's the way sunrise in the Rockies looks to H.A.D."

"Or to Harrison Anthony Drake," he said quietly.

Jenna looked from the painting to Harrison and back again. "This is yours?"

He nodded. "I've only done abstracts, but Tom always insists on hanging them in here with the Western art."

"You've done others? When do you find the time?"

"I usually manage to paint one a year when I'm on vacation, but when I came back from Montana I didn't want to wait with this one. I've been working on it at night, which has been difficult since we've been so busy at the office."

"Where are the others? I want to see them." She glanced around the gallery.

He laughed. "They're not here. Believe it or not, they actually sold."

"Of course I believe it. You're a wonderful artist. How long have you been painting?"

"I started painting seriously while I was in college. It gave my parents quite a scare, especially when I took a year off and studied art in Paris. That was when I used to see stars in my eyes instead of green dollars—a very unhealthy condition for a Drake." His tone held a hint of bitterness. "But, like a dutiful son, I returned to Yale, completed my graduate work in economics, and the rest is history." He impatiently tugged at his shirtsleeve to look at his watch. "It's getting late. We'd better get going. The kids will be home soon."

There was a finality to his words that told Jenna the subject was closed. Seeing the stern lines on his face, she made no further comment.

MOLLY AND CODY were already home by the time Jenna and Harrison returned. And just as Harrison had predicted, they had already eaten dinner and were anxious to leave for the dance at Molly's school. Jenna had to squelch the gasp that threatened to escape when she saw the way Cody was dressed. She knew that he hadn't wanted to look like a cowpoke from Montana, but she was unprepared for the drastic change from blue jeans to parachute pants with suspenders. Standing side by side, he and Molly looked like Madonna and Sean Penn clones. Molly's beautiful blond hair was sprayed red and Cody's dark head had a golden streak down the center. Unless Jenna was mistaken, her son looked distinctly uncomfortable.

"Cody, do you think I could talk to you for a few minutes before you leave?" she asked when she finally found her voice.

"I think Molly's worried we might be late, Mom," Cody objected.

"You've plenty of time," Harrison assured him, his eyes meeting Jenna's in understanding. "Did you want to ride along?" he asked her.

"No, I think I'll stay here and freshen up."

"Why don't Molly and I wait for Cody downstairs," he suggested, steering his daughter out of the room.

As soon as the elevator doors had closed, Jenna asked Cody, "Are you sure you want to go dressed like that?"

Cody looked down at his new clothes and shrugged. "Molly knows what everyone wears here, Mom. You know I don't want to look like a hick. After all, you haven't been wearing your usual clothes."

Jenna thought of the red gabardine suit and blue silk dress and knew she couldn't argue that point. "Are you having a good time?"

Again, he shrugged. "New York's a lot different than Red Lodge."

"Yes, it is," she concurred. "Well, if you're sure you're going to feel all right...."

"It's only for one night."

"Okay. Have fun." She gave him a quick hug.

"Thanks." He started to leave, then turned back toward her. "You're having a good time, aren't you, Mom?"

Jenna smiled and replied honestly, "Yes, I'm glad we came."

"Where did Mr. Drake take you today?"

"Oh, just out to lunch and to an art gallery. You'd better get going. We can talk tomorrow."

Jenna remembered Harrison telling her Molly's school was approximately an hour away, which meant he wouldn't be back for a couple of hours. Instead of a quick shower, she decided to soak in a scented bath before getting dressed for dinner. Molly had left her radio-cassette player on the double-basined vanity, and with a poke of her finger, Jenna hit a button and loud rock music echoed off the ceramic tiles at a near-deafening volume. Padding back into her bedroom, she dug deep into her carryall and found the George Strait tape she had listened to on her Walkman during their flight to New York. Minutes later, smothered in foaming mountains of bubbles in the elegant sunken bathtub, she went over the events of the past twenty-four hours while George Strait crooned songs about being crazy in love. Who would have thought she, Jenna Morgan, would be sitting in a rich man's bath preparing for an evening with a prominent member of New York society, or for that matter, wanting to spend an evening with a man like Harrison Drake?

Be honest with yourself, Jenna. You want to spend more than an evening with the man, a little voice told her. *If it weren't for Molly and Cody, you would be spending the entire night in the man's arms.* As the water began to cool, she reluctantly left her daydreams behind when the click signaled the end of side one of the tape. She climbed out and wrapped herself in a jumbo terry-cloth towel, letting the plush material soak up the drops of scented water on her skin like a large ink blotter. On her petite figure it fell to below her knees. Her room was directly across from the main bathroom, and as she crossed the thick carpet with feet bare, her eyes were drawn to the abstract painting hanging in the hallway.

Too curious to wait until she was dressed, she moved closer to the piece of art until she could read the signature. H.A.D. She stood back in critical appraisal and noticed the similarity to the painting at the gallery—the same dynamic lines, the same vibrancy of color that had sparked a warm feeling in her. She wondered how many of the other paintings hanging in the apartment were Harrison's. She tiptoed down the hallway to the guest room Cody occupied and stuck her head inside. Nothing but a couple of wildlife prints—two pheasants in flight and a solitary mallard afloat a pond. The walls in Molly's room, if she remembered correctly as she passed the closed door, were covered with posters. Harrison's room was around the corner—dare she look inside? She cautiously took the remaining few steps before having to turn left, poked her head around the corner and discovered the door to the master bedroom was slightly open.

Go ahead, take a peek, an impish voice inside her head urged. *He won't be back for at least another hour.* Jenna stepped around the corner as though she were testing unsafe ice. Through the crack in the door she could see the upper portion of a king-size bed, a brown satin quilt thrown over it.

With only the tips of her fingers pressing against the wooden door, she gave it a gentle shove. The rest of the room gradually came into view, as did the man standing in front of the closet.

At her startled gasp, Harrison turned and saw Jenna in the doorway. "Looking for someone?" he asked in a husky voice, his eyes wide at the sight she made standing in the doorway wrapped only in a towel.

"What are you doing here?" she demanded.

"This *is* my room," he managed to say with a slightly crooked grin.

"But you told me Molly's school was an hour away from here," she accused.

"It is. But the school dance is being held at a youth center about twenty minutes away."

"I wasn't expecting you for another hour."

"Then you didn't get my message?"

"What message?"

"The one I left on your bed. I knocked on the bathroom door to let you know I was back, but I think maybe the music was a little too loud for you to hear me—" He broke off as he realized that she hadn't come looking for him. "What are you doing in here, Jenna?"

A delicate blush covered her body. "I was looking to see if

you..." She paused as she realized that she was standing with only a towel wrapped around her otherwise naked body. Why did he think she had come into his room? *There's no one home; we're all alone,* she thought to herself. Unconsciously her hands went to the spot where she had folded the towel around her chest.

Harrison began moving toward her with such an intensity in his eyes it caused Jenna to tremble in anticipation. Slowly, his gaze never leaving hers, he reached around her shoulder and closed the door. Jenna stepped back against the wood as Harrison's right palm landed several inches above her head, taking the bulk of his weight as he leaned forward, trapping her between him and the door. Because of the height advantage, he was looking down and getting a delectable view of her cleavage.

"I've been waiting for you," he murmured.

Watching his lips move, Jenna thought that he had the sexiest voice she had ever heard. She was acutely aware of his gaze resting on the curve of her breasts. She turned her head to look at the arm extended close to her ear and saw blond hairs where his sleeve had been pushed back to his elbow. He had obviously just shaved, and the lemony scent of his shaving cream was like an aphrodisiac. When she raised her eyes to meet his, she saw the message that by now was becoming as familiar as his Robert Redford grin. The want, the need, the desire were all there for her to see. At that moment Jenna knew that they were going to make love. They were alone. They were alive.

"You smell like a tropical flower," he said thickly, his gaze passing slowly and deliberately down the column of her throat and over her shoulders, his breath a warm caress on her bare skin as he lowered his head and savored her scent. Jenna could feel the sudden tautness of her nipples as his eyes devoured the generous curve of her barely concealed breasts, the pink towel having slipped until only her nipples remained lost to his sight. A yearning such as she hadn't experienced in a long time rose up inside of her, triggering feelings that were threatening to overwhelm her. When he began to plant tiny hot kisses on the smooth skin just below her collarbone, she could feel her body responding with a lightning-quick reaction.

He was so close, yet the only part of him touching her was his mouth, trailing a path of kisses along the slender column of her neck until she felt his warm breath near her ear, and he whispered, "You taste even better than you smell...mmm... delicious," he murmured, kissing her cheek.

Jenna turned her head so that her lips met his, capturing his mouth with a soft, provocative kiss. With a groan of surrender, Harrison crushed her body against his, his lips parting and welcoming her tongue into his mouth. Tenderly at first, but then with a deepening passion that surprised even Harrison, he tasted her sweetness and responded by sliding his tongue forward, coaxing and teasing until Jenna was the one moaning in surrender. Each kiss became longer, deeper, more probing until they were both quivering with eagerness.

Harrison pulled back and searched her flushed face for a sign that she didn't want him as badly as he wanted her. But the only thing written on her face was the same emotion that was swelling his sensitive flesh and burning away his self-control. There was no mistaking the sensuous signals she was sending, and with a feeling of elation he lifted her into his arms and carried her to the bed.

Laying her back against the cool satin spread, he gazed into the dark brown eyes that reflected the sensuous abandonment he was feeling. She watched him shrug out of his sweatshirt and toss it somewhere behind him. When he started to unbuckle his belt, she rose to her knees and with a wanton pleasure replaced his hands with hers, unzipping his trousers and sliding them down over his hips. Harrison thought that had he not peeled off his clothes, the look in Jenna's eyes would have burned them away.

"Oh, Harrison!" Her exclamation at the sight of his nakedness made his heart beat even faster, and when she reached out to touch him, he closed his eyes and fought for self-control. He had been too long without a woman, and if her hands continued their erotic exploration he would rush what he wanted to be a slow journey to ecstasy. With a supreme effort, he caught her roving hands in his and kissed each fingertip. Then he hooked his finger inside the rolled edge of the towel and with a quick jerk Jenna's beauty unfolded before him—the high full breasts peaked with deep rose, the small waist, the curve of slender hips and the dark silken mound.

Harrison wanted to touch every inch of her perfect body—with his fingers, with his lips, with his skin. He wanted to move slowly, gently, to discover every erogenous spot on her tantalizing body. But the minute he bent and touched his lips to her skin, he knew the hunger pulsating inside him was only going to accelerate. With a groan he took her breast in his mouth, curling his tongue around the rosy tip until he felt it tighten in delight.

Wrapping his arm around her waist, he guided her back down onto the bed. Turning on his side so that his body half covered hers, he captured her mouth again, his tongue probing deep into its soft interior while his hands moved hungrily over her satiny flesh, tracing the smooth curves until they reached her thigh.

Feeling his hand slide down her body, Jenna's breath quickened when he moved his fingers to the softness of her inner thighs. Harrison began to stroke her intimately, savoring the softness, the moistness, the heat that caused her to shiver and moan until she could no longer hold back her passionate plea.

"Oh, Harrison, I want you so." It was a deep-throated whisper that had him nearly losing the last trace of control he possessed. He knew then that he was going to lose himself completely in this woman. She had a power over him that no woman had ever held, and although he didn't know why he should feel so completely under her control, he knew that he was going to make love to her so that she would never feel the same way again with any other man.

When she shifted her legs, he lifted his body and entered her with one swift movement, her softness parting to accommodate his hardness. A startled cry burst forth from Jenna, and Harrison paused until she began her own rhythmic movements. Then, moving as slowly as he could, he tried to savor every minute of ecstasy, as each stroke carried him further and further away from control and closer and closer to the explosion of pleasure he knew was coming.

What he hadn't expected was for Jenna's need to be as fierce as his, and try as hard as he might to control the tempo, the slow, steady rhythm quickly accelerated to a wild, driving explosion that carried them both to a shattering crescendo of convulsive caresses. Engulfed in waves of ecstasy, they clung to each other, their broken cries echoing the pulsating sensations that left them satiated with passion. For several minutes they remained locked together, as though they could somehow mesh their flesh together and prolong their union. The long, low moans of pleasure were replaced by contented murmurs of satisfaction and finally, reluctant sighs as Harrison began to stir.

"Don't leave," she whispered, making a small sound of protest when he would have eased away from her. Harrison responded by kissing her swollen lips tenderly; then, half lifting her, he rolled over to his side until they lay face-to-face.

"You took me by surprise, Mrs. Morgan," he said huskily, stroking her cheek with his fingertips. He brushed his lips over hers, taking pleasure in the contented murmurs that purred from her.

"In what way, Mr. Drake?" she murmured, enjoying the feel of his hands that were now sweeping across her naked flesh, caressing, reassuring and prolonging the afterglow of their lovemaking. With palms outstretched, she felt the damp thatch of hair covering his chest and absorbed the heat radiating there, wondering why the mere texture of him should be so gratifying.

"It was so good between us...." He felt her tightening and amended, "It *is* so good between us, isn't it?"

She laughed softly, sensuously. "You didn't think it would be?" Her finger was drawing a tiny circle about his nipple, and every so often her thumb would scrape across the hard nub.

"Not in my wildest dreams—and they were...pretty wild...last night." He was having trouble talking, hell, he was having trouble breathing, as Jenna's hips were moving against his once more, her pelvic muscles doing an erotic dance until he was steely hard and responding to her provocation. Then she was pulling him over her, and he was sinking deeper and deeper into her, and the hunger was there all over again, as though its fire had never been extinguished. As they rode the crest of exhilaration, Harrison thought that if he were to make love to Jenna a thousand times, he would never get enough of her. With a groan, he gave in to the fire that consumed them, and once again filled her sweetness with his warmth.

THEY LAY QUIETLY in each other's arms, listening to heartbeats slowly returning to normal, luxuriating in the afterglow of passion. Harrison pulled Jenna into the cradle of his arms and looked down at the face nuzzled contentedly next to his chest. She had been everything he had thought she would be. And more. She was just as daring and exciting in bed as she was when she rode her horse. She hadn't surprised him at all; the surprise had been his reaction to her, the intensity of his feelings for her—feelings that went far deeper than physical gratification, feelings that reached deep into his soul.

"This wasn't exactly the way I had it planned," Harrison finally said lazily.

"Good." She chuckled. "Your life is too well planned. You need to be more impetuous."

"We've missed our dinner reservations. I was expecting to take you to dinner at Lutèce, romance you over French cuisine, then bring you back here, and—"

"And?" she probed, her voice soft and intimate, like the hand that was sliding across his chest.

"Why did you come into my room?"

"To look for your paintings." As though suddenly remembering, she lifted her head and saw the large abstract across the room. "When did you do that one?"

"That was when I was in Paris."

"It's wonderful." She was off the bed and standing in front of the painting in seconds.

"So are you," he said, admiring her naked body from the back.

"Harrison, I'm serious. I don't understand why you aren't an artist rather than a money manager."

"And I don't understand why you don't have any tan lines. Do you sunbathe in the nude?" He didn't want her probing into his feelings about his art.

"I don't sunbathe at all," she snapped, then turned and gave him a capricious grin. "But I do skinny-dip in the lake on hot summer days." She picked up the shirt he had been wearing earlier and slipped it on. "There. Now you can tell me why you're not following in your uncle's footsteps." She sat beside him on the bed.

Harrison expelled a long sigh. "Jenna, a man has responsibilities and obligations. First, it was my parents, then it was a wife and child."

"And now?"

He shrugged. "I'm forty years old. A man my age doesn't toss a successful career out the door because he has dreams of becoming the next Picasso. Investing money is what I'm best at."

"How can you say that when you can create something as beautiful as this?" She swung around and pointed to his painting.

He sat forward and took her hands in his, then gently kissed each one. "We've only got a couple of hours alone. I don't want to spend them discussing my art." His hand slipped beneath the starched white shirt to find bare skin, and Jenna could feel herself yielding to his wish.

"I promised you dinner. We've missed Lutèce, but we could still go out."

"I'd rather stay here," she murmured as his fingers traced the hollow between her breasts. "We could raid the refrigerator and have a feast in bed."

"I'm afraid my refrigerator doesn't offer quite the same fare as Lutèce," he said apologetically.

Jenna gave him a big smile. "You forget, you're talking to a woman who thinks the four basic food groups are fast, junk, frozen and instant!"

CHAPTER TEN

SUNDAY BROUGHT A TORRENT of rain to New York City and Jenna hoped for Harrison's sake it would end before they arrived at the Bennet farm. She could see the disappointment in his eyes as he gazed out the plate-glass windows in the living room, tiny lines creasing his forehead. Molly appeared to be a bit sullen, and Jenna guessed that it was because Cody would be leaving after dinner. Today she had dressed in a pair of jeans and a leather jacket, French-braiding her hair except for the small tuft of spiked bangs. Jenna wondered if the heavy makeup was an attempt to cover the puffiness around her eyes.

Harrison had told Cody about the gelding, which Jenna figured as part of the reason for her son to return to his usual attire of Levi's and a plaid shirt. Only today his jeans were tucked into his boots—buckaroo style—as were Molly's. And when he donned his Stetson, all traces of the New York Cody were gone.

Harrison had told Molly they were going to take a drive into the country, stopping for brunch at an inn along the way. Although the two teenagers were unusually quiet, Jenna had no reason to suspect anything was wrong, for they sat huddled together in the car holding hands. They were doing exactly what she would have liked to be doing with Harrison. Once she caught Harrison noting the direction of her gaze and she knew that his eyes could read the message in hers—the message that said, *why aren't we snuggling side by side?* But this feeling with Harrison was too new, too special to share with anyone just yet, and she wasn't quite ready for their children's reactions to their relationship. She had told Harrison earlier that morning when he had kissed her on the sly in the kitchen that they were going to have to behave like parents today, not lovers.

Even though he had agreed, it didn't prevent him from getting close to her every chance he got. At the restaurant they sat side by side on the banquette, with Molly and Cody across the table. She could feel the warmth of him as he pressed closer to her, and several times he placed his hand on her thigh, gently caressing until she would inhale sharply. When he'd open the car door for her, he'd made a great effort to place his hand under her elbow and the other around her waist, helping her from the car in a gallant gesture.

If Molly had been sullen earlier in the day, there was no trace of unhappiness when Harrison pulled up to the Bennet farm and announced she was about to receive her birthday present. The joy in the girl's eyes at the sight of her very own horse rekindled feelings of nostalgia in Jenna, who could remember in vivid detail the day she got her first barrel horse. And just as she had expected, the horse suited the rider beautifully. Everyone but Harrison took a turn at riding the horse, which was called Red Fury. By the time they were ready to drive back to the city, Molly's cheeks were glowing, her eyes sparkling. As Jenna watched father and daughter hugging, she could see that the affection that had at one time seemed forced, now came naturally between the two of them. Molly's proclamation of love and appreciation made Jenna forget that the young girl had once said her father didn't care about her. This weekend Harrison had looked like the perfect everything—father, son, lover. Jenna hated to see the weekend come to an end, and she wondered how she would hide her emotions when it came time to say goodbye to Harrison at the airport.

But the only emotion she needed to hide was disappointment. When they arrived back at the penthouse, Harrison received an urgent phone call from Diana Elliot that caused not only worry lines on Harrison's face, but tears in Molly's eyes. An international monetary crisis—or something that sounded equally foreign to Jenna—necessitated his immediate attention and prompted him to arrange for Cody and Jenna to take a taxi to the airport while he went to the office. Although Molly begged her father to allow her to accompany them, he was adamant in his refusal, and Jenna saw Harrison Drake, financier, in action.

It was Sunday evening. Was twelve hours that critical in his profession or was Molly right in her insistence that work was the most important thing in his life? Jenna didn't want to confront the possibility that maybe he was a workaholic.

It had been frustrating not having any time alone with him today. Now Harrison's preoccupation with his business left her wondering if last night hadn't simply been a pleasant diversion for him. Instead of passionate kisses with promises for the future, their goodbyes were stilted and polite. Proper New York goodbyes, Jenna thought bitterly.

Cody was quiet on the flight home, but Jenna was too preoccupied with their abrupt departure to notice that he seemed relieved to be going home. In fact, Cody was grateful that his mother wasn't cross-examining him on the way back to Red Lodge. In his opinion, the weekend had been a bad scene. He had felt totally out of place in New York and he had hated the crowded streets and strange faces. But more than disappointment with the city, he had discovered that his mother had been right: he and Molly were opposites. She was so demanding, wanting him to do everything her way—even buy all those strange clothes. Most of her friends had treated him like some kind of nerd, and then when he had met a couple of girls who weren't stuck-up, Molly had thrown a fit, calling him a flirt and accusing him of being insensitive to her feelings.

For him, the highlight of the whole weekend had been going to see Molly's quarter horse, Red Fury. After seeing what the real Molly Drake was like, however, he personally didn't think she deserved such a beautiful animal. But that's what you got when your father was a rich banker. To think that he had almost moved to New York to be near her! He suppressed a shudder. Thank goodness he had listened to his mother and enrolled at the university. He looked sideways and saw that she had her eyes closed. Should he apologize for dragging her out East and making her spend the weekend with such a pretentious group of people? No, he might as well let her sleep. Before he left for college he would thank her for going along, but right now the feelings were too raw, and even though he knew she wouldn't say I told you so, he didn't want to discuss the subject of Molly Drake. Someday he'd tell her, but not now.

He reached up and turned off the overhead light beaming down on her, then draped his jacket over her. For a mom, she was quite a lady. He had been proud of the way she had fitted right in with all those society folks. But that was the one quality he had always appreciated in her, her ability to adjust to any situation, he reflected proudly. Lucky for him, his mother was one together lady. And on such a thought, he leaned back and drifted off to sleep.

IF JENNA EVER FELT as though she were not together, it was during the next few days. Packing up Cody's things and moving him up to Bozeman affected her in an unexpected manner. She told herself that had she gotten enough sleep she wouldn't have reacted so emotionally. But after their exhausting weekend in New York, she was operating on a short fuse, especially when she had to get up early Monday morning to drive to Bozeman. Although Cody was taking his old pickup to school, she and her father were driving behind to get a look at the campus and help him move in.

By the time they had carried all of his things into the dorm, Jenna could feel her emotions misbehaving. Until now, she hadn't really thought of Cody's going away to college as leaving home. But meeting his roommate and seeing his living accommodations reminded her that the dorm would now be his home. Knowing her son would be embarrassed if she launched into her "Don't forget to call me" sermon, she gave him a hug, wished him luck and said goodbye. She was her usual stoic self until she and her father got in the truck and began the return journey. They hadn't gone but a couple of miles when the tears broke loose.

"You'd better pull over and let me drive," her father insisted as her body began to shake with sobs.

"I'm f-f-ine," she said, sniffling.

"Jenna, you're not fine. Now pull over before you get us in an accident."

She slowed the truck down and eased it off the highway onto

the gravel shoulder, then slouched forward until her forehead rested on hands clasped tightly to the steering wheel.

"Don't you think you're overreacting a bit?" Hank said quietly.

"How am I supposed to react?" Her voice was muffled. "He's my baby...and he's g-g-gone."

"You're acting as if he's never coming back. You can call him every day if you like. Hell, you can call him soon as you get home," her father said. "Once you hear his voice you'll feel as good as new." But his words had no effect on the sobbing Jenna.

Hank could hardly believe that his strong, brave Jenna was falling apart. It was so unusual for her to cry. He leaned over and gently stroked her head. "Come on, honey, slide on over here. I can drive home."

Jenna straightened, then maneuvered her legs around the stick shift and slid across the bench seat. Hank wrapped an arm around her trembling shoulders and gave her a reassuring hug. "Now, listen to me, Jenna. Cody's not a baby and he's not gone for good. You're just feeling what every other mother feels when she discovers her nest is empty." He handed her his handkerchief.

"But I feel so alone," she mumbled into the white linen.

"I know, I know," he said soothingly. "Your mother went through the same thing when J.T. left home...and you know what a strong woman she was. Hell, she bawled for three days straight."

"Mom did?" Jenna looked up and hiccuped.

"Yup. Bawled after each one of you kids left. Only she never let me tell anyone. I could never understand it. I mean, here's a woman who was used to her kids being gone half the time, what with the rodeo circuit and all. But traveling and moving are two different things, I guess. You just go and have yourself a good cry and you'll feel better."

"I hate crying," Jenna said with self-derision, then blew her nose.

Her father gave her a gentle squeeze. "Well, I won't tell anyone if you won't." He climbed out of the pickup and walked around to the driver's side. "You're a lot like your mama, Jenna, and I'm mighty proud you're my daughter...crying or no crying."

"Thanks, Dad." Jenna leaned over and kissed the weather-roughened cheek. "But unless you've got another hankie you'd better not say any more."

Hank smiled as he shoved the truck in gear and headed for home.

JENNA HATED TO ADMIT IT, but her father was right. It had been a week since Cody had left and as determined as she was not to be a victim of the empty-nest syndrome, she was lonely as she had never been in her life. She didn't understand it and wished her mother were still alive, for it was at times like this that she needed her counsel.

It had been a week during which Jenna had felt at odds with the world. Although her father had done his best to lighten the atmosphere around the house, she missed Cody terribly and she just couldn't seem to shake off her melancholy. Her horses had always been a source of solace in the past, but even working out with J.T. and Tracey was more of a chore than a pleasure. Nor did it help that Snow Velvet had picked up a stone bruise. Or that the extra man she had hired to take Cody's share of ranch duties had been delayed because of a family emergency. Or that she hadn't heard from Harrison Drake. *That* was a major cause of her melancholy, although she was reluctant to admit it.

After a long day of stacking hay and feed bags, Jenna's back ached by the time she finished graining the horses. As they had so often during the past week, her thoughts turned once again to Harrison. When they had said goodbye he had told her he would call her. At thirty-six, she would have thought she wouldn't have fallen for that line. But in her heart she didn't want to believe it was a line. It might have been only forty-eight hours, but during this weekend together they had shared much more than passion. It seemed as though she had known him much longer than what the calendar would indicate. There was something between them that made her wish she could forget that east was east and west was west and never the twain shall meet. She thought again of the elegance of the Drake estate, then glanced down at her jeans covered with dirt, her boots caked with mud and manure, her hands rough and callused from having to take on the extra chores.

"Jenna, there's someone on the telephone for you." Her father's voice traveled through the crisp autumn air.

She dragged herself over to the open doorway and hollered back, "Can you take a message, Dad?"

"It's long-distance…Mr. Drake from New York."

Jenna immediately dropped the pitchfork and sprinted back to the house. Disregarding her father's clicking tongue as she crossed the kitchen floor without removing her boots, she paused to catch her breath before she picked up the receiver.

"Harrison, how are you?" She couldn't help smiling.

"Tired. I've been working twelve to sixteen hours a day all week long…which is why I haven't called."

To an exhausted Jenna, his voice was like a soft pillow. "Is the crisis over?"

"For the present time."

"I'm glad to hear that. I tried calling several times to say thank you for your hospitality, but there was no answer."

"I'm the one who should be thanking you. Especially for your help with Molly's horse."

"It was my pleasure. I had a great weekend, Harrison. So did Cody," she added.

"I hated to see it end…especially the way it did. I'm sorry about sending you to the airport in a cab."

"It all worked out just fine. I know how important your work is to you."

He heard the words, but he knew she really didn't understand his dedication to a job he didn't really want to be doing.

"How's Cody?" he found himself asking.

"Fine. He's away at college, so it's a little lonesome around here. And Molly?"

"She's fine. I don't see her much, what with her school activities and all. You know how busy teenagers are. Jenna, I didn't call to talk about my work or our kids." His voice softened. "I miss you."

She felt a warm flush inch its way over her body. Her father was eyeing her suspiciously, and when Jenna began making sharp finger gestures, indicating that he should leave the room, his eyebrows rose considerably.

"I miss you too, Harrison," she finally said when her father had left.

"I want to see you again...and soon," he said urgently. "If this weekend hadn't crept up so fast I would have flown out there."

The urgency in his voice sent familiar currents of excitement tingling down her spine. "We did a show in Idaho this past weekend," she pointed out.

He felt a little foolish. Here he was thinking that it was his schedule that was keeping them apart, forgetting that she had a career that was just as important to her. "What about next weekend?"

"I'm sorry, Harrison, but we're in Denver next weekend."

He stifled a groan. "You're on the road a lot, aren't you?"

"Right now we're booked every weekend until the first of November. During the winter the pace will slow down."

"I don't believe this!" He couldn't prevent the note of exasperation in his voice. "I'm tied up practically twenty-four hours a day during the week and you're gone on weekends. Jenna, when am I going to get to see you?"

"Maybe we're not supposed to see each other." She tried to make it sound flirtatious, but failed.

"I don't think you really believe that...not after last weekend," he said after a long pause, not wanting to think she could give him the brush-off after all that had happened between them. She wasn't the type of woman who took a lover for one night.

"I don't want to, but Harrison, there really is more than distance between us." *Please don't agree with me,* she silently prayed.

"Are you trying to tell me you don't want to see me again?" The thought was like a knife-sharp pain in his chest.

"I do want to see you, Harrison. I'd love to have another weekend like the last one. But..." She groped for the right words. How could she tell him she didn't want the complications of a long-distance love affair?

"Just answer me one question, Jenna."

"All right."

"Can you forget Saturday night?"

"No." It was a husky whisper. "I'll never forget it. It was wonderful."

"I agree." His voice was warm and sincere. "We've got a lot more in common than you give us credit for, Jenna. You'll see."

IN THE DAYS that followed, Jenna contemplated her conversation with Harrison, not understanding why she should feel their relationship was doomed when he had told her everything she wanted to hear. On Wednesday, a large manila envelope arrived by mail and Jenna immediately recognized the handwriting as Harrison's. Inside was a magazine article he had clipped out and sent to her with a note attached: "Tell J.T. you're simply ahead of the times…Harrison."

The title of the article was "Will the American Kitchen Become Extinct?" Jenna laughed out loud as she read about consumer trends toward conveniences that could eliminate home-cooked meals. She reached for the phone and dialed Harrison's office, only to discover that he was out of town until the following Monday.

As the trip to Denver approached, Jenna found herself lacking her usual enthusiasm for performing. She kept remembering that she could be spending the weekend with Harrison instead of working. Working? In all her years in rodeo she had never considered her riding as work. What was this discontent that was plaguing her? She wanted Cody to go to college, yet she didn't want Cody to go to college. She wanted to keep riding with the Flying Fosters, yet she didn't want to keep riding. She wanted a relationship with Harrison Drake, yet… The only reason she was unsure about their relationship was because she didn't know what their future held. Cody would always be her son whether at college or at home. Her riding would always be a source of income for her whether it was with J.T. and Tracey or teaching the barrels to young girls. But Harrison, would he always be there in her future?

There were two performances scheduled for the Flying Fosters in Denver, one Friday night and the other Saturday afternoon. Jenna had just finished brushing Snow Velvet after their first performance when one of the arena men came up to her and handed her a pink rose.

"You've got a fan, Jenna," he announced. "There's a cowboy out there who says he's come a long way to see you."

Jenna looked surprised and the man added, "Oh! I almost forgot. He also said to tell you anyone who looks as good as you do on a horse doesn't need to cook."

Jenna could feel the excitement bubbling up inside her. "J.T., I'll be right back." She turned to the arena man and gestured for him to lead. "You said a cowboy?"

"Yup." He led her to a secluded area in the indoor arena not far from the stock entrance. There, draped against a wooden fence, one foot up on the bottom board, stood Harrison, dressed in blue jeans, a jean jacket, cowboy boots and a Stetson.

"Howdy, Jenna," he said in a deep drawl.

She strutted over to him in her black leather pants with her red sequined top, raised herself up on tiptoe and pressed her body up close to his. When their brims collided, Harrison threw his hat to the ground and kissed her long and hard on the lips.

"I'm so happy you're here, Harrison." A couple of tears slipped down her cheeks.

"It's where I want to be, Jenna," he assured her, hugging her to him in a long embrace before letting her slip to the ground. "Tears?" he questioned, his finger smoothing over her cheek.

"No, they're not tears. My eyes are watering, that's all. Didn't you know—real cowgirls don't cry."

Harrison lifted her chin with his finger and forced her to meet his gaze. "I've missed you, Mrs. Morgan."

"I've missed you, too, Mr. Drake," she returned with a gamine grin. "When did you get here?"

"About an hour ago. I saw your act from way up at the top of the grandstand. You were wonderful," he said with a sexy caress, reminding Jenna of the way he had said those same words after they had made love.

"I'm glad you liked it." Again, there was a double meaning. "Is this the new Harrison Drake look or what?" she asked as she stepped back and appraised him.

"I call it my take-a-cowgirl-to-dinner look." He shifted his weight to one foot and hooked his thumbs into his belt. "A 'gen-u-wine' top-grade braided cowhide belt. Real cowboy boots with pointed toes. Denim. What do you think?"

Jenna reached down and picked up his black Stetson and set it on his head at an angle. Then she stepped back and put both hands on her hips. "The way you look in that hat—hell—a girl would have to be blind not to follow you to the moon."

"The salesclerk assured me that even my horse would love me in it." He grinned and raised both his eyebrows.

Jenna laughed. "Then it definitely was worth every penny you paid for it. Well, seeing you're dressed for dinner with a cowgirl, maybe I ought to change into my cowgirl clothes and meet you out front in say, half an hour?"

"Does that mean you're finished here?"

"I just have to check on the horses and tell Tracey and J.T. I've got a date."

"Can I come with you?"

"To check on the horses or to change my clothes?"

"Both."

She shook her head. "Uh-uh. I think I'd better meet you out front if we want to get any dinner tonight."

"Thirty minutes and not a minute more." Harrison removed his hat and leaned toward her but she interrupted his progress. Taking the hat from his hand she placed it back on his head, then tilted her head so that when she captured his mouth the brims didn't collide.

"Meet me out front," she said, then started back to the barn.

"By the way, I'm without wheels."

"Look for a red pickup," she called back over her shoulder.

Actually it was twenty-nine minutes later when Jenna pulled up to the curb in front of the arena entrance, and Harrison had been staring at his wristwatch all but five of those minutes. Jenna

had washed off the heavy stage makeup she used while performing and changed into a pair of black jeans with a red suede
jacket before pulling on the black boots and red hat to complete
her outfit.

"Do you want to drive?" she asked as he climbed up into
the cab.

"Not unless you want me to," he said. "It's been years since
I've driven a stick shift." His eyes made a sweeping scan of the
interior, noticing the aluminum horse-head knobs on the radio
and the small straw cowgirl dangling from the rearview mirror.

"Where to, Mr. Drake?"

"Heard of the Golden Steer Restaurant?"

"In the Plaza Hotel?"

"That's the one."

"Is that where you're staying?" She glanced at him out of
the corner of her eye.

"It just so happens it is." He grinned.

THEY SAT IN A SECLUDED corner of the restaurant, their fingers
linked across the table, sharing the intimate looks and secret
smiles of lovers. While they dined on chateaubriand for two,
Harrison filled her with stories about growing up in New York
City. Later, as they moved to the restaurant's lounge, he realized
that he had done all the talking. He didn't know how she had
accomplished it, but she had gotten him to talk about everything
from his political views to his favorite movie stars. He discovered that not only was she an interesting conversationalist, she
was also a good listener. And for once in his life he was happy
that he had told his secretary that he couldn't be reached for the
weekend.

"I tried calling you after I got the magazine clipping, but your
secretary said you were out of town until Monday," Jenna told
him as they danced cheek to cheek in the adjacent lounge.

"I was in L.A. on business until this morning. My secretary
has strict orders to tell anyone who calls that I am unavailable
this weekend."

"Does that mean you're staying all weekend?" Jenna could

feel the familiar desire running through her, the magic his presence stirred inside her.

"I want to spend every minute I can with you." His eyes darkened as his hands found the curve of her hips. "As long as you're in Denver, I want to be here, too."

"We're performing tomorrow afternoon, but we won't leave for home until Sunday morning."

"Then we'll just have to make the most of the next thirty-six hours." He led her from the dance floor and out of the lounge, past the lobby desk to the row of elevators leading to the guest rooms. "I think we agreed once before we shouldn't be slow-dancing in public," he whispered close to her ear.

Everything Jenna was feeling was written on her face. She was looking at him with such an expression of longing, he had trouble resisting the urge to crush her to him in the elevator. As soon as they reached his room, she went into his arms.

"I still can't believe you flew all the way here to be with me," she exclaimed in delight as her fingers found the snaps on his shirt and began undoing them.

Harrison reached for his Stetson and gave it a toss over his shoulder, then kissed her. Jenna steered him toward the bed where the hat had landed in the center of the blue patterned spread. She quickly snatched the Stetson from the bed, removed hers and placed both of them side by side on the dresser.

"Don't you know it's bad luck for a cowboy to put his hat on the bed?"

"I was aiming for the divan but I'm a lousy shot when I'm aroused." He gave her a boyish grin. "Maybe you should tell me what else a cowboy's not supposed to do. I wouldn't want any bad luck."

"Never eat peanuts before you ride.... I guess we don't need to worry about that one." Her fingers returned to the snaps. "Never wear a yellow shirt." She slipped his light blue shirt from his shoulders, allowing it to dangle from her index finger. "No problem here," she said before letting it drop to the floor.

"Is there more?" he asked huskily as her fingers reached inside the waistband of his jeans teasingly.

"Never make love to a lady who has her boots on."

Harrison could see his laughter reflected in her eyes. He pushed her down onto the bed and pulled off first one, then the other boot. Then he pulled her back up to her stocking feet and removed her clothes with deliberate care, kissing the naked flesh left by each item that fell to the floor. A flood of memories of how her body had instinctively responded to his lovemaking in New York threatened to overwhelm him. His hunger for her seemed insatiable and with a groan he pulled her into his arms, crushing her breasts against his chest, kissing her, stroking her, lifting her until they tumbled onto the bed.

The teasing, the smiles, the flirting disappeared. As Jenna helped Harrison finish undressing, the only emotion flowing between them was passion. They slid between the sheets, consumed by each other's needs, each other's desires. And they both knew, as their bodies moved together with an incredible sense of timing, that the enchantment they had felt in New York had been no passing affair. What was bonding them together now was much more than a wild desire sweeping them to ecstasy. When the rapturous explosion came that had them both shuddering in climax, they clung to each other fiercely, until every last shiver had ceased.

When Harrison rolled onto his back, Jenna slid her slender leg sensuously across his midsection. Wrapped in the circle of his arms, she let her body soak up the warmth flowing between them while Harrison gently nibbled on her earlobe.

"Sleepy?"

"Umm-hmm," Jenna purred contentedly as his hands softly stroked her flesh.

"This time we don't have to sleep in separate beds, and we can spend the whole night together. How does breakfast in bed sound?" His voice was barely a whisper.

"I love it," she returned sleepily.

"I love you," he breathed softly before kissing her goodnight.

HARRISON WOKE TO FIND Jenna putting on her clothes. Rolling over to his side, he propped himself up on one elbow and watched her wiggle her hips into the tight black jeans.

"I liked it better when they were going the other route," he murmured with a sleepy drawl.

"I thought you said you were a heavy sleeper," Jenna commented, her eyes meeting his in the mirror directly across from the bed.

"When I'm around you I'm a lot of things I'm not used to being...and I love all of them. What are you doing up so early, anyway?" He reached for his gold watch that was on the nightstand. "God, it's barely six o'clock," he groaned. "Why don't you come back to bed?" He patted the mattress beside him.

"I can't. I have to feed the horses."

"At six-thirty in the morning? Can't you hire someone to do that for you?"

Once again, Jenna was reminded of the differences in their backgrounds. Harrison simply hired someone to do the chores he didn't want to do—change the oil in his car, do his laundry, clean his apartment. "Harrison, I don't know of anyone on the rodeo circuit who doesn't take care of his own horse." She crossed the room to retrieve her red suede jacket.

"I just thought someone who had a stereo and a television in her horse trailer could hire someone to give her horses some oats."

"It's not just a case of giving a horse some oats. My horses need a balanced diet that includes sweet feed, bran, vitamin supplements and soybean meal, and on a regular schedule. As long as I'm with them, I feed them." Her tone was on the edge of being defensive. Jenna didn't want to snap at him, but this morning, after waking up in warm arms with a warm breath on her neck, she was feeling just a tiny bit guilty. It had been a long time since she had spent an entire night in a man's arms, and it was a bit disturbing to admit to herself that Jack had never made her feel the way Harrison could. She was going to have to close the door to the past, and she wasn't sure if she was prepared for such a step.

"Can I come with you?" he asked.

She sat down on the side of the bed and pulled on her boots. "Why don't you wait here? I'll be back," she promised, leaning over to capture his lips with hers. When she felt the flame of desire leap between them, she pulled back, but not before Harrison had reached inside the partially buttoned shirt and cupped her breast.

"What time is breakfast served at the Morgan stable?"

With his fingers inside her shirt and his eyes watching her as though she were about to answer some fascinating question, Jenna found she had just enough air to answer him. "Seven-thirty. It's best to keep the horses on a regular schedule." His hands were beginning to wander and she could feel her body tingling in all of its intimate places.

"The stable's only fifteen minutes from here," he whispered, his lips trailing kisses across her neck. "That leaves you forty-five minutes...and I said we'd have breakfast in bed." He had unbuttoned her shirt and had wrapped two fingers through her belt loop.

"You said a lot of things last night," Jenna returned.

"And I meant every one of them," he assured her.

"*Every* one?"

"*Every* one." He cupped her face in his hands. "I love you, Jenna. I never thought I'd find anyone who could make me feel the way you do. Now that I have, I don't want to let you out of my sight." He kissed her gently, then said, "Should we call room service or—"

"We can eat later." Jenna kicked off her boots and with a smile crawled in beside him.

For the remainder of the weekend there was hardly a minute when Jenna and Harrison weren't together. He wanted to know everything there was to know about her work, and was an eager listener as he followed her about her chores. It was a weekend that Jenna knew she would never forget; it was the weekend she fell in love with Harrison Drake.

CHAPTER ELEVEN

IN THE FOLLOWING WEEKS, Harrison materialized at four out of the five cities where Jenna was performing with the Flying Fosters. Each time they were together Jenna felt euphoric. She had forgotten the luxury of being in love, the way it could transfer the mundane things in life into glorious, happy times. Because their time together was always limited, they made each minute count; their relationship was exciting, romantic and felt so right. The long-distance phone bills that had once been created by their children were now due to tender, loving conversations taking place late at night, in soft, wistful voices—conversations that to other people might have sounded like small talk, but to Jenna and Harrison were intimate messages of longing.

Jenna wasn't quite sure where their relationship was heading or if she even wanted to know. She was content to accept what was happening between them without analyzing whether their feelings would have the same intensity if Harrison wasn't flying halfway across the country just to be with her. After five years of being alone, she wanted to bask in the exhilarating sensations of a love affair. They were weekend lovers—so unlike her relationship with Jack with whom she had shared every day-to-day detail, together on the road and at home. Since Jack's death she had learned to take life one day at a time, but as each day passed, she discovered Harrison was becoming a more important part of that life.

Although they made no secret of their relationship, the only people who knew of their involvement were J.T., Tracey and Hank Foster, who had taken one look at his daughter's flushed cheeks and knew there was a new man in her life. Jenna had to wonder if the svelte Diana Elliot didn't suspect Harrison was involved with another woman, especially since previously he had been at her disposal when it came to working weekends. The memory of her only meeting with the sophisticated redhead always managed to stir a twinge of jealousy in Jenna—a jealousy that disappeared when she was with Harrison.

With both Molly and Cody away at school, they had the freedom to spend their weekends together, to keep their feelings private. They had gotten to know each other because of their children, but they had fallen in love on their own. Telling their children of their feelings would be something to do in the future at the right time and place. Neither had presented itself so far.

By the beginning of November, Jenna knew that when country-and-western singers crooned about love making people do crazy things, they were right. Her craziness stretched as far as a yearning to be domestic—which maybe wasn't so crazy. After all, every time she and Harrison were together they were in some strange hotel eating restaurant food. With the thought of the Thanksgiving holiday approaching and visions of the family being together, she decided it might be the appropriate time to entertain Harrison and Molly.

"Trace, I've been thinking about doing the Thanksgiving dinner this year," Jenna told her sister-in-law one afternoon while they were having lunch at the Beartooth Café in Red Lodge.

"But, Jen, you have dinner at your place every year," Tracey said with a blank face.

"I don't just mean have it at the house. I mean do it. You know, cook the turkey and sweet potatoes and everything. I think it's time you had a break from all the preparations."

Tracey looked a little bemused. "You want to cook?"

"I do know how, Tracey," Jenna said with a wry grimace.

"Oh, Jen, I didn't mean to imply you didn't. I'm sorry." She placed her hand over Jenna's. "You're serious, aren't you? But I have to tell you I'm surprised. Your aversion to the kitchen is no secret in the Foster clan."

"I know, but Cody's been gone for almost two months now and it's his first time coming home. I really want this to be a special Thanksgiving."

Tracey studied Jenna's face thoughtfully. "Of course you do, and you can count on me to help make it special. Just tell me what you want me to do."

"This year you come as a guest. Of course, if you'd like to come as a pumpkin-pie bearing guest I wouldn't turn you away."

Tracey smiled. "Are you sure there's nothing else I could bring? A little coleslaw or cranberry salad?"

"No," Jenna insisted. "This year it's my dinner."

"If you're sure..." She hesitated, but Jenna gave no indication she wanted any help. "Gosh, it'll be good to see Cody again, won't it?"

"I had a more difficult time saying goodbye to him than I had expected," Jenna reflected on a sigh. "I wish now that Jack and I had had more children."

"Is that a hint of advice?" Tracey asked gently.

"Of course not. Just a lonesome mother's crazy sentimentality."

"You're definitely not crazy, and judging by the company you've been keeping the past month or so I don't think you qualify in the lonesome category, either," she teased. "Have you heard from Harrison lately?"

"He calls regularly." Jenna absently toyed with the straw in her soda. "I've invited him for dinner on Thanksgiving," she said nonchalantly.

"Dinner on Thanksgiving!" Tracey repeated in a knowing tone. "Now we get down to the true reason you are cooking dinner."

"Tracey!" Jenna's tone was indignant, her cheeks tinged with color.

"You know, Jenna, I never thought I'd see the day you'd be blushing over a man and wanting to cook dinner for him." Tracey's eyes danced in merriment.

"I already told you it's for Cody."

"Sure, Jen." She let out a dreamy sigh. "I think it's terribly romantic. Harrison is so handsome. He certainly is worth getting domesticated for, that's for sure."

"I am *not* getting domesticated for Harrison," Jenna pointed out. "Besides, he knows my feelings about the kitchen and he respects them. I just thought it would be nice to try to make it a special Thanksgiving, that's all. Actually, Harrison and I are planning the weekend as a surprise for the kids.''

"Are they still going together?'' She pushed her empty plate aside.

"Cody doesn't tell me much, but then he never has when it comes to Molly. I know they write regularly and Harrison said Molly's phone bill at school indicates she's been calling him. With both of them away at school, it's hard to tell how serious they still are. We thought this would be a great way to get them together again.''

"As well as the two of you,'' Tracey added. "I'm happy for you, Jen. Everything has worked out so well after the shaky start this summer, hasn't it?''

Jenna nodded in agreement. "Even Mrs. Fielding has consented to come to dinner. Maybe I should be groaning, but I'm pleased that Harrison was able to convince her to come. It's uncomfortable knowing that she dislikes the Fosters.''

"I never did understand what the problem was with her.''

Jenna shrugged. "All I know is what Dad told me. Something about she's been carrying a grudge for years. I always attributed her behavior to snootiness, but maybe once she spends a little time with us and sees that we don't lick our fingers at the dinner table she'll soften a little bit.''

"I hope you're right. Just being in her presence can be formidable. Will Molly and Harrison be staying with you?''

Jenna shook her head. "Harrison is telling Molly that this is a skiing trip and they're staying at Eleanor's for the holiday weekend.''

"Are you sure you don't want me to come over early and get the turkey in the oven for you? Harrison will never know.''

"Trace, trust me. I can cook a turkey. Besides, Dad's there if I need any help. Do you want more coffee or are you ready to go?'' she asked as the waitress hovered near their table with the coffeepot in hand.

"I think we'd better get going,'' Tracey said for the benefit of the waitress, then added in a near whisper, "Don't look now, Jenna, but Roy Cooper just walked into the café.'' Tracey knew of Roy's relentless pursuit of Jenna and did her best not to draw attention to their presence. "You're in luck. He sat down at the counter. You can probably get by with a quick hello on the way out. He isn't coming for dinner this year, is he?"

"Dad told me he was going to his sister's place in Idaho." There was a sigh of relief in her voice.

"The guy's stuck on you."

"Well, I wish he'd get unstuck. I've told him over and over, Tracey, that I think he's a nice guy, a great friend, but that's it. The more I say no to him the harder he tries to convince me how right we are for each other." Jenna glanced over toward the big broad back seated at the counter. "I suppose I'd better say hello. Are you ready to leave?"

Tracey stood up, picking up the check from the table. "I'll get this while you have a few words with Mr. Steamroller. Just keep saying over and over in your mind, 'I can smile and be gracious—he's not coming for Thanksgiving dinner.'"

Jenna simply rolled her eyes heavenward.

THE WEDNESDAY before Thanksgiving saw a winter snowstorm whip through southwestern Montana, closing roads and highways, stranding holiday travelers and delighting skiing enthusiasts in the area. The storm also delayed Cody's departure, forcing him to wait until Thanksgiving morning before leaving for home.

Early Thursday morning, Jenna found herself cramming stuffing into a twenty-pound turkey and hollering for her father. When he came shuffling into the kitchen, she attacked him with a vengeance.

"How am I supposed to get this damn thing to stay together?" she snapped as her fingers fumbled with the stuffing skewers. "And I can't find the roasting pan. I don't know where you keep it hidden."

"Little short of patience, are we this morning, Jenna?" her father commented pleasantly, reaching into a cupboard and extracting the large blue enamel roaster.

"I'm sorry, Dad." She accepted the pan with an apology.

"They're not royalty, you know." Jenna couldn't help but smile. Her father was never one to be subtle.

"I know. It's just that I wanted everything to be perfect and then this darn snowstorm had to happen. It's bad enough that I've got the cooking to contend with. I don't need to worry about Cody getting home safely."

"Look." He pulled the yellow checkered curtain back from the window. "The sun is shining. The highways are being cleared and Cody knows better than to leave until the roads are in good driving condition. We'll just have to eat a little bit later, that's all. Try to relax. After all the time you've spent preparing this meal it'll be great." He patted her shoulder reassuringly.

"But you know I'm not very good at this," she said, rubbing her hands on her apron as her father took over threading the skewers through the turkey.

"Bah! You can do anything you put your mind to. Always could. You're a Foster."

She placed her arms around his shoulders and squeezed. "You're right, as usual."

"There. She's ready for the oven." He carried the turkey over to the stove while Jenna held the door open.

"Now, why don't you let me clean up the kitchen and you go make yourself pretty." He eyed the huge stack of dirty dishes in the sink.

"Thanks, Dad." She untied the apron and tossed it on the counter.

"Oh, by the way," Hank said just as she was about to pass through the door. "The table looks great but you're going to have to add one more setting. Roy wasn't able to drive to Idaho because of the snow, so I've invited him over here."

"You what!" Jenna whirled around.

"I invited Roy to dinner," he repeated in his dulcet tone.

"How could you?" she groaned, still absorbing the shock of his words.

"How could I what? Invite a good neighbor to spend Thanksgiving dinner with friends?"

If she hadn't stayed up past midnight polishing the silverware and putting together fancy hors d'oeuvres, and if she hadn't spent the past three days scrubbing every nook and cranny in the house and if she hadn't spent half of yesterday worrying that neither Harrison nor Cody would make it to dinner, then maybe she would have had a smidgen of remorse for her attitude. But in her present frame of mind, she had no conscience when it came to Roy Cooper.

"I can't believe you went and invited him, Dad! If he embarrasses me in front of the Drakes..." She could hear her voice rising.

"Would you rather I let the man sit home alone on Thanksgiving Day? Or maybe I should have suggested he go to one of them fancy restaurants in town and eat by himself," he said with heavy sarcasm.

"This can't be happening!" She shook her head in dismay. "Dad, if he comes, he'll probably be difficult."

"No more difficult than Eleanor Fielding."

"Too bad he's not her age instead of mine," she groaned in exasperation.

"Roy has been a good friend and neighbor for too long for you to be acting this way, Jenna," he admonished. "This home has always been a welcome stop for any of our friends."

Jenna released a long sigh of resignation. "I guess you're right, Dad. But I have this awful feeling that something's going to go wrong today. Ever since that snowstorm hit so unexpectedly last night I've been on edge. First Cody can't get home, then you tell me Roy's coming to dinner.... I hope that's the last of my surprises.

A HUNDRED AND FIFTY MILES from Red Lodge, Cody was loading several suitcases into the back of his pickup. According to the radio reports, the highways were clear, but travelers were advised to drive with caution. He opened the door, climbed up into the cab, tapping each toe on the chrome running board to get rid of any excess snow before sitting behind the steering wheel. He pulled off the cowhide gloves and rubbed his hands together, then turned to the dark-haired girl sitting beside him.

"All set?" Seeing her nod, he added, "Why don't you slide that cute little bod of yours over here next to mine? You can always slide back over when we pull up in the driveway at Mom's."

"Oh, Cody." She giggled and did as he suggested, snuggling up close to his side. "I hope you know what you're doing, bringing me home with you like this."

"Kristy, I've already told you. My mom is going to like you just fine." He gave her a gentle kiss. "And once she gets to really know you like I do, she's going to love you."

"Cody, you're so sweet." She laid her head on his shoulder. "I just wish you had told her you were bringing me home with you. I don't want to be an imposition."

"You're *not* an imposition. You're my girl. And I've already told you—the Lost Creek has got a welcome mat as big as the blue sky of Montana. If I know Mom, she's probably invited all sorts of friends and neighbors to dinner. And you are just the kind of girl she would pick for me to bring home to dinner. When she hears you were the state champion in girls' high school rodeo, she'll flip out. So just relax, put that Alabama tape in the player and let me take you home."

J.T. AND TRACEY were the first ones to arrive for dinner.

"Holy mackerel, Sis, who's coming to dinner—the president? I hope you're passing out diagrams as to what to use when. I haven't seen so much silverware and china since that fancy wedding Tracey and I went to in Dallas."

Tracey gave J.T. a playful slug. "Will you cut it out? Pay no attention to him, Jenna. The table looks beautiful."

"You don't think the linens look too dated?" Jenna asked, rubbing her fingertips over the ivory damask cloth that had been her grandmother's.

"The tablecloth is gorgeous and so are you. I love your dress." She gave her sister-in-law a hug.

"Thanks." Jenna warmed at the compliment. She had purposely chosen the blue dress she had worn in New York because she knew how much Harrison liked it.

"So where's the big college kid?" J.T. asked.

"He should be on his way. He called and talked to Dad this morning," Jenna replied.

"What about Harrison and Molly?" Tracey asked.

"Their plane arrived before it started snowing yesterday—thank goodness. We do have an unexpected guest, though." She paused while Tracey looked at her inquisitively. "Because of the snow, Roy decided not to visit his sister, so Dad invited him here."

"Good grief!" Tracey shared a sympathetic look with Jenna. "Well, there's only one solution. J.T. will simply have to keep him entertained."

"Me?" J.T. exclaimed just as the doorbell rang.

Tracey ran over to the window and lifted a corner of the voile curtain. "That's him now. Wouldn't you know he'd come early," she groaned. "Get the door, J.T. Jenna and I have work to do."

Jenna allowed herself to be propelled back into the kitchen, where she and Tracey busied themselves with the last-minute preparations. It was only moments before Roy popped his head through the swinging kitchen door.

"It sure smells great in here. How are my two favorite cooks doing?" he asked, sniffing appreciatively.

"Hi, Roy," they returned in unison.

He strolled into the kitchen and presented Jenna with two bottles of sparkling wine. "Thanks for inviting me, Jenna. I thought maybe this would go good with your dinner. Happy Thanksgiving."

"Thank you, Roy." She accepted the wine, glancing at the label before giving him a kiss on the cheek. "How nice of you. This is my favorite."

"Hey, Roy, how about a beer?" J.T. asked, having followed him into the kitchen. "I bet you could use one after that job you did."

"What job was that?" Jenna asked.

"Roy plowed the road for you, Sis."

"I figured since Cody wasn't home yet, I'd do it for you. It'll make it easier for the rest of your guests to get through," Roy explained. "Plus, I wanted to say thank you for inviting me to dinner."

"That was very thoughtful of you, Roy. Thank you," Jenna said politely, noting the lift to Tracey's eyebrows.

"Roy, I think we'd better leave these women alone or we won't see dinner," J.T. teased, steering the big man out of the kitchen. After they had gone, Tracey turned to Jenna.

"Harrison's going to be seeing red if Roy looks at you like that all day."

Jenna frowned. "I'm beginning to think I made a mistake in thinking this dinner would work out. Harrison and I looked at it as an opportunity to tell Molly and Cody about us, but I don't think Eleanor Fielding has any idea that Harrison and I are seeing each other, nor Roy."

"Well, you won't be able to keep it a secret much longer. Anyone who's around you two can see that you're crazy about each other. Do you want me to put these sweet potatoes in the oven?" she asked, looking in the refrigerator.

"Oh, I almost forgot them. And the vegetable casserole has to go in, too."

"I'll take care of them," Tracey assured her, stepping around Jenna to place the dishes in the oven. "It's times like this I sure envy you your kitchen space...and this wonderful old stove. I'd love to have a big old kitchen like this one," she said wistfully.

"It certainly is old," Jenna acknowledged, her eyes taking in the fading paint of the cupboards and scuff marks on the floor.

"Jenna, don't you dare look scornfully upon this wonderful kitchen," Tracey warned.

"I can't help but compare it to Harrison's chrome and glass one."

"But I bet it doesn't have the warmth of this room."

"I think I could forsake warmth for convenience."

"Not me. Oh! There's the doorbell. Jenna, you'd better go. It's probably Harrison."

Unconsciously Jenna's hand flew to the dark curls swept back from her face. "I'll just say hello, then I'll be back in to help," she told Tracey who was nodding in understanding.

Jenna knew the moment she entered the room that Harrison's eyes were on her. She wanted to rush to him, wrap her arms around him and kiss him passionately. Instead, she extended both hands and turned her cheek for his kiss as they met halfway into the room.

"Happy Thanksgiving, Jenna," he said in a husky voice, his fingers tightening on hers as he reluctantly kissed her cheek. Keeping one of her hands in his, he turned and introduced his aunt.

"Aunt Eleanor, you remember Jenna Morgan? Jenna, my aunt, Eleanor Fielding."

"I'm happy you could share this holiday with us, Mrs. Fielding," Jenna said graciously, extending her free hand to the older woman. "Happy Thanksgiving."

A frail, wrinkled hand appeared beneath the thick mink coat sleeve and Jenna caught the scent of expensive perfume. "It was very kind of you to invite me, Mrs. Morgan," Eleanor said stiffly.

"Oh, please call me Jenna."

Eleanor gave her a weak smile, then moved aside as Molly stepped forward.

"Hi, Mrs. Morgan." She stood before Jenna looking like the demure debutante in a classical yet trendy two-piece sweater dress.

"Molly!" Jenna dropped Harrison's hand and hugged the girl close.

"I could hardly believe it when Dad told me we were coming here for dinner today," she said excitedly. "It's great to be back."

"It's good to see you, too," Jenna replied. "How have you been? And how's Red Fury?"

"Great to both questions," Molly said with a smile.

"I want to hear all about both of you after dinner. But right now, please come sit down and J.T. will make the introductions and see that everyone gets something to drink." Jenna watched Harrison's expression change from anticipation to irritation upon discovering Roy's presence.

"But where's Cody?" Molly asked, looking around the room.

"He called this morning and said he's on his way," Jenna replied. "I'm afraid this snowstorm had him grounded temporarily, but he is coming." While everyone made small talk,

Jenna excused herself to get the hors d'oeuvres. She was just about to rejoin her guests when she heard Cody's truck horn.

"There he is now, Jenna," Tracey called out excitedly. "Here, let me take those in," she said, taking the silver tray out of Jenna's grasp. "You'll want to welcome Cody home privately."

Jenna's heart was thumping madly. This was going to be the best Thanksgiving ever. Although Harrison looked a bit annoyed, the group in the other room was getting along just fine, her dinner smelled delicious and Cody was home. Swinging open the back door, Jenna could feel her smile sinking, just like the feeling in the pit of her stomach. Cody was striding up the walk with a girl—a short, dark-haired girl he held carefully by the arm so she wouldn't slip on the icy path. When they reached the stoop, Cody relinquished his protective hold and rushed to open the storm door.

"Mom! It's good to be home." He grabbed his mother around the waist.

Jenna hugged him tightly, savoring the feel of him, the familiar sound of his voice. She remembered how much she had missed him, how difficult it had been when he had left, and nothing else mattered at the moment except her son was home. She choked back her tears and said, "Welcome home, Cody." When she finally released him, he stepped back and pulled Kristy forward.

"Mom, I'd like you to meet Kristy Parrish. Kristy, this is my mom."

Jenna didn't remember responding, but she must have, for Kristy was smiling and saying all sorts of polite things. In the meantime, Cody was looking at the girl the same way he had looked at Molly last summer.

Molly. Jenna's mind raced ahead as to what was going to happen when Cody took his girlfriend into the other room. All the work she and Harrison had gone to to arrange for the two lovebirds to meet, and this lovebird already had a new turtledove. Oh, God, how was she going to handle this? Jenna sank down onto the ladder-back chair.

"Who all's here for dinner, Mom?" Cody asked after retrieving the luggage from the truck. "For a minute I thought I saw Mrs. Fielding's car."

"You did," Jenna said sadly.

"What's she doing here?" He looked puzzled.

"I invited her...along with her nephew and great-niece."

"Molly's here?" His voice rose an octave in a whisper. "Mom, how could you do this to me?"

"Me do it to you?" Jenna stood up and faced him. "I thought I was doing it *for* you. I thought it was what you wanted. Never once when you phoned did you tell me you weren't still interested in her. Harrison and I thought the only thing keeping you apart was distance and we—" Jenna stopped when she saw the look of distress on Kristy's face.

"I'm sorry, I shouldn't have come," Kristy apologized. "I tried to tell Cody it would be an imposition." As she spoke she was slowly backtracking toward the door, on the verge of tears.

Jenna walked over to her and put her arm around her shoulder. "I'm the one who's sorry, Kristy. Here you are a guest in my home and I haven't even shown you where to put your things. Forgive me...please. I know Cody wouldn't have brought you home if you weren't a special friend."

"Maybe it would be better if we left," Cody suggested.

"Cody, it's Thanksgiving. J.T., Tracey, Grandpa...they're all looking forward to spending it with you. Why don't you take Kristy upstairs so she can freshen up."

"I would like to change," she added, eyeing Jenna's fancy dress.

At that moment the buzzer sounded, indicating the potatoes were done. "She can use the room next to mine," Jenna told Cody, turning off the burner on the stove. "Everything will be all right." She tried to give them a reassuring smile.

When Tracey returned, Jenna nearly pounced on her. "Thank God you're back. The potatoes are done. I can't tell with the turkey, the vegetable dish looks like it's almost done and I think I should get Dad to make the gravy, and Cody brought a girl home from school," she said in a rush.

"He did what?" Tracey exclaimed.

"Cody has a new girlfriend. Kristy something. Cute. Sweet.

Just the kind of girl I always expected him to bring home. And Cody's face lights up every time he looks at her—just like it did when he looked at Molly last summer.''

''And Molly's waiting in there for him!'' Both of her hands flew to her forehead. ''Oh, my goodness! Jenna, what are we going to do?''

''What can we do? Lock the girl up in the closet?'' Jenna began to laugh, but stopped when she saw Harrison in the doorway, an ice bucket in his hands. He stared at her for several seconds before he spoke.

''J.T. sent me for more ice.''

Tracey and Jenna couldn't help but look like two kids caught with their hands in the cookie jar. Jenna took the ice bucket from him and filled it while Tracey made several trivial comments about dinner. As soon as Jenna handed back the bucket, he mumbled an abrupt thanks and left.

''He certainly looked annoyed about something. I told you he wouldn't be pleased about Roy,'' Tracey observed.

''I think he might have heard my comment about locking Kristy in the closet. Maybe he thought I meant Molly. Oh, God, what am I going to do?'' Jenna sighed in exasperation.

''First you're going to get this dinner on the table,'' Tracey told her in her take-charge voice. ''Look at all the time and preparation you've put into it. And it smells wonderful. We'll get Hank to carve and I'll do the gravy. Cody and Molly will have to work out their own difficulties.''

''How could this have happened? Dad invites Roy, and Cody invites Kristy, and neither one of them think about asking me!''

''Foster men are unpredictable, Jen,'' she sympathized. ''Let's get everything ready to go on the table, then if there's a dead silence after Cody introduces his girl we can announce dinner. There's nothing like good food to ease awkwardness among guests.''

Jenna would have liked to disappear, but she knew she had to accompany Cody and Kristy into the living room. At first Molly didn't realize there was another person trailing behind Jenna and Cody. The minute they walked through the swinging door, she was on her feet and rushing into Cody's arms. It was only as Cody turned his face to accept her kiss on his cheek that she saw the girl lagging behind Jenna. A spasm of pain transformed the look on Molly's face from one of exuberance to distress and Jenna could cheerfully have booted her son in the pants. Why hadn't he told her he had a new girlfriend?

"Molly, I'd like you to meet a friend of mine, Kristy Parrish," Cody said as smoothly as was possible under the circumstances. "I invited Kristy home for the long holiday weekend so she could meet Mom. Kristy does barrels, too."

After a silence that was almost deadly, Jenna continued to make the introductions until she was certain her smile would crack. If she thought Harrison had glared at her in the kitchen, now his gaze could have frozen her solid. Molly looked stunned and Eleanor simply looked as uncomfortable as she had ever since her arrival. Jenna quickly invited everyone to be seated for dinner, but Molly was whispering something in her father's ear. Harrison in turn drew Eleanor aside, had a few words with her, then faced Jenna.

"I'm sorry, Jenna, but Molly's not feeling well. We're going to have to leave."

CHAPTER TWELVE

"LEAVE! YOU MEAN you're not staying for dinner?" she asked incredulously, following Harrison up the stairs as he went to retrieve their coats. He didn't say another word until they had reached her room where half a dozen coats lay across the bed.

"Molly's not feeling well," he repeated, turning around to face her.

"What you really mean is she just doesn't want to face an awkward situation. Why don't you just come right out and say she's embarrassed because Cody brought another girl home?"

"All right, she doesn't want to stay and I can understand why," he said grimly, his paternal instincts rushing to his daughter's defense. "For God's sake, she's just found out her boyfriend's been two-timing her. It's obvious your son has been making all sorts of promises he never intended to keep, and I, for one, don't intend to stay here and let her be humiliated one moment longer."

"Now wait just a minute, Harrison," Jenna snapped, resenting the way he had automatically assumed her son was to blame for the fiasco in the living room. "What makes you so sure that all of this is Cody's fault? He told me that things haven't been the same between the two of them since our weekend in New York, only Molly won't accept the fact that it's over."

"Jenna, if that were the case, don't you think we would have known about it?"

"You mean like the way our children know about us? Or is there still an 'us' for them to know about? The way you've been glaring at me anyone would think you're having second thoughts."

"Maybe I'm the one who should be asking you that."

"What's that supposed to mean?" She stood with her hands on her hips.

"It means what the hell is Roy Cooper doing here? And don't try to tell me that he's just a friend."

"He *is* just a friend and he's here because he's our neighbor," she vehemently protested. "And *I* didn't invite the man, my dad did."

"Some neighbor," he mocked. "He's all over you every chance he gets. I suppose Thanksgiving just wouldn't be the same without 'good neighbor Roy' at the dinner table."

"At least he wants to be at my dinner table," she retorted.

"I don't believe this." He threw up his hands in exasperation. "Not only do you expect Molly to sit and watch another girl fawn all over Cody, I'm supposed to idly stand by while Roy Cooper foams at the mouth every time you look in his direction."

Jenna couldn't believe that Harrison was jealous of someone like Roy or that he could be so insensitive to her feelings. Couldn't he see how hard she had worked to make this dinner special? This was to have been their surprise together and now he was acting as though she were to blame for situations beyond her control.

"Don't you think you're exaggerating just a bit?" She swallowed back her disappointment and anger. "Come on, Harrison. It's Thanksgiving." She gave him what she thought was an appealing grin, but he didn't take it that way.

"I don't find a young girl's heart being broken amusing, Jenna."

"You think I do? I feel awful about the whole situation, but Molly's not the only one who's feeling awkward, you know. How do you suppose Cody must feel under the circumstances? Or for that matter, Kristy? It's embarrassing for all of us, but leaving isn't going to solve anything."

"We'll just have to see about that, won't we?" He slipped his arms into his camel cashmere coat.

"But what about all the food I've prepared? And what about after dinner? What am I going to do then?" She tried to keep the frustration from overwhelming her, but she hated to think that all her preparations were for nothing and their plans to spend the day together were being shattered.

"Don't worry. If you get bored you can always sit around and watch the rise and fall of Cooper's Adam's apple for entertainment." Without waiting for her response, he grabbed the other two coats off the bed and disappeared out the door.

She didn't know how she managed to play the gracious hostess after that. But somehow she carried out her duties, offering Mrs. Fielding an apologetic goodbye despite the glint of triumph she saw flickering in the older woman's eyes. By the time the dinner was actually served, most of the food was cool. Thanks to J.T.'s effervescent personality, however, the day was not a total failure. But for Jenna, Harrison's departure was too bitter a disappointment to be swept away with humor and laughter. When dinner was over, while everyone gathered around the oak dining room table to play cards, Jenna, preferring solitude, insisted she'd take care of the dishes alone.

When Roy followed her into the kitchen and picked up a dish towel, she tried not to lose the little patience she still possessed.

"Roy, I wish you would join the others in the card game. Guests don't belong in the kitchen and I really think I need this time to myself," she said wearily, giving him a sideways glance.

"But I hate to see you so strung out like this, Jenna—especially over the likes of Eleanor Fielding and her hoity-toity relations. I think it serves them right they left. They missed a wonderful dinner."

Jenna counted slowly to ten before answering. "Roy, I appreciate what you're trying to do, but I'd rather not discuss the Drakes right now."

"That's fine by me. As far as I'm concerned, they aren't worth talking about. I came out here because I wanted to talk about us."

"Please, Roy...not now." Jenna bit down on her lip, keeping her eyes on the sink full of soapy water.

"I know it hasn't been a good day for you, Jenna. You went to all that trouble for dinner and then look what happens. But didn't it at least show you that those society people will never be like us?"

"Roy…"

"Please, just hear me out, Jenna. I know you're always saying you don't need a man to lean on. But you and I are the same kind of people. We love the land out here, we love ranching. And you know I've always tried to be around for Cody ever since Jack died."

"Roy, you've got to stop." Jenna finally looked up at him. "You're a wonderful friend, and I appreciate having you for a neighbor, but I'm in love with Harrison Drake." When she saw the expression on his face, she immediately felt contrite. She hadn't intended to be so blunt, but it seemed the only way to reach him. "I'm sorry, Roy."

"Me, too, Jenna. Me, too," he repeated, then stared at her thoughtfully for several seconds. "A man like that will never fit in with your life-style, Jenna." He folded the dish towel and draped it over the back of a chair, then left without another word.

Minutes later, Cody was in the kitchen.

"Mom, what did you say to Roy? He left without saying a word to anyone."

"I don't think it's any of your business, Cody." Jenna didn't want to snap at him, but she had reached her emotional limit for one day.

"What's going on with you, Mom?"

"What's going on with me?" She spun around to face him. "I'll tell you what's going on with me. I spent three days cleaning and cooking, trying to make this the best Thanksgiving we've ever had. Why? Because you've been away at school for over two months. Because I wanted to share the holiday with someone I love. Because I wanted to give you a surprise that I thought you wanted—to be with the girl you told me you were in love with. And what happens? The whole thing blows up in my face. You know how you felt when you saw Molly here now that you're dating Kristy? Well, that's how I felt having Roy Cooper here, because you see, I've been seeing Harrison Drake."

"What?" Cody shrieked. "You and Harrison Drake? You hardly know the guy and he's not your type at all."

"Oh, yes, he is my type," Jenna assured him. "At least he

was until this whole fiasco today. And I know him quite well, believe me.''

"And so you've dumped Roy Cooper for Mr. Drake?'' There was censure in his tone and his face registered his disbelief.

"I didn't *dump* anyone, Cody. Roy's never been anything other than a friend and I certainly never encouraged him to believe anything else. It was you and Dad who were doing that matchmaking. I didn't want to hurt Roy, but I had to tell him about Harrison.''

"My God, you're serious!'' He was pacing the floor by now. "This is crazy. I go away for two months and I come home to find you're cooking dinner, putting all that mousse stuff on your hair, and all for a city slicker like Drake. What's happening, Mom? Are you going through some kind of midlife crisis or what?''

"Cody, I'm only thirty-six and do I have to remind you that you didn't have any objections to falling in love with a city slicker's daughter last summer?'' she said irritably.

"But why didn't you tell me about him?''

"I guess it was the same reason you didn't tell me about Kristy. I think it's called a lack of communication, wouldn't you agree? It's obvious we could have eased the shock for both of us.''

There was a short silence before Cody apologized. "I'm sorry about springing Kristy on you like this. I had no idea that you had planned to have Molly here.''

"It wouldn't have happened if you had only told me you weren't interested in her anymore.'' Jenna sank down wearily onto a chair. "You gave me the impression you were still crazy about her.''

"I didn't want you to think that our trip to New York had been a big waste,'' he confessed, seating himself across from her. "Right after I started school I told Molly I wanted to date other girls, but she acted as though everything was the same as it was last summer. She'd say things like, 'Isn't it great that your mom and I have become such good friends.' I decided to wait until I came home for the holidays before I told you about it.''

"And I was waiting for you to come home before I told you about Harrison."

"Jeez, Mom," he drawled, "of all men, why Mr. Drake? You've seen how he lives—it's like he's from another planet."

"Cody, I don't feel like defending myself right now so let's just let it go for tonight." She got up and returned to washing dishes.

"Well, how serious is this thing with Mr. Drake?"

"I really think it's better if we talk in the morning when our guests aren't sitting in the other room waiting for us," she said firmly.

Cody shrugged. "Tracey told me to ask you if you would accept any help yet."

"I'm just about finished," she assured him. "Tell everyone I'll be in shortly."

He got up from the chair. "Despite everything that happened, the meal was great, Mom."

"I could have served TV dinners and no one would have cared," she said dejectedly.

"Come on, Mom. It wasn't that bad."

Jenna forced half a smile. "You'd better get back in there. Kristy's probably wondering what happened to you."

"What do you think of her?"

"I like her. But then you knew I would, didn't you?"

"She's our kind of people, Mom," he told her, then slipped through the swinging door.

Jenna resisted the urge to scream in frustration. First Roy, now Cody. What kind of people did they think *she* was? When she and Harrison were together on the weekends, she most definitely was his kind of people. *But what about the other five days of the week?* a little voice inside her head demanded. She didn't want to think about those other five days. Right now all she wanted was for Harrison to be with her for the rest of this holiday weekend.

But he wasn't going to be. Later that evening in the quiet of her room, Jenna was staring moodily at the ruffled canopy over the four-poster bed when he phoned.

"I think we've had our first fight…. Will you forgive me?" His voice was husky, seductively pleading.

"You mean our first fight since we've been more than Molly's father and Cody's mother," she corrected, relieved to hear the tenderness in his tone.

"I'm sorry, Jenna. I behaved like an ass today."

"I'm sorry, too. I wasn't exactly Miss Prudence. I could see how upset Molly was, yet I wanted so much to spend the day with you."

"If it weren't for our kids…" His voice trailed off in exasperation.

"They did bring us together," she reminded him while silently she was wondering if they wouldn't drive them apart.

As if he sensed the direction of her thoughts, he said, "Just because our kids break up doesn't mean we can't see each other."

"You don't think there will be problems? How did Molly take it when you told her about us?"

"I haven't told her yet. She was so emotionally drained after today I thought it best if I waited."

Molly was emotionally drained, Jenna repeated silently, biting down on her lip. Didn't he realize how emotionally drained she was? Her disappointment put a cool edge on her words. "You might not want to wait too long. I've already told Cody, and if by chance he and Molly speak before the weekend's over…" Jenna hesitated, then asked, "You are staying for the rest of the weekend, aren't you, Harrison?"

"Molly wants to go back tomorrow," he reluctantly admitted. "Maybe it would be better if we put this weekend behind us and start the next one on a fresh note."

Jenna said nothing for a moment. "Then you've already decided to return to New York," she managed to say when she'd swallowed her disappointment long enough to speak calmly.

"I don't want to, Jenna."

"But Molly does."

"There will be other weekends."

"And probably more problems with our children."

"None we can't overcome," he said firmly.

"If it were just the kids, I'd agree. But there's also the distance, your career, my career."

"You sound as though you're giving up on us." God, he wanted to keep the anger out of his voice, but how could she think such a thing after all they had shared the past six weeks?

Jenna felt the lump rising in her throat. "It's been wonderful, Harrison, but the reality is you're an executive and I'm a cowgirl. We come from two different worlds."

"You're just saying that because of what happened today between our kids. We're good together, Jenna...you know it and I know it."

"That's because on weekends we can shut out the rest of the world and be whatever we want to be. But look at what happened to us today when the outside world reached in." Her voice broke.

"You're tired," he said soothingly. "Why don't I call you tomorrow when I get back to New York. Just because I'm leaving doesn't mean I'm saying goodbye. I love you, Jenna." He thought he heard her whisper "I love you, too," before the final click of the receiver.

EACH DAY THEREAFTER a single red rose arrived for Jenna. No message, no card, just a rose. And each day Jenna tried to call Harrison, to hear his voice, to thank him for the flowers, but she was unable to reach him. He was either in a board meeting, at a seminar, with an important client or simply unavailable. She wondered how their relationship could possibly work when she couldn't even talk to him. It was as though they were playing telephone tag; neither one was usually home when the other phoned. In the week that followed, she managed to speak to him once, and that conversation had been cut short because of his work.

The first week in December, Jenna had planned to fly to Las Vegas to attend the National Finals Rodeo with J.T. and Tracey. For months, the three of them had been anxiously looking forward to the trip, as it was the grand finale of the rodeo season and many of their friends would be competing for world-championship titles. Tracey had taken Jenna shopping, insisting the two of them buy enough clothes to look as though they had won at the gaming tables before they even arrived. Jenna didn't want to admit that her previous enthusiasm for the trip was dimmed because of the uncertainty in her relationship with Harrison. If she was going to take a vacation, she'd rather spend the time alone with him. Instead, she'd found herself amid hundreds of cowboys in a city that never seemed to sleep.

As she walked along the brightly lit streets with Tracey and J.T., Cody's words came back to her. Maybe she was going through some kind of midlife crisis. Her once fervent interest in the rodeo seemed to be waning. Normally, she'd be the one inviting people to her hotel room for a party; now she didn't even care if she saw anyone outside the arena.

"WHEW! IT SURE IS GOOD to get away from those neon lights for a bit, isn't it?" J.T. said as they sat down at a square table.

"I didn't think they'd have a place like this in Las Vegas," Jenna commented, looking about the rustic bar with its dim lights and soft music. Except for a couple of slot machines near the entry, there were no other gambling tables. They had walked quite a distance from the main strip in order to meet several of J.T.'s friends. "Are you sure this is the right place, J.T.? I don't recognize any of the people in here." She cast an inquisitive glance at the small crowd that consisted mostly of Westerners, judging by their appearance, but no one Jenna recognized from the rodeo.

"Have you ever known me to be wrong?"

Jenna arched one eyebrow delicately.

"Trust me, I'm not this time," he said, taking the pitcher of beer the waitress had left and pouring each of them a glass.

"I think I should have passed on tonight," Jenna stated flatly. "Do you realize how late it was when we finally went to bed last night? We're going to have to crawl back to Montana if we keep up this pace."

"Come on, Jen, it's only nine-thirty," J.T. reminded her. "You're not that old."

Nine-thirty and twelve-thirty in New York. Jenna mentally figured out the difference, then winced at the way her mind was always returning to Harrison. "Old enough to know better than to play slots till four in the morning."

"How does it feel to be a spectator rather than a contestant in the finals?" J.T. asked, changing the subject.

Jenna shrugged. "I shouldn't be competing with those young girls. I'm too old."

"Shoot!" J.T. exclaimed. "You could have beat any of those times, had you been out there. And you know perfectly well that if you went back on the circuit you'd easily qualify for the finals."

"I must be losing my competitive edge. I'd rather be trick riding than competing," she said honestly.

"Will you listen to that music?" J.T. made a face. "You girls wait here. I'm going to the jukebox and show these people what real music is about." He rose and sauntered over to the other end of the bar.

"You're not having a good time, are you?" Tracey asked as soon as J.T. was out of hearing range.

"What makes you say that?" Jenna answered.

"Usually we can't get you to leave the arena because you're talking to everyone that passes by."

"The finals don't seem the same this year. Maybe it's because Cody isn't with us."

"Are you sure it's not because Harrison's not here?"

"Oh, Tracey, if it were only that simple." Jenna sighed heavily.

"What's wrong, Jen?"

"You mean besides the fiasco I created on Thanksgiving?"

"It wasn't your fault. And I thought you said Harrison had apologized for what happened."

"He did. But there're so many obstacles blocking our way."

"Like what?"

"Well, besides our children, there's the fact that he lives three thousand miles away, never mind his fear of horses."

"Just because he doesn't live in the same town doesn't mean the relationship can't work. Look at how much J.T. and I were separated when we were dating. And everything turned out fine."

Jenna smiled gently at the younger girl's optimism.

"Where's the Jenna Morgan who I'm always complaining takes too many risks? I've never known you to be afraid to take a chance," Tracey challenged.

"Which just goes to show you I'm not myself when it comes to Harrison."

"Women in love seldom are."

J.T. returned to his seat and sat down just seconds before the jukebox switched to another number. "Now this is much better," he announced as the sound of a country-and-western song filled the room.

"That's all we need. Another woeful love song. J.T., couldn't you have found something a little bit snappier?" Tracey asked.

"This is beer-drinking music," he said, refilling each of their glasses, then signaling for the waitress to bring another pitcher of beer.

But the words of the song were soon drowned out by the eruption of a commotion in the bar. Jenna turned around at the sound of chairs and tables being shoved across the floor while laughter and surprised cries filled the room. Many of the bar's patrons were standing on chairs, craning their necks toward the entrance. Being short, Jenna couldn't see what was the object of so much attention.

"What in the world is going on?" she asked aloud to no one in particular as she rose to her tiptoes.

"There's some guy on a horse," a man with a pot belly and a handlebar mustache relayed down from the chair he was standing on.

Jenna turned to her brother. "What kind of a nut rides a horse into a bar in Las Vegas? J.T., don't tell me this is one of your buddies who's been drinking too much and thinks he's still in Cheyenne?"

The potbellied man looked at J.T., then at Jenna. "This guy doesn't look like he's a rodeo cowboy to me. He doesn't even look like he knows how to ride a horse!"

Jenna felt a sudden lurching of her stomach. She was about to climb up onto her chair when the potbellied man jumped down and exclaimed, "Better move! He's coming this way."

Suddenly coming straight toward her was a stranger on horse-back—at least in the dimly lit room she thought it was a stranger until she heard a familiar voice calling out her name. The man on the horse was none other than Harrison! His eyes were frantically searching the room, both hands clinging to the saddle horn as he rode through the bar, sitting ramrod straight on the slowly moving animal. When he saw Jenna's startled expression, his eyes lit up and a big smile spread across his face.

"Harrison! What are you doing?" Jenna cried out in surprise.

"I've come to ask you to marry me!" He rode right on over to the table and then right on by the table as the horse refused to stop.

"Pull on the reins," J.T. called out, scrambling toward the horse.

But Jenna was quicker. With lightning-swift reflexes and years of practice, she stopped the horse, then climbed up in front of Harrison, gently easing his fists from the saddle horn. Harrison gave her a big kiss for her efforts. Amid whistles, cheers and shouts of encouragement, she rode the horse back out onto the street while Harrison tipped his Stetson triumphantly to the well-wishers. Jenna could feel his other arm clenched around her waist in near panic. As they exited, he murmured, "Is this a yes?"

As soon as they were out in the street, Jenna half turned and looked at him. "Do you know you're crazy?"

"Crazy in love with you," he said close to her lips.

"You could have been arrested for this! Harrison, this isn't Cheyenne Frontier Days!"

"No, it's Las Vegas, Nevada, which means we can get married right away in one of the twenty-four-hour wedding chapels."

"You mean you want to get married *now?*"

"I've missed three appointments in the past two weeks, ignored several important financial meetings and when I have been at work I've been useless. Since I've met you I've discovered that my work and all it involves is not the most important thing in my life. I don't need the board meetings and the social obligations. What I need is you, Jenna. I need you to be my wife."

"But—"

He stopped her protestations with a finger on her lips. "Don't think about our children. Don't think about our backgrounds. Don't think of being practical. I'm tired of being practical and doing what is expected of me. For once in my life I'm going to do what I want. Please say you'll marry me, Jenna."

Jenna looked into eyes the color of aquamarines, eyes that were strong, sincere and full of love. "Where's the closest JP?" she asked before kissing him so hard they both nearly fell off the horse.

Harrison might have been impulsive in his decision to marry her but just as Jenna suspected, he had carefully planned the arrangements. He had checked out the local wedding chapels and reserved a honeymoon suite at one of the poshest hotels in Las Vegas. Had Harrison had his way, they would have ridden horseback to the chapel and been married immediately. But Jenna insisted that she change into something more appropriate than blue jeans, and after hearing that J.T. had helped orchestrate Harrison's dramatic proposal, asked that her brother and his wife be their witnesses. Tracey accompanied Jenna back to her hotel room to help her prepare while J.T. saw that the horse was returned to its owner, one of his friends. It was agreed upon that the four of them would meet in the lobby of Harrison's hotel, as it was only a block away from the Chapel of Love.

Jenna felt as though she were walking in someone's dream as she changed into a white leather dress with a fringed neckline that plunged to a V where a beaded butterfly graced the bodice. Tracey arranged her hair in a French twist, securing the dark tresses with a jeweled comb. Then she wove sprigs of baby's breath into the curls that fell in wisps around her face. Since Jenna had only brought boots along on the trip, Tracey lent her a pair of silver high heels, reminding her of the something borrowed necessary for good luck. Jenna thought the younger girl was much more nervous than she was, fussing over Jenna's appearance and chatting incessantly. By the time J.T. knocked on the door, both women were ready to walk the short distance to Harrison's hotel.

Jenna's heart caught in her throat when she saw Harrison

waiting in the red velvet furnishings of the lobby. He wore a Western-style black tuxedo with a crisp white shirt and a black ribbon tie. In his hands was his black Stetson and when he caught sight of Jenna, he smiled and walked toward them.

"You came," he said quietly, his eyes taking in every inch of her appearance.

His uncertainty touched her. "Of course. You think I'm going to let you get away from me now?" She flashed him a possessive smile and placed her arm through his.

"You look beautiful," he said huskily. "And I've forgotten your corsage upstairs. Maybe we should all go up and have a drink," he suggested.

"Why don't you go on up and Tracey and I will try out the slot machines here," J.T. offered, slanting a knowing look in their direction.

"Just don't be gone too long," Tracey added. "He's already lost his shirt once today."

As soon as Harrison got Jenna into the elevator, he pulled her into his arms and took her mouth in a slow, satisfyingly sweet kiss. "I think they knew the corsage was a ruse to get you to myself," he said on a ragged breath.

"You're going to have all night for that, Mr. Drake," she murmured before brushing her lips over his just as the elevator doors slid open. He led her to the door at the end of the hallway, then kissed her once more before inserting the key. When he reached for her again, she said, "If you don't stop, you're going to ruin my makeup and then Tracey and J.T. will know they were right."

The elegance of the room took Jenna's breath away. "Oh, my God, Harrison, it's beautiful!" she exclaimed in delight as her eyes discovered the heart-shaped bed covered in red satin with white roses strewn across the pillows. Everywhere Jenna looked there were mirrors. "It's positively decadent!"

"It's ours for tonight," he said grabbing her from behind and burying his face in her neck. "You should have seen the look on the bellboy's face when I checked in alone. Come. I want you to see the bathroom." He pulled her by the hand into another room where a small pool bubbled gently.

"Our very own pool?" she gasped.

"With a bar, stereo, color TV." He ran his hand along a remote control panel and chuckled. "As if a honeymooning couple would need a TV."

Jenna walked like a star-struck child around the large suite, her hand skimming the surfaces of the exquisite furnishings. Harrison followed her, enjoying her pleasure and happy that he had made the right decision.

"I'd better get you that corsage before J.T. and Tracey come pounding on our door." He crossed to the portable refrigerator and pulled out a florist's box. Inside was a large orchid, and with trembling fingers Harrison pinned it to her dress. Jenna's lashes were thick, dark fans across her cheeks as she looked down at the flower. She was so busy admiring the orchid, she didn't notice he had extracted another box from his pocket, this one bearing a jeweler's insignia. He flipped open the lid and on a cushion of black velvet sat a large diamond solitaire. Jenna's breath caught in her throat.

Harrison plucked the ring off its velvety bed and reached for her hand. "I know it's going to be a short engagement, but consider yourself officially engaged." He placed the ring on her finger, then brought her hand to his lips.

Everything in Jenna's heart told her she was doing the right thing. She loved Harrison and he loved her. And if there were problems they would be able to solve them together. She wrapped her arms around his neck and kissed him—a long, passionate kiss that said more to him than any words could have expressed. It was the ringing of the phone that forced them apart. They both looked at each other and laughed and said, "J.T. and Tracey" in unison.

While Harrison went to answer the phone, Jenna reached into her white clutch purse for her lipstick. After glossing on another coat of Passionate Plum, she snapped the bag shut and walked out into the sitting room. Harrison had his back to her, but she could see that he was tense, and catching snippets of his end of the conversation she heard Molly's name. The look on his face as he turned and saw her, confirmed her suspicions that it was not her brother but his daughter on the phone. Harrison casually turned away from her and lowered his voice. Jenna had the distinct feeling that he didn't want her to hear his end of the conversation. Retreating back into the bedroom, she closed the door and waited for his return.

It was a sober-faced Harrison who finally opened the door and walked over to her.

"That was Molly, wasn't it?" Jenna asked, getting up off the bed.

Harrison nodded. "Diana didn't realize I hadn't told my family about our plans and when Molly came home from school unexpectedly, she told her the news."

"And?" Jenna prodded.

"And naturally Molly was upset. Especially hearing it from someone other than me. Jenna, it's only to be expected that she would be apprehensive over my getting remarried."

"What is 'apprehensive'?" she asked cautiously.

"You know how dramatic Molly can be."

"Obviously it has upset you."

"Jenna, I'm not letting my seventeen-year-old daughter tell me what to do," he stated firmly. "I love you, and Molly is going to have to accept that. Ever since her mother died I've avoided getting involved with anyone because she always reacted so strongly. But no more. She's feeling what every daughter feels when her father decides to remarry—it's probably what you would feel if Hank were to remarry. The thought of a stepmother is threatening, and she's expressing that fear by being difficult."

Jenna stood silently pondering Harrison's words.

"She just needs some time, Jenna." She felt his hands close over hers. "After all, when you were simply Cody's mother she was very fond of you...sang your praises night and day." He gave her a crooked grin. "Trust me. Once you move in with us and she sees how we can be a family, it'll all work out."

"After I move in with you?" Jenna stepped back and extricated herself from his grip. "Harrison, what makes you think I want to move to New York?"

"We're going to be married. I'm not exactly old-fashioned but I do believe in a husband and wife living together. Did you think we would have a commuter marriage?'' He looked surprised.

"Of course not!''

"Then where did you think we were going to live?'' he asked, then answered his own question before she could. "In Montana?'' His voice was incredulous.

"What's wrong with Montana?'' she demanded. "You told me you realized that you don't need the board meetings and all the headaches of your job. I thought you meant you were giving them up to move out here on the ranch.''

"And what would I do on the ranch? I don't know a thing about raising horses. Hell, I can barely sit on one,'' he protested.

"You could paint.''

"Painting is my fantasy, Jenna. Managing money is my business, whether I like it or not.''

"Well, the ranch is my business. I'd suffocate in the city, Harrison. I can't take all those hordes of people and the continual traffic and the tall buildings blocking the sky.''

"We wouldn't have to stay in New York year-round. We could get a house in the country for the weekends. Molly needs a place to keep her horse and you could bring Snow Velvet and any of the others you want.''

"It's not going to work, Harrison.'' She was shaking her head as she sank down onto the heart-shaped bed.

"It will work,'' he declared, dropping down beside her. "I'm not letting you go, Jenna. I love you and I want to marry you.''

"Can't you see what we're doing here? We've only known each other a short time, yet we're ready to rush headlong, starry-eyed into a lifetime commitment. We're acting just like our kids did a couple of months ago! We're actually worse than the kids were. At least they thought about their future; we haven't even considered our responsibilities or talked about where we're going to live. We're not inexperienced teenagers who don't know the first thing about marriage.''

She could see that Harrison was thinking over her words carefully. He rubbed the back of his neck with his hand and muttered an expletive.

"I can't believe this is happening, Jenna. What happened to

the two people who met downstairs and waltzed up here on a cloud of happiness?''

''They were jerked back to reality. And that reality is we aren't free to rush into marriage without considering the consequences.'' She looked down at the large diamond sparkling on her finger and gently twisted it.

''Don't you dare remove that ring,'' Harrison said vehemently. ''The timing may be wrong for us right now, Jenna, but our feelings aren't. One way or another, I'm going to find a way for us to be together.''

Jenna didn't trust herself to speak. She knew that they shouldn't get married tonight. Then why was she feeling betrayed because he had agreed with her? With as much courage as she could summon, she mumbled some noncommittal response and walked toward the door. The only thing she left behind was the orchid.

CHAPTER THIRTEEN

HARRISON GLANCED AROUND the honeymoon suite and grimaced, knowing there was no way he could spend the night in this room. He dialed the airlines and arranged for a flight home, then decided to spend the rest of the night in the casino lounge. While tourists pumped coins into the one-armed bandits he drank cup after cup of black coffee, staring indifferently at the eclectic crowd that wandered in and out. Las Vegas, the city that never sleeps, was alive with excitement and he was morose with regret. He hadn't expected to be sleeping either—but not because he had planned on gambling all night.

Maybe he should have done things differently—like pushed Jenna back onto the heart-shaped bed and kissed her until she no longer cared that they were behaving impetuously. And the thought that he could have done just that nagged at him. In his arms she was soft and yielding, as he had always dreamed the woman he loved would be. The irony of it was that for the first time in his life he was ready to act without methodically weighing the pros and cons in his usual conservative manner only to have Jenna, the most daring, impulsive woman he had ever known, behave with caution.

It was also ironic that seventeen years ago, when he hadn't wanted to take his place in the fast lane of high finance, he had done so because of what it meant to Rita. She had been the one who was the social ladder climber, convincing him of the advantages the position would give not only them, but their unborn child. Now, that position was a hindrance in his relationship with Jenna and she expected him to give in to his yearning to be an artist, the occupation Rita had looked upon distastefully. Jenna didn't seem to recognize that the same loyalty that bound her to the rodeo bound him to his work. Could he break those bonds? Did he even want to? How could he make her understand, when he himself wasn't sure?

While Harrison passed the night away in the lounge, Jenna lay tossing and turning in a hotel bed only a block away. Her mind kept playing over and over the highlights of the past twelve hours; Harrison riding into the bar; his gallant marriage proposal; her elation as she prepared for their wedding; the large orchid; the diamond ring. It all seemed like a big bubble of joy that Molly had been able to burst with a single prick of her finger.

Tracey had spent hours trying to assure Jenna that everything would work out for her and Harrison, but Jenna was not convinced. She had left much more than the large orchid in Harrison's room; she had left her hopes and her dreams.

The following day they sat through the final round of the championship rodeo, and if Jenna didn't jump up and scream when J.T.'s best friend won the bull-riding event and one of her former students won the barrel-racing title, no one commented. In between sympathetic glances Tracey tried to steer their conversation toward the mundane, the trivial. But that night, when they were invited to a victory party at one of the hotels, Jenna declined. Tracey offered to keep her company, but Jenna insisted that she would rather be alone. In her room, she stared at the plate of cold food room service had delivered. She sipped on a wine cooler and sang along to the words of a country-and-western song that lamented the pain of being in love.

DURING THE NEXT FEW DAYS, while Harrison and Jenna searched for answers within themselves, their children were seeking some answers of their own. Molly was beginning to panic over what she called her father's obsession with a cowgirl, and phoned Cody to elicit his help.

"Cody, I don't think you realize what is happening!" she insisted.

Cody switched the receiver from one ear to the other, wishing Molly hadn't called him at the dorm. He disliked standing in the hallway and trying to carry on a conversation while the rest of the guys in the dorm filed noisily past.

"Molly, could I call you back tomorrow? I'm in the middle of studying for my exams and this really isn't a good time for me to be on the phone."

"Fine!" The word was as sharp as the crack of a whip. "If you don't want to hear how your mother's about to ruin her life, I can hang up and call you back when you have the time," she said sarcastically.

He sighed in exasperation. "And just how is my mother about to ruin her life?"

"You know she's been dating my father."

"Yeah."

"And that doesn't bother you? Cody, they're total opposites!"

"Hey! I don't like it any better than you do, but what good is it going to do to say anything? I already had a big fight with my mom over it."

"I'm not talking about a family discussion on the subject," she said dryly. "Believe me, I've cried and talked till I was blue in the face and the best I could do was to get Dad to postpone the marriage."

"Marriage!" Cody raised his voice, prompting several heads to turn in his direction. "They're getting married?" he squeaked in a near whisper.

"You mean you didn't know that your mom almost married my dad in Las Vegas last weekend?" She made an exaggerated sound of disbelief. "If I hadn't wormed the truth out of Diana Elliot I wouldn't have even found out about it, and by this time we would have been related—as in brother and sister."

Cody couldn't believe his mother would do such a thing without talking to him first. "Are you sure about this, Molly?"

"I wish I wasn't. They were getting ready to leave for one of those all-night wedding chapels in Las Vegas when I called my dad's hotel. Luckily, I caught him just in the nick of time. I cried my heart out and fortunately, Dad saw reason. The wedding's been postponed, but Cody, if we don't do something, I'm afraid they'll go through with it. They're acting like a couple of teenagers instead of parents."

"God, I just can't believe my mom didn't tell me she wanted

to marry him. If it's that serious, I don't see how anything we say is going to make a difference."

"Cody, you know talking to parents is like next to impossible. We're going to have to *do* something."

"Like what?" he asked cautiously.

"Like try to make them less available to each other."

"And how do you propose to do that?"

"Look what happened to us," she began, swallowing back the lump in her throat. "We thought what we had was the real thing, but once we were apart for a while, we realized that it wasn't. Well, the same thing will probably happen to our parents, but what we have to do is keep them apart so that it's not too late when they do finally see the light.

"For example," she continued, "Christmas vacation. We'll both be home from school, right? Well, when my dad calls for your mom, you can say she's not in the house and I'll do the same if your mom calls for my dad. It would be even better if you said she was at that Roy's ranch—my dad turns green every time the guy's name is mentioned. I could tell your mom my dad's working with Diana."

"I don't know, Molly. That sounds so underhanded."

"Underhanded? *They*'re the ones who tried to sneak off to Las Vegas and get married without telling their own children. Do you really think it would be better if the two of them got married and then had to go through a painful divorce?" Molly sighed. "I'm not asking you to deliberately lie to your mom. You can just hint to my dad that she's over at Roy Cooper's. Come on, Cody, isn't it worth a try? When they thought we were wrong for each other, they didn't hesitate in doing everything in their power to break us up."

There was silence on the phone until Cody reluctantly said, "I'll think about it."

"Good. And you can also think about this: do you honestly believe your mom would be happy if she sold the ranch and moved to New York?"

"She'd never sell the ranch," Cody vehemently objected.

"People in love do all sorts of things we never expect them to do. I heard Dad calling some real-estate agent about finding a hobby farm here in New York. He said he wanted a place where he and his wife could spend weekends, a place where they would be able to keep horses.''

Cody swore under his breath.

"Look, you know I like your mom. She's one of the nicest ladies I've ever known and she taught me so much about horses I'll always be grateful to her. But she'll never fit in here in New York. And I'm not saying that to be mean. She belongs out West in the mountains...just like you do.''

"I'm not disagreeing with you about that. It's just that I don't like what you're suggesting we do.''

"And if we do nothing, you just might be watching the lights flash in Times Square rather than the rodeo arena scoreboard during the school break. Doesn't it bug you at all that you could be getting a new father?''

"All right, Molly, you've made your point,'' he snapped. "I've said I'll think about it and I will. Listen, I've got to go. Someone's waiting to use the phone.'' He glanced over his shoulder at the kid leaning up against the banister, a book open in his hands while he waited his turn at the telephone.

"It would only be for a couple of weeks,'' she coaxed. "When are you going home?''

"The day after tomorrow. How do you know they're not spending Christmas together?'' he asked curiously.

"December is Dad's busiest month at work. He barely finds time to take Christmas Day off. This isn't going to be as bad as you think.''

Cody hung up the phone and returned to his room. He opened his biology book but found he couldn't concentrate, and snapped it shut derisively before tossing it on his bed. As much as he hated Molly's suggestion, he couldn't help but shudder at the thought of his mother marrying a man like Harrison Drake and leaving everything behind to go live in New York.

God, he couldn't believe his mother was acting like this. He raked back the dark hair on his forehead and stared out at the murky December sky. How could she seriously consider marrying a man without even telling her own son about it? What was wrong with her, running off to elope like an infatuated teenager? And with a city slicker who was afraid of horses, no less. Heck, of all the cowboys on the rodeo circuit she could date, she had to go and pick a stuffy office jock from out East.

Molly probably was right. If they did get married, chances were they'd end up getting divorced once they realized how unsuited they were. No matter how his mother might have deluded herself, he knew she couldn't live anywhere except the mountains. Maybe Drake could convince her to give up rodeoing, but she'd never leave the ranch. If he and Molly could stall the wedding, then maybe it would only be a matter of time until his mother would come to her senses. Maybe time was all that was needed.

So Molly and Cody put their little plan into action. If Jenna thought it strange that Cody raced for the telephone every time it rang, she kept it to herself. Cody guessed that his mother suspected he was waiting for Kristy to call. He had been home for three days when the first call from Harrison came through. He hadn't known if he would be able to lie in front of his mother, but as luck would have it, Jenna wasn't home. Ironically she was at a neighboring ranch, but not Roy Cooper's. So when he told Harrison that his mother had gone to keep a sick neighbor company, he conveniently forgot to add that the neighbor was eighty-year-old Mrs. Killian. Cody made sure his mother knew of Harrison's call. What he didn't tell her was that Harrison had told him he would be out the rest of the evening and would call her the following day.

Consequently when Jenna returned Harrison's call, it was Molly who answered. She informed Jenna that her father had gone out to dinner with Diana Elliot to celebrate the holiday season—neglecting to add that it was the office Christmas party they were attending.

For several days luck seemed to be on the side of the two teenagers, as they were able to intercept several calls meant for their respective parents. Cody felt only a twinge of guilt as he informed Harrison of his mother's absence due to the fact that she had gone to help Roy Cooper look at brood mares. Likewise, the remorse was fleeting for Molly as she told Jenna her father was helping Diana move into her new apartment. In actuality,

Jenna was offering professional advice to Roy's niece who was choosing a barrel horse, and Harrison was having some new file cabinets moved into Diana's office.

After a week of success with the plan, Molly called Cody to suggest they risk being a little bit more elaborate with their stories. Cody decided that rather than lie, he would plead ignorance. The next time Harrison called, he simply told him that he didn't know where his mother was. Molly came right out and told Jenna that her father was with Diana on a date.

One night when Cody returned home after being out with his friends, he found Jenna waiting up for him.

"Hi, Mom. What are you doing up so late?" he asked, shrugging out of his sheepskin-lined parka.

"I thought it was time we had a little talk, Cody."

He dropped down onto the sofa next to her, reaching for a handful of peanuts from the dish on the coffee table.

"I talked to Harrison this evening," Jenna said quietly and saw Cody wince.

"You finally connected, huh?"

"Yes, we *connected*. You sound disappointed."

"Who, me? Why would I be disappointed?" he asked innocently.

"You know, it's real strange, Cody. Harrison had the impression that I've been spending a lot of time with Roy. Now what would have caused him to think that, do you suppose?"

Cody shrugged. "Maybe the guy's got a fertile imagination."

"I can tell you it wasn't my imagination that Molly was trying to insinuate her father was dating Diana Elliot."

There was silence in the room except for the crackling of embers that still flickered in the fireplace.

"Diana Elliot's his assistant, Mom," he finally said, avoiding her eyes.

"And you're my son and Molly is Harrison's daughter and Roy Cooper is just a neighbor. So why did the two of you think that you could do or say anything to change that? What were you hoping to accomplish? Did you think that I'd be so jealous I'd tell Harrison to go to hell?" She finally stood and confronted him with hands on her hips. "It really was quite childish, Cody, and I don't know why you didn't come and tell me how you felt about my relationship with Harrison instead of plotting with Molly behind my back.''

"Don't you?" Cody stood up, his lean frame towering over hers. "What about when you went behind my back and got engaged to Harrison Drake? I've been home over a week, Mom, and you haven't once explained that rock on your finger." He pointed accusingly at the diamond on Jenna's finger.

"That's why you've been cool toward me, isn't it?" she surmised. "I told you when you were home for Thanksgiving what was happening between me and Harrison."

"Wrong, Ma. You told me you were seeing each other. You never told me you were planning on getting married. I had to hear it from Molly, who took great pleasure in telling me that my mom had run off to Las Vegas with her father—or maybe I should say *our* father."

"But we didn't get married. I certainly would have told you if it had happened."

"When? After you had moved to New York?"

"I wasn't planning on moving to New York." She heaved a sigh of frustration. "I can see that Molly has added two and two and come up with five."

"So what is the correct answer?"

Jenna sank down onto the sofa, gesturing for Cody to sit beside her. "The reason I haven't explained about this ring is because I'm not sure myself if I should even be wearing it." Her eyes were fixed on the diamond solitaire. "Harrison and I did almost get married in Las Vegas, but when we realized how we were rushing into it without having made plans for the future, we decided to wait. Cody, I'm not blind to the fact that Harrison and I come from two different worlds. Our careers are as different as night and day; he doesn't want to leave New York and I don't want to leave Montana. But I don't want to be apart from him, either. All I can hope for is that in time we'll find some answers, because our marriage doesn't involve just the two of us, but all four of us.''

"Three of you, maybe, but you don't need to worry about me. I don't need a new father at my age," he said defensively.

"Harrison doesn't want to take the place of your father, Cody, and I certainly don't expect to take the place of Molly's mother. I know it's a little awkward, considering your past relationship with Molly, and technically you'd be stepbrother and stepsister, but you two aren't children anymore. You've got your whole lives ahead of you and each of you will go a separate way. Surely you don't begrudge me not wanting to spend the rest of my life alone?"

"You wouldn't have to be alone a day in your life. There are lots of guys on the rodeo circuit who'd jump at the chance to date you."

"I don't want any of the guys on the rodeo circuit. I happen to have fallen in love with Harrison Drake. For the first time since your father died I've found someone who makes me happy. He's a good man, Cody. Can't you at least give him a chance? Will you try to accept my feelings for him?"

She watched him gaze into the dying fire, his eyebrows knit close together as though he were thinking over her words. After several minutes of silence, he brought his eyes back to hers.

"I do want you to be happy, Mom, but I don't want to see you make any mistakes, either. I don't think you realize what you're doing. I mean, marriage is serious stuff."

"Oh, Cody." She sighed. "Why do you sound like the parent and I feel like the teenager?"

He gave her a half grin. "Just a few minutes ago you were calling me childish," he reminded her. "I'm sorry about going along with Molly's little scheme, Mom. It was awfully childish, but I was angry that you hadn't told me about marrying Mr. Drake. And it didn't help that Molly was rubbing it in every chance she got."

"It's hard for her to accept the idea that her father wants to remarry."

"Are you going to marry him, Mom?"

Jenna leaned her head back against the cushions and sighed once more. "I wish I knew the answer to that myself."

In New York, Harrison and Molly had discussed the same topic, only Molly had found it more difficult to accept her father's relationship with Jenna than Cody had, and subsequently, had done her best to play upon her father's paternal heartstrings. The result was for Jenna and Harrison to agree that the most sensible thing to do would be to spend the Christmas holiday with their children rather than with each other.

Jenna found herself wishing Harrison wasn't so sensible and walked around the house singing "Blue Christmas" as she decorated the house with holly and mistletoe. And before she went to bed, she tried not to notice the lone package lying under the Christmas tree, its silver foil concealing a hand-tailored red satin shirt with a black yoke. She had thought it would be the perfect shirt for Harrison to wear for a Western Christmas. But that was before she had learned he'd be spending the holidays in New York.

Jenna was not alone in her misery. Harrison went through the motions of enjoying the holiday dinner purely for his mother's benefit. He would gladly have traded champagne-roasted duck for hot dogs and beans if it had meant being with Jenna. And after successfully resisting the temptation to fly out and be with her for the holidays, he decided that being separated from her was not solving anything and he was going to do something about it.

He wanted Jenna with him in New York. He wanted to take her to the jazz clubs, to the art galleries, to the theater. He wanted to show her his New York, one that hopefully she could become accustomed to. The only way they were ever going to work out the obstacles between them would be for her to come and stay with him. And it was with such thoughts in his mind that he called her, repeating all the arguments he had mentally prepared including the possibility she would be able to check out the horse clubs in the area.

After her miserable Christmas, Jenna readily agreed to Harrison's suggestion. The day after Cody returned to college, she caught a plane to New York. The first few days of her visit were like paradise. Molly was away at boarding school and with the exception of the housekeeper, Jenna had the apartment to herself during the days and Harrison to herself during the nights. She went window shopping at Tiffany's, visited a masseuse who managed to work a kink out of her calf that had been bothering her for weeks, and was pampered by a leading New York stylist who sent a chauffeured car to pick her up, then shampooed and styled her hair while she sipped cappuccino. Harrison took her to the theater to see a Tony Award-winning play, to dinner at a chic but intimate French restaurant, and on a harbor cruise around the Statue of Liberty. Although she still felt crowded by the city, being with Harrison she felt she could tolerate anything—until Molly came home for the weekend.

The minute the teenager walked in the door, Jenna knew that their paradise would never be the same. Molly had a determined look in her eye and her confident stance indicated she was accustomed to getting her way, especially on home turf. Jenna went to bed that evening feeling frustrated and a bit alienated—and the weekend had only just begun.

After a night of considerable tossing and turning, she decided the only course of action was to ignore the girl's pointed barbs and wait patiently for the Molly she had grown fond of in Montana to return. But the Molly who greeted Jenna Saturday morning bore little resemblance to the girl who had followed her around the ranch and helped her care for the horses. Some of the optimism she had awoken with began to fade.

"Good morning," Jenna said pleasantly, trying not to act surprised to find Molly busy making breakfast. "What are you cooking? It smells delicious." She caught a glimpse of the dining room table glistening with formal dinnerware.

"It's probably the scones in the oven," she said in a tone that sounded to Jenna like a young Eleanor Fielding.

"Scones?"

"Yes. They're Dad's favorite. I thought you'd know that by now. Every time he and my mother would visit London he'd come home and talk of nothing else for weeks, so Mom decided she would make them a part of our weekend breakfasts."

"I see." Jenna forced a smile to her lips.

"Actually, the scones were a concession on Mother's part. Her specialty was French cuisine, which you probably already know my father absolutely adores. She'd make the most wonderful French dishes."

Jenna thought Molly appeared a bit nervous as she flitted

around the kitchen, but she seemed to have everything under control.

"Is there anything I can do? Make some juice or butter some toast?"

Molly shot her a look that could have had Jack Nicklaus questioning his ability to sink a putt. "We don't make juice from a can, Mrs. Morgan. Dad likes it freshly squeezed and I've already told you we're having scones, not toast."

Just then Harrison strolled into the kitchen and planted a kiss on Jenna's mouth, which prompted Molly to use a bit more force than was necessary to close the cupboard. Jenna didn't enjoy the kiss. She didn't want Harrison showing her any affection in front of Molly, which she knew was absurd and only added to her growing frustration.

"You're cooking breakfast, Molly? What a nice surprise!" Harrison gave his daughter's shoulder an affectionate squeeze.

"I figured it had been much too long since anyone had cooked you a decent breakfast," Molly explained, casting a defiant glance in Jenna's direction.

Harrison looked suspiciously from his daughter to Jenna. "Well, whatever the reason, it was awfully sweet of you."

Jenna had to bite her tongue and remind herself that patience was indeed a virtue.

"Everything's ready if you want to sit down," Molly suggested.

If Molly intended to follow in her mother's footsteps when it came to cooking, she was going to have to spend a lot more time in the kitchen, Jenna thought as she managed to swallow herbed scrambled eggs that appeared to have more herbs than eggs. Harrison kept the conversation light by asking his daughter about school, and when he announced that he wanted to take them to the stables, Jenna saw Molly relax for the first time.

"Your father tells me you've been working on reining patterns," she commented as they cleared away the breakfast dishes.

"Yeah, but I've switched to hunt seat." Although Molly's tone was patronizing, Jenna detected the enthusiasm and love of horses they had in common.

Later, as Molly demonstrated her skills at the indoor arena, Jenna could see how hard the teenager had worked and complimented her on her efforts. As long as they were around horses, there seemed to be a good rapport between them, but as soon as they returned to the city, Molly reverted to her sullen disposition. By Saturday evening Jenna was ready to board the first available plane for Montana, except she knew that if she could weather one more day of Molly's stormy behavior, school would resume and she and Harrison would be alone again.

Harrison had managed to get hold of a couple of tickets to the New York Knicks basketball game for Sunday afternoon. Jenna had never been to a professional basketball game in her life—another shortcoming Molly took great pleasure in accentuating, especially since she knew her father was an avid fan. When Molly heard there were only two tickets, she groaned and carried on as though she were missing the school prom. Jenna, in a self-sacrificing manner inherent in mothers, suggested Harrison take Molly. After all, she reasoned, Molly would be returning to school, she would be staying. After she made the suggestion, however, she felt instant remorse, for Molly looked positively triumphant. Short of making a scene, she couldn't retract her generous but idiotic offer.

After they had gone, Jenna prowled around the apartment restlessly, disgusted with herself for having been manipulated by a seventeen-year-old. What had made her think this trip to New York would work? She shouldn't have come. Even without the added complication of Molly, she simply didn't fit in a city like New York. She flicked on the television; she flicked it off. She picked up a book; she put it down. She put a compact disc in the player; she took it out. Spreading two pleats of the vertical blinds, she peeked out at the gloomy New York skyline, surprised to see intermittent snowflakes falling.

Having the sudden urge to feel those snowflakes on her face, she quickly pulled on her jacket, grabbed her purse, then rode the elevator down to the first floor. She hurried across the lobby and out into the crisp January air. As soon as she stepped out from under the entrance awning, she looked up at the sky and stuck out her tongue, trying to catch one of the large flakes that seemed to fall so effortlessly. With a sense of freedom, she started walking, the now steadily falling snow a tranquil sight, softening the angles and planes of the city. She breathed deeply, letting the brisk air fill her lungs, ignoring the smell of bus fumes and the sounds of the steady stream of traffic.

By the time she reached Central Park, the ground wore a blanket of white. Taking one of the hikers' paths that wound through the center of the park, she marveled at the beauty of the wooded terrain with its statues and fountains. She hadn't expected to see parents with sled-toting children or horse-drawn carriages in the park. It was so invigorating to discover such a natural setting in the midst of the city, she didn't realize how far or how long she had been walking until she noticed the yellow lights glowing in the apartment windows and twilight darkening the sky.

She turned around and started to retrace her steps, only this time she passed fewer people, and as evening set in, she became aware of her cold toes, her cowboy boots insufficient protection against the wet snow. All of a sudden she felt someone grab at her shoulder bag from behind. Instinctively she tightened her grip on the purse and spun around to meet a large object being thrust in her face. It was only as she fell backward that she realized the large object was a man's fist, and that he was still trying to wrestle the purse from her grip. Kicking at his shins, Jenna struggled to keep the mugger away from her, but as she fell to the ground he was on top of her, his bearded face close to hers. Twisting her head, she managed to scream as loud as she could, at the same time continually kicking him. Her attacker reeled back in pain, but not before he had struck another blow to her body. He scrambled to his feet and then fled out of sight. Winded, Jenna lay trembling on the ground, too shocked to even cry.

Suddenly there was a small crowd of people gathered around her, giving her looks of both pity and curiosity. As she sat up, she felt a bit dizzy, and only fragments of conversation were coming her way.

"He went off like a scared rabbit."

"Did somebody call the police?"

"Why didn't she just give him the purse?"

"She's lucky she didn't get killed."

"Are you okay, Miss?" one tall man in a ski jacket asked, bending down on one knee.

"I...I think so," she stammered, looking down at her blood-stained hands. It was only as the man handed her a handkerchief she realized it was her blood—her nose that was bleeding.

Then the police were escorting her to an ambulance that whisked her off to an emergency room in a hospital that reminded Jenna of something she had seen on television, with lots of commotion and people all hurrying in different directions. After being X-rayed and examined by a doctor, she was diagnosed as being "badly bruised with several contusions but no broken bones or lacerations requiring further treatment." When she was asked if she was alone in New York, she gave them Harrison's name and address. While she waited for him to come to get her at the hospital, the police went over her story several times, then asked her if she would stop at the police station later and look at mug shots. Jenna nodded absently, wondering how long professional basketball games were. The numbness was beginning to wear off and replacing it were definite aches and pains, as well as a feeling of melancholy. She longed for her bed at home, and in an effort to replace the memories of the violent attack with the images of her mountain valley, she closed her eyes.

"Jenna, sweetheart, it's me, Harrison."

Someone was gently tugging on her shoulder, a shoulder that felt stiff and sore. Rolling over, she opened her eyes and saw a horrified look on Harrison's face.

"My God, Jenna, what happened?"

Jenna propped herself up on one elbow, grimacing at the pain the slight movement brought to her bandaged wrist. "I got mugged, Harrison. I thought the police would have told you." Was that her voice sounding as though she were miles away?

"I don't understand. How did you get mugged?"

"I went for a walk in Central Park and one of the finer citizens of New York City decided he wanted my purse."

"You went for a walk in Central Park?" he repeated, his

voice rising. "My God, Jenna, everyone in the whole United States knows you don't go walking alone in Central Park, especially after dark. You could have been raped, even murdered."

Jenna looked at him in bewilderment. What was wrong with Harrison? She was the one who was the victim and he was acting as though it were her fault. "I was trying to get some *fresh* air. Trying to look up at the sky and see snow instead of skyscrapers. Trying to remember what it's like to see land that doesn't have every square inch accounted for. What good is a park if people can't even use it?"

"Jenna, this is New York City, not Montana. You can't behave the same way you do out West."

"That's what I've been trying to tell you all along." She swung her legs over the edge of the bed. "Harrison, just get me out of here...please."

He helped her stand, his arm reassuring and consoling. "They said you can leave?"

Jenna nodded. "I just need my jacket and my purse. They're on that hook over there." She pointed to the back of a door.

"Your purse? You're not going to tell me you fought with the man over your purse?" For the second time, she thought his expression was one of horror.

"It was an instinctive reaction. I'm not some pampered socialite, Harrison. I've been around bucking stock and rough men all my life and I know how to take care of myself."

"A mugger in New York City is hardly the equivalent of some bucking animal. For heaven's sake, Jenna, what if the guy had been armed with a gun or a knife? Was it worth risking your life for a goddamned purse?" His ears were turning red.

"My life wouldn't have been in any danger had I not come to this stupid city," she flared. "I don't belong here and I never should have let you talk me into coming. Now look at me! I can't even put on my own coat." She was close to tears as she struggled to get her bandaged wrist into her jacket. Harrison finally helped her get her healthy arm through the sleeve, then draped the jacket around her injured shoulder.

"I'm just going to have to take care of you," he said, his anger dissolving at her helpless vulnerability. Jenna allowed herself to lean into his cashmere coat for several minutes as he murmured words of comfort. "You belong in bed—my bed. Let me take you home, sweetheart."

She straightened and moved away from him. "It isn't going to work, Harrison. I'm going home."

"Jenna, please don't say that. Look, all newcomers to New York need time to get used to the differences. This is not a normal city. I'm sorry I got so upset, but it drives me crazy to think of you walking around unprotected."

"I don't want to stay in a city where I need protection."

"Please, Jenna. One week is hardly a fair chance."

"It was enough for me to be temporarily put out of action." She raised her bandaged wrist. "Now I can't even ride! If I stay, I might end up permanently disabled," she said sarcastically.

"You're upset. Please let me take you home and get some rest. We can talk in the morning."

"The only place I will ever rest is in Red Lodge, Montana. I'll go back to the penthouse with you, but only to collect my luggage. I'm going home!"

CHAPTER FOURTEEN

"HARRISON, WE'RE WAITING on you for the daily strategy meeting," Diana Elliot reminded her boss a bit impatiently as she waltzed into his office with a copy of the *Wall Street Journal* tucked under her arm.

Harrison glanced at his watch and scooped up the papers in front of him on his desk. "Everyone else is present?" he asked, slipping into his suit coat.

"Yes. Harrison, is anything wrong?" She looked suspiciously at the blank computer screen that normally displayed rows of figures.

"Everything's fine," he assured her, guiding her out of his office, understanding her concern. Ordinarily he was the first one at the teleconference room, eager to connect with the London, Tokyo and San Francisco offices, but lately, strategizing about the stock market no longer held the same fascination for him.

As they walked the short distance to the conference room, Diana gave him a rundown of the analysts who were scheduled to give presentations later that day—a task she normally wouldn't think of doing, but lately she found necessary if she wanted her boss to be present.

"Can you cover for me with the oil analysts this afternoon?" Harrison asked as they entered the conference room.

Diana gave him a puzzled look. "Of course I can, but Harrison—"

"The hookup's completed, Mr. Drake," the secretary cut in, prompting Diana and Harrison to settle into sleek leather chairs around the polished mahogany table. And for the next forty-five minutes, Diana saw the intense investment manager lead a mind-twisting session analyzing what could happen during the day's trading.

As soon as the meeting was finished, Harrison quickly dealt with his urgent appointments, then hustled out of the office before anyone else could detain him. While Diana took care of the oil analysts, he pored over back issues of every rodeo paper and periodical he could get his hands on at the library. He made photocopies of the articles featuring Jenna Morgan, world-champion barrel racer, then took his stack of copies home where he perched himself on a bar stool and began sketching.

That first night he sketched until the wee hours of the morning, unable to stop his pencil once he began. The following evenings he'd eat a quick dinner, then begin sketching again, plugging in his answering machine to keep from being interrupted. His sketching started to become more important than his work at the office, and soon he found himself half listening at meetings, not fulfilling what his mother referred to as his "social obligations," and becoming very short-tempered with anyone who disturbed him in the evening. He was a man with a purpose, only this time his tenacity wasn't directed toward the financial world, but to the art world.

Meanwhile the subject of Harrison's sketchings felt like a woman without a purpose. Ever since Jenna had returned to Red Lodge, she had been trying to figure out what direction her life was taking. Despite what she had told Harrison, her injuries in New York hadn't prevented her from getting right back on Snow Velvet the minute she had come home. Riding was about the only thing she felt she had under control in her life. It was like eating and sleeping; her body craved it. After a rigorous workout one February afternoon, she returned to the house to find Tracey and J.T. having coffee with her father.

"You look whipped," J.T. told her as she kicked off her boots near the doorway. "What are you trying to do, kill yourself?"

"J.T.," Tracey said pointedly, placing a warning hand on her husband's arm. "Don't pay any attention to him, Jen. He's about as subtle as a tank."

Jenna pulled off her jacket and ran her hands through her loose hair as she glanced in the oval mirror beside the coatrack.

Not even the cold, crisp winter air had put any color in her cheeks, and she knew J.T. spoke the truth. "He's probably right, Trace. I'm hitting that age where I should be putting on makeup every day or else I'm going to start scaring people."

"You need makeup to enhance your beauty like I need another nose on my face," Tracey said, looking at the unblemished skin that never seemed to lose its golden hue. "Your body is still recovering from that incident in New York, that's all."

"I wish you would take it a little easier on your workouts, Sis," J.T. added.

"Listen, you two, I'm fine," Jenna replied a bit impatiently, dropping down onto the vacant chair at the table.

Hank poured her a cup of coffee and set it down in front of her. "Why don't you have a caramel roll?" He pushed a serving tray in her direction. "Tracey brought these over."

Jenna took a sip of the hot coffee, but ignored the rolls. "So what brings you two out on such a blustery cold day?"

"Tracey's got some news she wants to share." J.T. eyed his wife affectionately, as his pinkie reached over to entwine with Tracey's forefinger.

Jenna glanced at Tracey and thought of how vibrant she looked, how much in love she and J.T. were, and felt a stab of envy. Their future held so much promise because they both wanted the same things out of life and were working together toward common goals.

"Well?" Jenna looked expectantly from one to the other.

Tracey reached across the wooden table and took J.T.'s hand in between her palms, then said shyly, "I'm pregnant."

"But that's wonderful!" Jenna exclaimed, getting up to give her sister-in-law a hug. "No wonder you're glowing." She stood back and looked at Tracey from arm's length, then turned to give her brother a hug. "Congratulations, J.T. I'm happy for both of you. You'll make terrific parents."

"Thanks, Sis. We wanted you to be the first one to know, since it means some decisions are going to have to be made concerning the specialty act."

"Of course some decisions are going to have to be made. And the first one is putting Tracey officially on maternity leave.

Her only responsibility is to see that the next Flying Foster is healthy."

"Then you don't mind that it'll only be the two of you?" Tracey asked.

Jenna saw the hesitation in the younger girl's eyes. "You weren't thinking I'd be disappointed because you're going to have a baby, were you?" She patted Tracey's hand. "This is the best news I've heard in a long time. You don't need to worry about me or the specialty act," Jenna assured her. "We'll work something out."

"What would you think about getting another rider?" J.T. suggested.

"Until Tracey comes back, or permanently?"

"I was thinking more as a backup than a replacement. You know how much both Tracey and I love to perform, Jen, but after the baby's born, I think we might want to cut back on our engagements, stay at home a little more."

"Whatever you decide will be fine with me." Jenna forced a smile to her lips, but inwardly she felt troubled. She had been searching for a reason to trim the schedule of performances, but now that the opportunity presented itself, she found herself reluctant to do so.

"It doesn't have to be decided right this minute, does it?" Hank interjected, pushing his chair away from the table to rise. "I'm pleased as punch that I'm going to have another grandchild, but right now you're going to have to excuse me. I've got to go out and look at that pump that's been giving us trouble."

"I'll come with you, Dad," J.T. offered, getting up from the table. "This way you two women can sit and talk about babies or whatever your little old hearts desire." He planted a noisy kiss on Tracey's cheek, then led his father outdoors.

"So when's the littlest Foster going to make his public appearance?" Jenna asked, getting the coffeepot and refilling Tracey's cup.

"His?" Tracey echoed. "*She* is due around the first week in September."

"You want a girl, don't you," Jenna concluded, sitting down opposite Tracey.

"Oh, I'd be happy enough with a son, but I must confess I want a daughter. I know everyone says it doesn't matter as long as it's healthy, but I can't help myself. I want a girl so badly."

"I know what you mean." She smiled in understanding. "When I was pregnant with Cody I felt the same way. They have all those cute little clothes for girls—the frills and the bows and the barrettes and ribbons. But I can promise you this, Trace. Once that little baby is born it won't matter whether it be boy or girl, because it will be yours."

"I'm sure you're right," Tracey agreed, her normally ivory complexion rosy with excitement. "Boy or girl, one thing is certain. This child will know how to ride a horse." The blue eyes staring at Jenna were sparkling blissfully.

"I don't think I've ever seen you looking this happy."

"Oh, I am, Jenna. I really am. It's going to be hard for me to be away from performing, but I want this baby so much. I just wish I could spread this happiness around. I hate to see you looking so…so…"

"Miserable?" Jenna supplied. "It's okay, Tracey. Why should I say I'm fine when I'm not. I am miserable." She leaned back in her chair and sighed.

"You haven't heard from Harrison since you came back from New York?"

"Our phone calls seem to be fewer and fewer. He works so much I'm beginning to wonder if he isn't a workaholic. When we do talk, we can't seem to get past our usual stumbling block—his career is in New York, mine is in Montana. I used to think obstacles were only weaknesses in the mind, but they seem to be concrete in my life."

"Then it isn't just Molly?"

"Molly is practically an adult and even though there's some tension in our relationship, I'm optimistic enough to believe time could take care of that problem. It's Harrison I can't understand. Tracey, you should see what a wonderful artist he is."

"Harrison's an artist?" A look of amazement swept across Tracey's face.

Jenna nodded. "I was just as surprised when I found out. He's always wanted to be an artist—he even studied in Paris—but his family put a lot of pressure on him to take his place in the business world. And I'm certain from our conversations that Molly's mother enjoyed the prestige of being married to one of the top financiers in the country and didn't encourage him to pursue his creative talent. Instead of following his heart and taking up painting as a full-time occupation, he went to some dreary office to be overworked and stressed out. In New York City, no less. A man who hates crowds, yet he tolerates that cement jungle."

"But Jenna, when you consider his background, it would be hard for anyone to give all that up to become an artist. I'm not very familiar with the art world, but it must take some time to establish a reputation."

"But he's already established his name as an artist. Every year he spends his vacation painting and his work sells as soon as it's hung in the gallery."

"Yes, but he's also established a name for himself in high finance," Tracey pointed out. "Do you honestly believe he could be happy as an artist?"

"Yes, I do," she insisted firmly, trying to convince herself as much as Tracey. "He's a completely different person when he's away from New York. He's told me himself that he's in the financial world because of his strong sense of responsibility and loyalty to his family. Drakes become financiers, not artists."

"And Foster women became trick riders, not socialites? Jenna, haven't you ever wondered what would have happened if you had wanted to become a pencil pusher instead of a rodeo star? Wouldn't that same family loyalty that has Harrison working in the business world have kept you working in the rodeo?"

Jenna looked at her pensively. "I never wanted to be a pencil pusher. All I've ever wanted is to be around horses. I don't think Harrison loves his job but he does love painting."

"What if Cody came to you and told you he didn't want to ranch?"

"But Cody does want to ranch."

"Are you sure?" she asked gently.

"Now you're starting to sound like Harrison." She sipped her coffee thoughtfully. "After Jack died I didn't think I'd ever want to get married again. I had it in my head that Cody and I would continue on with his dream—to eventually be stock contractors. Ever since Cody was a little boy the three of us had planned on that happening some day. I thought my future was crystal clear. Then I met Harrison, and now I find myself wondering if ranching is even as important to me as I thought it was all my life.''

''So where does that leave the two of you?''

''I wish I knew, Tracey. Somewhere between the altar and New York City, I guess. I hope Harrison's having better luck at figuring it out. I feel as though I've been walking around in a fog lately. Remember that feeling you had when you graduated from high school and you realized for the first time in your life that you were in charge of your future?''

''Uh-huh,'' Tracey murmured reflectively.

''That's a little like how I feel right now. Like I've graduated from motherhood and once more I'm free to choose what I want to be doing with the rest of my life. To be honest with you, Tracey, it's a little scary.''

''Jenna, are you trying to tell me you're afraid to make a commitment to Harrison?''

''I know it sounds crazy. All of my life I've been impulsive, daring, always ready to meet the next challenge.''

''I think it sounds real normal. But where's the Jenna who takes risks? Remember, she's the Jenna Morgan that Harrison fell in love with. You're expecting him to take all the risks, but what about you?''

''I want to, but I'm afraid we're not going to make it,'' she reluctantly admitted.

''Is that why you've still got those dead roses?''

Jenna looked across the room to where a hand-painted vase held the dried remains of the red roses Harrison had sent her for Valentine's Day. ''I'm hoping that's not what our relationship is going to look like before too long.''

''Flowers die, but love doesn't. Just give yourselves some time, Jen.'' Tracey reached across the table and squeezed her arm reassuringly. ''Is Harrison coming out for the reopening of the Fielding Gallery?''

Jenna looked up from her cup. "Mrs. Fielding is reopening the art gallery next to the courthouse?"

"You didn't hear about it?" Tracey asked.

Jenna shook her head. "I wonder what prompted her to do that? That place has been closed ever since Charles Fielding died."

"J.T. heard about it from one of the councilmen. Apparently Charles Fielding had quite an extensive collection that no one's seen. She's planning a gala showing sometime next month, sending out engraved invitations and everything. I just assumed Harrison would be coming."

"I don't think so, Tracey. I'm sure he would have told me if he were going to be there. I know he's been working night and day to wrap up a special project he's involved with. And I can assure you I didn't get an engraved invitation. Considering the way Eleanor Fielding feels toward me, it's no surprise."

"I still can't figure that woman out. The vibes she sent out Thanksgiving Day were positively hostile." Tracey looked nonplussed. "Maybe you ought to go see her, Jen…make a gesture of friendship."

Jenna nearly choked on her coffee. "I'd rather make friends with a rattlesnake. As long as she doesn't come between my relationship with Harrison, I prefer to leave well enough alone. It's obvious that I antagonize the woman just by breathing. It's probably easier if we simply don't see each other."

But one bright March afternoon when the sun was melting away the winter snow, Eleanor Fielding made a point of speaking to her. Jenna had paused outside the bootery in Red Lodge to read a notice advertising an upcoming horse auction when she heard a haughty voice call out to her.

"Good afternoon, Mrs. Morgan."

"Mrs. Fielding," Jenna acknowledged, throwing an artificial smile over her shoulder before returning her gaze to the poster. When she realized that Eleanor was expecting her to engage in conversation, she straightened and faced the older woman.

"Isn't this a lovely day," Eleanor commented pleasantly. "One can almost smell springtime in the air."

"Yes, it is nice," Jenna agreed. "How are you, Mrs. Fielding?"

"I'm simply marvelous, thank you. But then you've probably heard that I'm reopening the gallery?"

"Yes. I hope it'll be very successful. Your husband was a wonderful artist and I'm sure his work will be greatly received."

"Thank you. Harrison tells me I shouldn't worry, but it is a big venture for me. Of course I couldn't have done it without his help. Well, I don't need to tell you how busy he is, yet he came all the way out here to help me select which paintings to display."

"Harrison was here?" The words were out before Jenna could even attempt to stifle them.

"Yes. Oh! I'm sorry, I thought you knew he was in town. I had just assumed he had contacted you." She made a great pretense of looking apologetic, but Jenna saw the gleam in her eye and guessed that Eleanor knew Harrison hadn't called her.

"Well, you know how dreadfully busy he is with his work. In fact, there'll be quite a few important people coming from New York...art collectors, dealers... Oh, and I believe Harrison said he was bringing his lovely young lady, Diana Elliot."

The arrow hit its mark as Jenna's face clearly revealed, and Eleanor, as if pleased with the result, continued. "I told him I didn't want this to be a working visit, and he assured me Diana was coming along for pleasure. She has a degree in art history besides her economics degree, and she's always been interested in Charles's work."

"Your husband's work is very respected." The words were like cotton in Jenna's mouth. Just as Eleanor had intended, the information imparted had Jenna wondering about Diana and Harrison's true relationship. Images of Harrison escorting Diana through the Uptown Gallery flitted painfully across her mind. "If you'll excuse me, Mrs. Fielding, I'm afraid I have an appointment," she said, squinting at her watch.

"Of course. I wouldn't want you to be late on my account," Eleanor said smugly, then smiled as Jenna hurried away.

When Jenna reached the pickup, she took several deep breaths before starting the engine. Why was she letting that woman upset her so? she thought. She knew Harrison's relationship with Diana Elliot was professional, so why did she let an old woman plant seeds of doubt? Probably because she hadn't seen Harrison for over a month and because she herself had been feeling insecure about their relationship. Harrison had been working long hours with the beautiful and sophisticated Diana Elliot. Maybe he had realized that she was the kind of woman he needed, not some cowgirl from Montana who didn't know enough not to go walking alone in Central Park. And it had hurt to hear that he had come to Red Lodge and hadn't even picked up the phone to say hello. If he was planning on attending the gallery opening, why hadn't he mentioned it to her?

When she arrived home she stared at the telephone, debating whether she should call him. After several minutes of indecision, she finally made the call. However, when his secretary informed her that Ms Elliot was receiving all of Mr. Drake's calls, she promptly hung up, feeling worse than ever. She spent the next few days wondering if she was about to be jilted, especially after the invitation arrived, an ornately engraved invitation with gold lettering on parchment inviting her to join in the celebration at the Fielding Gallery. Why would Mrs. Fielding invite her unless she knew for certain that Harrison and Diana were coming together?

When Harrison did finally call, she wasn't home to ask him about all the things troubling her. Her father had scribbled a message on the notepad next to the phone. It said: "Harrison says your time is up. Can you meet him at the gallery Friday night?"

Jenna quickly found her father, who told her Harrison would be at the reopening celebration but had asked Hank to drop her off at the gallery, as he wasn't sure if he'd be on time.

Jenna felt some of her confidence return as she thought about the message. When she had left New York, Harrison had told her he would give her time to think without pressuring her into any decisions. Did this mean he now wanted her to make a commitment? Of one thing she was certain: Diana Elliot was not going to be his date for the showing.

The night of the opening, Jenna took extreme care with her

appearance until she was completely satisfied with the image in the mirror. She walked over to her dresser and removed the diamond solitaire from the wooden jewelry box. Ever since the invitation had arrived, she had been going to bed with Vaseline on her hands to soften the roughened areas, and earlier in the day she had treated herself to a manicure while at the hair-stylist's. Now, dressed in her black suede skirt and sequined top, she slid the diamond onto her finger, determined to chase away any traces of her cowgirl blues. Her appearance drew a whistle from her father when she walked into the living room, and she smiled as she thought about Harrison's reaction to what her father called her "fine feathers."

Jenna recognized many familiar faces as she walked into the Fielding Gallery and it was obvious that besides the local residents, Mrs. Fielding had many influential friends. Every time Jenna glanced in Eleanor's direction, there was a small crowd gathered around her. The older woman looked extremely pleased, and Jenna could understand why. Charles Fielding's work was exceptional and very valuable. She was about to approach Mrs. Fielding when she saw Harrison enter the gallery...alone.

He was dressed in his Western-cut tuxedo, and the memories of the last time he had worn the dark suit washed over Jenna like melting snow swelling the mountain streams. At first he didn't see her, and Jenna drank in the sight of him, her heart rate increasing as she saw his gaze frantically searching the room. Then their eyes met...and all of her doubts disappeared.

She began to walk toward him, and just as they were about to meet, Mrs. Fielding intercepted their plans, embracing Harrison in a formal hug. She offered him her cheek, then thrust her arm through his in a possessive gesture. She began making introductions among the small entourage that had followed her progress across the room, and Jenna stood back, smiling to herself at Harrison's obvious impatience. When he was finally able to excuse himself, Jenna could see the anger in Mrs. Fielding's eyes as he walked toward her.

"Hello, stranger," she said huskily as he took both of her hands in his.

"If we weren't in a room full of people I'd show you how inappropriate that name is," he murmured, raising her fingers to his lips. "I've missed you, Jenna."

"I've missed you, too." She looked up at him with a smile that was both seductive and innocent, bemusing Harrison completely.

"What do you think of the paintings?" he asked, releasing his hold on her and shoving his hands into his pockets as he looked around the room.

"They're wonderful. The one of the U.S. Cavalry in the canyon is my favorite. The shading and lighting are superb."

Jenna allowed Harrison to escort her through the gallery as together they viewed the art, sharing their thoughts and feelings on each piece, until they had seen the entire collection.

"I don't understand it." Harrison glanced around with a puzzled expression on his face. "Not all the paintings are here."

"Why is that, do you suppose?"

He shot an ambiguous look in his aunt's direction.

"Come. I want to show you something." He led her out of the gallery, stopping to retrieve her fur wrap from the coat check before escorting her outside. Although the temperature had climbed to springlike mildness that afternoon, the nighttime air was frosty, and Jenna could see her breath as they walked the short distance to Eleanor's home.

Jenna followed Harrison into the house and up the grand staircase, her eyes hurriedly taking in the elegant furnishings as they sped by. At the top of the second flight of stairs, Harrison pushed open the door and flicked a switch that sent a flood of light into Charles Fielding's studio.

"I wonder where she put them?" Harrison mumbled, looking around the room impatiently.

"Put what, Harrison?"

"The other paintings." He was moving crates and boxes, until Jenna heard an "Aha." Pulling several canvases out from behind a closet door, he leaned them against the wall, carefully watching Jenna's expression as he did so.

"It's Grandmother!" she exclaimed, moving closer to study the portraits. "Oh, my God, Harrison. They're beautiful! How come they're not with the rest? I know the Fosters aren't her favorite family, but..." She paused in awe of the works. "He's captured her perfectly. She was so beautiful."

"So are you," Harrison said quietly, coming up behind her and turning her around. "The first time I saw them I almost thought it was you. You have her dark eyes, and that daring look in them, as though you could tackle the whole world if necessary. But she's got that tiny mole below her left eye." His finger trailed along the soft contour of her cheek.

Jenna looked again at the paintings. "He must have known her quite well to have painted her that way," she said thoughtfully. "Do you think he was in love with her?"

"It's obvious that he had very strong feelings for her." He lifted her chin with his finger. "I can relate to that." His eyes seemed to devour every inch of her face. "I've wanted to paint you, but I wasn't sure I could do you justice. You're the most beautiful woman I've ever known, Jenna, and I love you so much it frightens me," he admitted solemnly, then slowly lowered his mouth to hers. His lips were warm and lingering, echoing his words, as he kissed her deeply.

"Oh, Harrison, I love you, too," Jenna murmured, her body trembling as he pulled her against him.

"What is going on up here?"

The sound of Eleanor Fielding's scratchy voice had Harrison and Jenna pulling apart and looking toward the doorway.

"How could you bring that woman here—in Charles's sanctuary, of all places?" Eleanor demanded of Harrison, her face flushed with anger.

"I felt she should see the portraits of her grandmother," Harrison calmly replied. "Why weren't they on display with the others?" he asked, walking toward the older woman.

Eleanor stepped around him and glared at Jenna. "You have no right to be in this room. You're just like she was, and this family doesn't need another Foster woman tarnishing its reputation." Her buxom chest was heaving in agitation as her voice rose hysterically.

"Eleanor, stop this immediately," Harrison said firmly, trying to still the hand whose finger was pointing accusingly at Jenna. "You owe Jenna an apology. I invited her up here."

"Apology?" Eleanor looked horrified. "She's the one who should be apologizing for what that grandmother of hers did to me. She ruined my life, but does anyone care about that?" she shouted, shaking her hands free of Harrison's hold. "Just look at those pictures of her—he made her look as though butter wouldn't melt in her mouth. If he had had his way, the whole world would have looked at her as beautiful and virtuous, but I knew she was immoral. Turn them around," she demanded, "I can't bear to see her laughing at me." She began turning the canvases to the wall, her voice cracking with emotion, her face twisted with pain. "I should have destroyed them years ago," she cried.

"Eleanor, stop this." Harrison drew her sobbing figure into his arms, then led her to the sofa. "She's not laughing at you." His voice was soothing, as he gently made her sit down.

"Oh, yes, she is," the older woman sobbed. "Just like she did the day I found out that Charles was in love with her."

Harrison exchanged startled glances with Jenna. "Are you saying that Uncle Charles had an affair with Harriet Foster?"

"He chased her all over the country, while she traipsed from coast to coast, riding in those rodeos just like one of the men."

"Why didn't you go back to New York?"

"And tell my friends that my husband had left me for a cowgirl? I was trapped. I had to stay in Red Lodge and suffer the humiliation of all who knew about it."

"I can't believe my grandmother would have done such a thing," Jenna interjected. "She was in love with my grandfather."

"She hadn't met your grandfather at that time," Eleanor said brokenly. "Your grandfather was the reason Charles didn't divorce me. He had told me he couldn't live without her anymore and followed her to California, but came home feeling despondent. Apparently Harriet had met your grandfather, fallen in love with him and sent Charles home."

"And you never told anyone about this?" Harrison gently prodded.

"How could I? My father had disowned me after I married Charles. I certainly couldn't go back to New York. Everyone in Red Lodge already knew about the affair. It was humiliating."

"I'm sorry, Aunt Eleanor, that you've been carrying around all this hostility for so many years. But I know for a fact that Uncle Charles loved you."

Eleanor's weeping was now a subdued sobbing, and Jenna decided to give her some time alone with her nephew. "Harrison, I think I'll wait downstairs for you," she said in a near whisper. But before she left she added, "I'm sorry, Mrs. Fielding, that you had to suffer because of my grandmother."

Later, when Harrison came downstairs, he was alone. "She's going to go to bed," he told Jenna. "I'll have to take care of closing the gallery. Do you feel like going back with me?"

"All right."

He placed his hands on her waist and drew her close. "I'm sorry, but I had no idea she harbored such feelings. To be honest, I thought the reason she disapproved of our relationship was because she was a snob."

"I almost wish that was the reason," Jenna answered. "I can't believe my grandmother would have been involved with a married man. I've been trying to come up with some explanation that would absolve her from any blame...like maybe your uncle had an obsession with my grandmother that she didn't reciprocate. It's obvious from the paintings that he was in love with her, but maybe that love was one-sided."

"Jenna, we don't know all of the circumstances, and certainly Eleanor's perception is clouded. After harboring all those bitter feelings for so many years she may be embellishing the actual facts. It's your memories of your grandmother that you should treasure; you know the kind of person she was."

"She was a lady, Harrison. I know that sounds odd, considering she roped and tied steers. She also played Chopin and knew practically all of Elizabeth Barrett Browning's poems by heart. And she loved to get all dressed up in fancy clothes and play the gracious lady of the house. After women were barred from the men's rodeos she and her brothers joined a wild West show, putting on riding and roping contests. I used to listen to her talk for hours about those old shows. They played all over the world, you know, from Madison Square Garden to Buckingham Palace.'' A wistful expression crossed her face. "She was such a warmhearted and fair-minded person I can't believe she would knowingly have become involved with your uncle."

"It doesn't matter what's happened in the past; you do realize that, don't you? All we have is Eleanor's word that there even was an affair."

"It certainly explains all the hostility she's harbored toward the Fosters."

"It was irrational for her to blame you," Harrison said seriously. "To be honest, I can't say I blame Uncle Charles. I'm not sure I would have been able to stay away from you under the same circumstances."

Jenna looked up and found his eyes were studying her intently, his hands warm on her hips. "An affair today is hardly the scandal it would have been back then."

"And neither one of us is married, so why aren't we together?" He sighed impatiently. "How much time do you need to decide you want to become my wife?"

Jenna stiffened at his words. "That's not fair, Harrison," she replied, stepping out of his embrace. "You know I want to get married."

"Sure, as long as I agree to give up my career and move to Montana. Jenna, you're not being practical. Do you realize the income I have in my profession?"

"Money isn't everything in life, Harrison," she criticized.

"Oh, that's choice coming from someone who can't even balance her own checkbook," he bit back.

"Look what it's done for you," she snapped. "It's kept you chained to a job you don't want to be doing in a crowded city you hate. Oh, yes, it would be awful to be an artist...after all, you might have to give up those weekend yachting parties and dinners with the governor," she drawled in an affected New York accent.

"You talk about me being chained to a job!" he exclaimed. "I've told you we'd get a place in the country where you could raise your horses and teach riding, but it's the rodeo you can't leave behind. It's that fiercely competitive spirit of yours. You have to be a winner no matter what you do, and that goes for our relationship as well, doesn't it? Heaven forbid a Foster should have to concede defeat—and that's how you see marriage to me, isn't it?''

"No, you're wrong!" she vehemently denied. "It's just that I know we'd be much happier here in Montana."

"Why? Because then you could still run off and do your rodeos? Jenna, you're thirty-six years old. How much longer do you think you're going to be able to keep up the demanding pace? You say there's more to life than money? Well, I say there's more to life than rodeo." He took her hands in his and looked into her eyes, his voice dropping. "You know what it's like when we're together, Jenna. I don't want us to be apart any longer. Won't you come back with me to New York and we'll look for a house in the country?"

Jenna wanted to say yes—every nerve in her body was crying yes—but he had reached deep into her soul and uncovered vulnerable feelings. And it was disturbing to think that another person could see so far into her very being.

"I'm leaving tomorrow on a road trip with J.T. and Tracey," she said flatly. "We have to see how the act's going to work without Tracey riding."

Harrison dropped her hands. "I see."

But Jenna knew at that moment that he had spoken the truth.

CHAPTER FIFTEEN

So ONCE MORE Harrison went back to New York alone and Jenna went on the road with J.T. and Tracey—a pregnant Tracey who, despite a bad case of morning sickness, beamed with happiness. For the first time since the three of them had been performing together, Jenna felt like a third wheel. It wasn't that J.T. and Tracey were behaving any differently, just that she was more aware of the love and devotion the two shared; and it was a painful reminder of what she was missing. She wanted that kind of a relationship with Harrison.

The Flying Fosters were traveling across the southwestern part of the United States on one of their longest road trips of the year. Jenna was happy to be away from Red Lodge. In her present state of mind, she didn't need to be running into Eleanor Fielding in town. Spring had blossomed in the Rockies, and after a long winter, she felt not unlike the flowers struggling to push their heads through the cold ground to reach the warmth of the sun. Only Harrison was her sun, and she wasn't sure she was going to be able to break through the barrier that was keeping her from reaching his warmth.

Jenna had told Tracey only part of what had happened the night of the gallery opening. She purposely omitted any of the story concerning her grandmother, allowing Tracey to assume that she and Harrison had simply had another argument. Jenna suspected that her brother and sister-in-law thought she was brooding over that quarrel. Besides carefully avoiding bringing up his name, they discreetly gave her time to be alone without asking a lot of questions. Jenna wouldn't have called it brooding, but she appreciated their sensitivity.

In her heart she knew that many of the things Harrison had

said were true. She did have a fierce competitiveness, but rather than hating the idea of losing, she feared becoming dependent on a man. Ever since she had been a child, people had always thought of her as independent, able to take care of herself. But the truth was, it was an impressionable seventeen-year-old girl looking for a fairy-tale love and a man to take care of her that had married Jack Morgan. If she had appeared to be feisty and independent, it was because he had allowed her to be. It was only after his death that she realized how dependent upon him she had become, and having to suffer through losing him taught her never to allow herself to lean on a man to that extent again.

In the five years since his death she had discovered she was as strong as everyone had always said she was. Now, with Harrison, she could feel herself succumbing to that temptation to let a man take care of her again. If she were to marry him, would she be giving up that part of herself she had fought so hard to find? Why was she so hesitant about taking that risk?

After three weeks of being on the road during which time she had missed several easy jumps in her routine, Jenna knew that she was ready to take that risk. There was only one place she wanted to be, and that was with Harrison. On the day of their last performance before they were scheduled to return home, she and J.T. ate breakfast alone since Tracey was suffering from her usual morning sickness.

"Jenna, do you remember Cindy Williams, the bridesmaid at our wedding who had the long blond hair?" he asked as he spread honey on his biscuits.

"Sure, she was one of my students." Jenna was having her usual breakfast, a cup of black coffee, while J.T. ate sausage and eggs.

"She's here in Albuquerque. Tracey and I ran into her after dinner last night at the lounge where we went to hear that country-and-western singer. What would you think of her as a part of the act?"

"I thought she was performing with a Canadian specialty act."

"She was up until a couple of weeks ago, but apparently

they've split up. She's a heck of a rider, and I know she's look-ing for a job.''

''Are you thinking of her as a temporary replacement or a permanent addition?''

''She knows we're looking for someone to replace Tracey until she's ready to ride again, but if she's as good as I remember her to be, I think we might seriously consider taking her on as a fourth rider.''

''I was hoping Cody might be interested in filling in from time to time, but with college and the rodeo circuit this summer, we'll be lucky if we even get to see his face.''

''Then you don't mind if Tracey and I offer her the job?''

''Do you think the three of you can work well together?''

''The three of *us?*'' J.T.'s fork, laden with scrambled eggs, stopped in midair.

''It's not a decision for me to make, J.T.'' She hesitated, studying the coffee cup in her hands. ''I've been wanting to talk to you and Tracey, but I haven't been able to take a firm stand until today. I've decided to move to New York.''

''Whoa, Sis! Are you telling me you're giving up riding?''

''J.T., my heart's not in it anymore. I didn't think I'd ever be saying that—you know how much I love performing—but I have to follow my heart, and my heart's in New York.''

''Does this mean you and Harrison have worked out your problems?''

''The problem was my riding and I'm eliminating it. Well, not exactly eliminating it. I'm just not going down the road anymore.'' Seeing the concern on J.T.'s face, she asked, ''You think I'm acting crazy, don't you?''

''I think Harrison's a lucky guy—that's what I think,'' he told her, giving her a brotherly grin. ''I'm happy for both of you, and you can be sure I'll welcome Harrison into the family. So tell me what plans you've made.''

''So far, nothing's definite. You're the first one I've told,'' she admitted nervously. ''I haven't even told Harrison.''

''What about Cody and Dad?'' he asked. ''Is this going to catch them like a bolt out of the blue?''

''My relationship with Harrison is a delicate subject with

Cody. But I've told him I'd never sell the ranch," she said firmly. "Until the day when Cody wants to take over, I'll hire someone to help Dad. Besides, we'll need a place to take a vacation...Harrison loves the mountains."

"There's no chance the two of you could live in Montana?"

"J.T., that's been one of the major stumbling blocks to our getting married. Harrison has a very important position in New York and I've accepted that. Maybe someday we'll be able to move back home, but for now, I just want to be where he is."

J.T. threw her a bemused look. "God, I can't believe you're sitting here telling me you're leaving. I'm going to miss you, Sis." He reached across the table and took both of her hands in his.

"I'm going to miss you, too." She squeezed his callused hands tightly. "Harrison's promised to find us a place in the country where I can have my horses, and you know I won't be able to stay away from trick riding, even if it is only for exercise. And I'm going to continue teaching."

"Do you have any idea when you'll be leaving?"

"I want to fly to New York just as soon as I can, but first I have to talk to Harrison." She looked at her watch. "I should try to reach him now while he's in his office. I'm also going to call Dad to make sure everything's okay back home, and I've got a couple of errands to do before lunch. Do you think Tracey will feel like eating by then?"

"Once she gets past this early-morning sickness, she's fine."

"Then don't tell her my news," she instructed. "I want to be the one. Why don't I meet you both at the Sundowner Café at noon?" She reached up and grabbed their hats from the hooks on the end of the booth.

"Thanks for the moral support," she said, then plopped J.T.'s Stetson on his head and kissed his cheek.

"Anytime, Sis. Say hello to Harrison for us and give Dad our love," he called out to her departing figure.

Jenna would have loved to say hello to Harrison for them had she been able to locate him. But when she dialed his office in Manhattan, to her surprise she was told that he was no longer an employee at the firm. His secretary would give out no further information, and Jenna debated whether she should speak to Diana Elliot or not. *Come on, Jenna, where's your nerve?* a voice inside her questioned and she found herself asking for Diana, then immediately regretting doing so, for she learned the indispensable Ms Elliot had also left the firm's employment. Jenna's heart sank lower than she dreamed possible. Could both Harrison and Diana have been fired? But where would they have gone? Off together to start their own company? When the secretary would offer no further information, Jenna reluctantly hung up.

She quickly dialed Harrison's home only to hear the rings repeating as no one answered, as he hadn't even left on his answering machine. Digging down into the bottom of her purse, she found Mrs. Drake's number and once more dialed New York. This time she reached Mrs. Drake's housekeeper, who told her Harrison's mother was vacationing with friends on a yacht in the Mediterranean and wouldn't be back for several weeks. Jenna asked several questions to which the woman politely responded. No, Mr. Drake had not accompanied his mother; no, she did not have any information concerning Mr. Drake's employment status; and no, she did not have Ms Elliot's home phone number. Jenna mentally berated herself for asking that last question. She didn't want to call Diana's apartment, and hung up the receiver feeling extremely frustrated. Where on earth could Harrison be?

Finally she called her father and asked him if Harrison had tried calling in her absence. But according to Hank Foster, there had been no long-distance phone calls from Harrison. She told her father to expect her home in three days, then despondently went to find J.T. and Tracey.

JENNA FELT A QUIVER of homesickness when she rounded the final curve in the highway leading to the Lost Creek Ranch. The winter snows had melted away, leaving the ground soggy in the valley, but the fragrance of thawed meadows carried a promise of warmth and growth. Soon wildflowers would be tossing their saucy heads in the spring breeze, filling her vision with a riot of color. As she turned off the main highway onto the gravel driveway, she felt such a rush of emotion, she began to think maybe it was best that she hadn't been able to contact Harrison. When the big white house came into view, she admired its old but stately design, remembering how often she'd sat on the porch swing and gazed at the stars, grateful for her small piece of heaven here in the valley. It was home, sweet home. Could she really leave it?

Everything looked so dearly familiar as she drove past the house down to the corrals—everything except the barn door. Painted across the large double doors was a life-size mural of a woman riding a horse around the barrels, her dark hair flying, her eyes flashing. Jenna gasped at the portrait of herself. She brought the pickup to a stop and leaped from the cab to stand staring at the beautiful scene.

"Welcome home, Jenna." It was her father's voice she heard over her shoulder.

Turning around, she stammered, "Wh-what? Wh-where did this come from?" Her arm made a sweeping gesture toward the barn.

Hank scratched at the stubble of gray whiskers on his chin. "Well, one day I was out in the barn and this fellow pulls up in that Jeep over there." He paused to point to a red vehicle that was parked next to the house. "He was looking for work. Seems he had just up and left a good job in the city. I thought he meant ranch work, but this is what happened. Mighty pretty, isn't it?" He smiled at Jenna who stood momentarily paralyzed, gazing at the barn. "He's a hard worker, this man. Worked from sunrise to sunset, which is why I let him have the guest room in the house. Why don't you go on up and—" His words were lost on Jenna who went racing across the ground, her boots leaving deep imprints in the mud as she ran to the house. She leaped the porch steps in one jump and was in the house before Hank could even finish his sentence. He smiled as he went to the back of the trailer to unload Jenna's horses, mumbling to himself, "And she yelled at Cody for neglecting the horses."

Jenna ran through the kitchen, past the living room and into the family room, searching frantically. Discovering the first floor empty, she took the stairs two at a time, and she was definitely out of breath by the time she reached the landing. Her cheeks flushed, her eyes wide, she saw Harrison lazily leaning against the doorjamb of the guest bedroom. Not far from him on the hallway wall was one of Charles Fielding's portraits of her grandmother, but Jenna didn't notice the painting. All she could see was a cowboy dressed in denim jeans, a plaid long-sleeved shirt, boots and a Robert Redford grin.

"You're here!" she squealed.

"I'm glad you're home, Jenna. I've been waiting for you," he said in the New York accent she had grown to love.

"Oh, Harrison!" She ran into his arms and covered his lips with hers, kissing him until she heard him groan. "The barn is beautiful," she cried, unable to stem the flood of tears that had begun. "It's the most beautiful thing anyone's ever done for me."

"Hey, what's this?" He wiped at the tears with his thumbs. "I thought you told me real cowgirls don't cry."

"Maybe I don't want to be a cowgirl anymore." She hiccuped and Harrison smiled.

"Now that would be a real shame since I had it all planned to become a cowboy." He held her chin in his fingers, his eyes studying every inch of her face.

"You mean you really did quit your job to come out here and be with me?"

"I was a lousy weekend cowboy," he confessed. "I figured if I was going to do it right I needed to be here the other five days as well."

"But quitting your job! Harrison, what about the money?"

"You're the one who told me money isn't everything."

"But what will your family think?"

"They'll think I'm having a midlife crisis." He laughed.

"That's what Cody thought was happening to me when he found out we were dating," she confessed with a grin.

"I prefer to call it early retirement." His thumb traced the line of her cheekbone.

"But you didn't need to retire. I was coming to New York. *I* quit the Flying Fosters!" she exclaimed.

Harrison's eyes gleamed. "You really were giving it all up for me?"

She nodded. "I told J.T. right before we left for home. Then I tried calling your office, your home—even your mother—and I couldn't find you. I was worried you had run off with Diana Elliot."

"Diana?" He laughed. "Diana's on her honeymoon, which is where I wish I was right this minute. She and I have been friends for years, as well as business associates, but that's all it's ever been. You weren't really jealous of her, were you?"

"Of course I was. The woman is gorgeous and you were spending almost every waking moment of your day with her. Plus, both Molly and Mrs. Fielding implied there was more to your relationship than work. And why didn't you call me when you came to help your aunt select the paintings for the showing?"

"I tried several times but there was no answer. It was a last-minute decision to even fly out here and then I returned the very same day."

"Well, absence may make the heart grow fonder but it can also create a few insecurities," Jenna pointed out.

"Well, I don't plan on us being apart any longer and I'm going to do my best to show you I love only you, Jenna." His arms tightened around her and he began to move slowly, inching his way into the bedroom.

"Then you really are going to live out here and paint seriously?"

"Living with you is what's important. If I'm successful as an artist, I'll owe it to you. You're the one who showed me how important it is to take risks." He brushed kisses over her eyes, her mouth, her forehead and her cheeks, gentle kisses that made Jenna tremble with emotion. "There's nothing we can't solve together."

"What about Molly and Cody?"

"I've explained my feelings to Molly and she's been pretty fair about accepting them." Seeing Jenna's skeptical look, he added, "Please be patient with her, Jenna."

"Of course I will," she assured him. "Because I know Cody probably feels the same way."

"He does. He came home last weekend and we talked about a lot of things—college, his future, the stock market."

"The stock market?" She raised her eyebrows. "Cody doesn't know anything about the stock market."

"He sure does. He's been investing and trading ever since he took a class in economics at the university. Actually, he's got a great head for figures."

"He always did like to help Dad with the paperwork for the ranch," she said thoughtfully.

"It might take a little time, but I do believe that both of our children will be happy for us. At any rate, they're not really children anymore. Molly is graduating next month and she's been accepted at Wellesley—much to her grandmother's delight. Mother's already told her she can spend summers with her, but I've got a feeling she'll be visiting us frequently. She really does love it out here."

"Harrison, are you sure this is what you want?"

He kissed her deeply, his tongue parting her lips with a hunger that brought a low moaning sound from Jenna's throat. When he lifted his mouth, his eyes were sparkling with desire. "For the first time in my life I'm doing what I want instead of what's expected of me, and I feel wonderful doing it. Jenna, this is not an impulsive decision."

Jenna smiled to herself, knowing that Harrison could change his career but never his well-regulated mind. It was one of the things she loved about him. Everything he did was well thought out—well, almost everything, as his hands were telling her now. They were slowly working her shirt free of her jeans.

"It doesn't have to be a final decision. Until this morning I was ready to live in New York. You know I'd follow you anywhere, Harrison." They both moved toward the bed, where Harrison gently eased her down beside him.

"This is where I want to be, Jenna." His fingers unbuttoned her blouse, and the soft cotton parted to reveal her lacy camisole. When he slid the shirt off her shoulders, her hand stopped his.

"Dad's outside—he could come in any minute."

"No, he's not," Harrison expelled on a deep sigh of yearning as her nipples tightened beneath his touch.

"He's not?" she whispered, heat radiating her skin until it nearly glowed.

"He's not," he repeated, catching her nipple between his thumb and forefinger, his light touch making her gasp with pleasure. "He told me he would be gone all afternoon as soon as he unloaded your horses."

"My horses!" she exclaimed. "Harrison Drake, look what you do to me! This is the first time in my life I've forgotten to take care of my horses!"

"I think Hank was expecting it." He smiled and continued to tease the fullness of her breasts. "I have to admit, it certainly did something for my ego to see you come racing toward the house without thinking first of your horses."

"They're not as important to me as you think," she told him.

"I never expected you to give up riding for me." His eyes darkened for a moment.

"Not riding, just competing," she amended. "But you were right about my competitive spirit. Only I wasn't competing against you, but with myself. I was afraid of losing a part of me—not my freedom—just a part of me that I wasn't sure I was ready to lose. But you made me realize that without you, that part of me I was trying so hard to protect isn't worth much." She watched Harrison's eyes gleam in understanding and his lips part in a smile.

"Will you marry me now, Jenna?"

"How soon is now?" she asked shyly.

"Just as soon as we can arrange a small wedding with our children in attendance."

"I will." She made a sound of pleasure and stretched her arms toward the sky.

Harrison brought her down on top of him on the bed, laughing and kissing her at the same time. Her hands flew to his shirt buttons and he groaned. "Easy, I've got a stiff back and saddle sores."

"You've been riding?"

"Hank taught me. Actually, I've gotten to be quite good at it," he admitted with false modesty. "Would you like me to show you?"

She stared into the face that had become as dear to her as the air that she breathed. She saw the man who had fallen off a horse and come back to apologize. The man who had given up a career to be with her. The man who had overcome his fear of horses and learned to ride for her. Her heart swelled with love.

"Tomorrow," she said, unbuckling his belt. "Or the day after that...or the day after that."

Harlequin Romance®

Delightful
Affectionate
Romantic
Emotional

Tender
Original

Daring
Riveting
Enchanting
Adventurous
Moving

Harlequin Romance®—
capturing the world you dream of...

HARLEQUIN®
Makes any time special®

HARLEQUIN *Super*ROMANCE®

...there's more to the story!

Superromance.
A *big* satisfying read about unforgettable
characters. Each month we offer *six* very different
stories that range from family drama to adventure
and mystery, from highly emotional stories to
romantic comedies—and much more! Stories
about people you'll believe in and care about.
Stories too compelling to put down....

Our authors are among today's *best* romance
writers. You'll find familiar names and talented
newcomers. Many of them are award winners—
and you'll see why!

If you want the biggest and best
in romance fiction, you'll get it
from Superromance!

Emotional, Exciting, Unexpected...

HARLEQUIN®
*M*akes any time special ®

HARLEQUIN *Presents*

**The world's bestselling romance series...
The series that brings you your favorite authors,
month after month:**

Helen Bianchin...Emma Darcy
Lynne Graham...Penny Jordan
Miranda Lee...Sandra Marton
Anne Mather...Carole Mortimer
Susan Napier...Michelle Reid

and many more uniquely talented authors!

Wealthy, powerful, gorgeous men...
Women who have feelings just like your own...
The stories you love, set in exotic, glamorous locations...

HARLEQUIN *Presents*

Seduction and passion guaranteed!

HPDIR1

HARLEQUIN®
INTRIGUE

WE'LL LEAVE YOU BREATHLESS!

If you've been looking for thrilling tales of
contemporary passion and sensuous love stories
with taut, edge-of-the-seat suspense—then
you'll love Harlequin Intrigue!

Every month, you'll meet four new heroes
who are guaranteed to make your spine tingle
and your pulse pound. With them you'll enter
into the exciting world of Harlequin Intrigue—
where your life is on the line
and so is your heart!

THAT'S INTRIGUE—
ROMANTIC SUSPENSE
AT ITS BEST!

HARLEQUIN®
Makes any time special ®

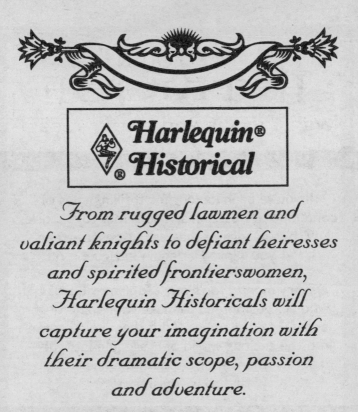

Harlequin® Historical

From rugged lawmen and valiant knights to defiant heiresses and spirited frontierswomen, Harlequin Historicals will capture your imagination with their dramatic scope, passion and adventure.

Harlequin Historicals . . . they're too good to miss!

HHDIR1

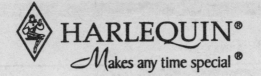

HARLEQUIN®
Makes any time special ®

Upbeat, All-American Romances

HARLEQUIN®
Duets™

Romantic Comedy

Historical, Romantic Adventure

HARLEQUIN®
INTRIGUE

Romantic Suspense

Harlequin Romance ®

Capturing the World You Dream Of

HARLEQUIN® *Presents*~

Seduction and passion guaranteed

HARLEQUIN® *Super*ROMANCE®

Emotional, Exciting, Unexpected

HARLEQUIN®
Temptation

Sassy, Sexy, Seductive!